CLARITY

A Young Adult Dystopian Thriller (Clarity Chronicles, Book 1)

J Lynn Hicks

J Lynn Hicks

CHAPTER 1

W arm sunlight filters through the bay windows, and the moon is steady over the eastern horizon. The container ship horn blows, signaling its arrival and the start of the new day. And though the cottage houses are quiet. Inside, people are busy with their morning routines.

It's unusual for me to see this early part of the day, everything so still. It makes me think of how lucky I am to live here in Sol Luna-Nueva, where beauty abounds.

A glint of light catches my eye, and I strain past the bright rays of sunrise to see what has caught my attention. Almost invisible, a girl stands in the middle of the road. The barrette in her black hair catches the sunlight as she faces our house. When she looks up as if she's seen me, I wave.

The girl doesn't move. I can't tell if she can see me for sure, but after a few moments, she turns and walks back up the street. Strange. She must not have seen me for the lights reflecting off the windows.

When she's out of sight, I return to my morning routine. I'm up early this morning, eager for my art aptitude test at the academy and much too excited to sleep. The creative field is competitive for jobs, but I'm optimistic. I know how important it is to Clarisse, my mom. (Yes, that's what she has me call her.). Clarisse is one of the leading designers in the fashion industry, and she wants me to follow in her fashionable footsteps. To be honest, I would rather paint and draw, but she doesn't want to hear about that.

I've laid my clothes out on the window seat, so I slip on my blouse and skirt. They're already enhanced through PR (or Personal Reality, for those who prefer the longer term), but they still need a little pop. Using the neural projector embedded in my brain, I look to the left, and the dials for aesthetics come up in my lower field of vision. I increase the yellow and adjust the color saturation until it's right. Then I do the same to my cheeks—a touch more red in each. Not too much, but just enough. Perfect.

When I'm satisfied, I grab my bag off the hook on the landing and run barefoot down the stairs to the kitchen. Clarisse is sitting at the wide wooden table with all sorts of breakfast meats and pastries piled in front of her. As soon as she sees me, she points to the counter where she's poured me a large glass of juice.

"Morning, Libby." She takes a sip of her coffee as she looks over her fashion panels. "Did you sleep well?"

I nod, though I didn't. I don't want her to know about my aptitude test, or she'll inundate me with questions. You'd think she has as much invested in the outcome as I do.

I glance around the unusually quiet kitchen as I put small portions on my plate and sit. I'm too nervous to eat, but if Clarisse notices, she says nothing.

"Where's Dad?" I ask. It's surprising for me to beat him to breakfast. He's usually up and ready for work early.

Dad works as a balancer for PR; he's even more important than Clarisse, at least to most of the community. They both are important, though, and counterbalance each other well. Left brain, right brain. They make a great team.

"Elizeus is in his study. He's got some work to do at home before he leaves for the office." She stands and slides the panels into her portfolio. "Eat what you want, but don't be late for the academy.

This close to the end of the testing, your art aptitude test should be soon. I want you to be punctual."

I don't respond. She didn't ask me a question.

"How do I look?" she asks, grabbing her keys.

As always, she's the fashion guru. Her hair is a deep red, and her makeup is flawless. She's wearing a red-and-white striped blouse with a red sash around the waist. Her skirt is white with red stripes on the sides.

"You look amazing, Clarisse." Once I told her she looked fine. I'll never make that mistake again.

Clarisse nods, looks me over, and sighs. Apparently, I don't look amazing.

"Dial up your contrast and color saturation, dear. You're looking somewhat pale."

Doing as I'm told, I don't argue. It would do no good. Clarisse knows everything about beauty, and I am but her protégé.

I bite my lip to keep from grimacing. Being on display gets annoying. She thinks if I don't look my best, I'll reflect badly on her. And I probably do.

"Much better." She flattens her skirt with her hands. "Ta-ta!"

With that, Clarisse bangs the door behind her. She does everything with a flourish.

Before I can turn around, I feel something hit the back of my head. I scan the floor, trying to find it. Just under the dining table is a small cloth ball with a butterfly on it. I pick it up and tuck against the wall.

A quiet click, and Dad peeks from behind his study door, and I hurl the ball back at him, hitting him in the face.

He grabs his head and dramatically falls to the ground, heaving his last breath, and dies nobly. He lies there until my giggles cause him to open one eye.

It's good to see Dad like this. He's looked tired the past few weeks, but now his eyes are bright and he's tufted his hair is tufted from running his hands through it.

"You're getting good at this," he says. "I may have to retire."

He stands up with a sheepish grin and ducks back into his study. Curious.

When he comes back out, he's wearing his light work coat and fumbling with something in the pocket. He makes his way to the table. "Is your mother gone?" he asks, as if that's not obvious.

I nod, and he takes a deep breath and smiles.

Dad is no slave to fashion. He wears the same clothes most days. He looks comfortable, if unkempt. But I love him just the way he is.

"That's enough fooling around. We've got about fifteen minutes. If you're done eating, I'd like to talk to you a minute, Liberty."

I love the way he says my name, like we're equals, though we most certainly are not. He always says my full name—never Lib, Libby, or Libs like others do. Always Liberty. It makes sense, as he's the one who named me.

With no explanation for our talk, he walks over to the red angular couch and pats the seat beside him. Weird.

I take my space next to him. "What's going on?"

"I'm trying to think how to start, where to begin..." He pauses for a moment, staring at me. Then, as if waking up, he says, "I want to tell you something about PR and PREP."

"What's PREP?" I crook my head to the side.

"Yes, well... Let me put that aside and focus on the main thing for the moment. I have something for you."

He reaches back into his pocket and pulls out an envelope with my name written on the front. He holds it out for me.

I take it but look up for an explanation, but once I see the sparkle in his eyes, all the weird vibes disappear. He's excited about his gift, so I am, too.

"Go on. Open it," he says. "I've waited a long time to give this to you. Too long, really."

Something weighty slides as I move the envelope, so I open the top end and pour the contents into my other hand.

At first, I don't know what to think. It's a cord, almost invisible. On it is a clasp and a long pink pendant. It's a necklace.

"It's for you, as long as you want to wear it." He smiles nervously.

I'm hesitant. After all, it's an unusual gift. Still, it's lovely.

The pendant must be a crystal. It's opaque and fashioned into a teardrop shape. It's much nicer than the necklaces Clarisse wears.

But I'm confused. Clarisse wears jewelry—not me. When I look at him, my questions fade. His eyes shine with pride, and I smile at him. "Thanks, Dad."

"Here, let me help you put it on." He takes the necklace back. "Now, turn around."

I do as I'm told, facing the side window as he drapes the cord around my neck and fastens it in the back. Then he reaches around to adjust the pendant.

The window.

What was clear and whole a moment ago is marred by a jagged crack. The glass looks cloudy and dirty, and a light streams through it like a spotlight—so bright that I have to blink. I glance down at the pendant just as my father lets go. When I look up again, everything is back to normal.

I turn my attention back to Dad. "Did you see that? The window—it changed."

"Nothing changed, Liberty." He shakes his head, his eyes looking tired again. "You have my word on that."

I'm quiet. I think I saw it, but it makes little sense for things to look one way one minute and completely different the next. Sure, what we see is enhanced, but the beauty comes from somewhere. It's not that far off reality...

But I'm not about to argue with Dad. He's an expert, and if he said nothing changed, then it didn't. It must have been a trick of the eye. I let go of the necklace and look around the room. Everything looks as it always has.

"Behind this crystal is a story, something I want to tell you." Dad shakes his head and changes course. "It's also valuable. There are only three that I've seen, but I'm told there are three more. Though I can't say for sure."

My face must show my confusion, because he laughs nervously. "I'm getting ahead of myself. I can explain the rest later. The most important thing you need to know for now is that this is our secret. Wear it today under your blouse, get used to it, but don't show it to anyone. I'll explain the rest to you after work."

"If you don't want anyone to see it, why should I wear it at all?"

His face falls, and I worry I've hurt his feelings. I tilt my head down and smile at him. Thankfully, he rebounds quickly.

"I'll tell you tonight, but not here, okay? Promise."

I nod but am at a loss for words as Dad rises from the couch and locks his study door. He pauses before he leaves the house. "Oh yes, whatever happens, don't tell your mother. This is between you and me."

That's enough to stop any further questions. I've always viewed my parents as a team, and now he wants to keep a secret from Clarisse. I'm torn, both thrilled to have his trust and wary of what the secret might mean.

"Promise?" He's eying me from the front door.

I put my hand on the necklace, sliding it between my fingers. Not sure, but deciding to trust Dad, I say, "I promise."

Chapter 2

When I walk out of the academy, the sun warms my shoulders. The afternoon is crisp and clean, the beginning of spring. In front of the building is a flag post mounted on an enormous concrete block. It's a nice place to sit and enjoy the afternoon and the perfect place to continue my drawing until Dad gets home and tells me why he gave me this necklace.

I pull the pendant up to watch the light glimmer from it, forgetting that I'm supposed to keep it hidden until a boy passes by and gives me a strange look.

Hopping up on the block as others flood out of the academy, I pull out my sketchbook to work on the butterfly sketch I started during art aptitude testing.

I have a lot to live up to with both of my parents being so valued in the community, so doing well in testing is important to me. I worry the assessors won't place me in a prominent role. All of this is aggravated by the fact that I didn't do as well as I'd hoped today. Others tested much better than I did, so I need all the practice I can get. I did my best, but today my best wasn't good enough. I knew I should have worked harder on design theory.

As I work on perfecting the butterfly's wings, I look up, and my heartbeat skips: Aden Cade is at the bike rack by the academy gate.

He won the PR Achievement award last year, given to the most promising graduate of the academy, and I've been crushing on him since then. With light-brown hair and wide-set green eyes, he's gorgeous, but also really smart. Of course, I'm not the only one who thinks so. He's got a following, as evidenced by the crowd that instantly forms around him.

These days, I only catch a glimpse of him now and then doing his afternoon deliveries. After he tested out of the academy, he went to work full time on his father's farm. They grow food for the entire town, but they also do experimental farming, finding additional food sources and using enhancement treatments on different produce.

He doesn't stop for his admirers. Instead, he smiles and collects his bike from the rack. When he looks my way, and it's obvious that I'm staring, I'm mortified. I flip my head so quickly that I almost fall off the block.

While the blush warms my cheeks, I attempt to return to my sketch, but my curiosity gets the better of me. I look up to see if Aden is gone. He is not. He's staring my way, steadily walking his bike toward the flagpole.

I turn around to see if there's someone behind me, but the crowd of testers had scattered while I sketched.

"You're not supposed to sit there," he says, though where that authority comes from, I don't know.

"Why not?" I ask.

"It's the flag, Lib. It's supposed to stand alone."

Never mind about the flag; Aden Cade knows my name. With my mouth open but unable to form words, I stare at him.

"Hello?" he says, jarring me from my stupor.

"I know of no rule that keeps me from sitting here, but I'm done, so I'll grant your wish." I stand and tuck my sketchbook back in my bag, avoiding eye contact at all costs.

"Can I see?" he asks.

I accidentally snap my gaze to his. "What?"

For a second, I'm sure he's joking, but those green eyes hold mine as he repeats, "Your artwork. Can I see?"

Without a word, I open my sketchbook to my butterfly and pass it over. I don't know why I did; it's not my finest work. But who could resist those eyes?

He studies it, then glances at me, his eyebrows raised. I move to snatch it away when he thumbs through the other pages.

He pulls it out of my reach. "These are great! You had your aptitude test yet?"

"Yeah, today." I finally grab the book and hold it to my chest. "I didn't do as well as I hoped, so I'm practicing now. Besides, drawing relaxes me."

"You don't seem relaxed."

Well, duh. Of course I don't. I'm talking to Aden Cade. He knows my name, and he likes my artwork. I'm a jangle of nerves as I put the sketchbook in my bag.

"Anyway," he says. "I have to get back home soon, but I can walk you to the carousel."

I have to replay his words in my head twice to make sure I heard right. The butterfly from my sketchbook has moved to my stomach and is fluttering its wings restlessly. I have to force myself to answer.

"Okay... we can do that."

He nods and holds his hand out, gesturing for me to lead the way, so I do until he walks beside me, pushing his bike at his other side.

The city center isn't far, maybe a ten-minute walk, but my feet are not cooperating. It's like I've forgotten how to walk for a few steps. If he notices, he says nothing about it.

I'm shaky about filling our walk with idle conversation and worried about saying or doing something wrong. But he acts casual, and after a few minutes of walking, I chill out. A little.

"I haven't ridden the carousel in years," he volunteers. "Have you?"

The rush of blood to my cheeks is immediate. I rode it last fall with Dad. Seventeen is much too old to ride, but it sounded fun.

"It's been a while," I say. Technically true.

He glances at me and readjusts his hands on the handlebars of his bike. "Really? Did you ride with someone or alone?"

I'm not about to tell him I rode with Dad, so I keep it simple. "Yeah, with someone else."

"Oh." He continues walking with me, but I must have said something off, because the conversation comes to a complete stop.

Then, out of nowhere, he asks, "Do you have a boyfriend?"

The content of my stomach has given up its tight quarters and leaped into my throat. Is he going to ask me to be his girlfriend? *Cool, play it cool.* "No, why?"

He shrugs. "I thought you might have one." His voice sounds canned, distant.

My nerves get the best of me, and I let out a nervous giggle. "Not yet."

Okay, could I be a tad more obvious?

"Oh." And the conversation stops again.

As we get closer to the carousel, the tall buildings on Main Street poke above the palm trees. Most of the businesses are within this area, although a few are scattered about elsewhere. To the right, the moon glows, reflecting the light of the sun. It's not too hot or too cool. The temperature is ideal, but it doesn't keep my hands from sweating.

A girl darts across my path, forcing me to abruptly slow my steps. She appeared to come out of nowhere, and I can't be sure, but I think it's the same girl from the street this morning. She's wearing a metallic barrette in her hair.

"You okay?" Aden asks.

"Huh? Oh." I glance at Aden and quickly move forward, not realizing I'd stopped in the middle of the path. And he is two steps ahead of me.

"Why'd you stop?"

"Just a... er... stone in my shoe." I shrug. I'm not about to relinquish Aden's attention over to this girl, whoever she is.

And yet I'm curious enough to scan the area for her, finding her some distance away now. Watching her, I see that no one else seems to take notice of her—one man almost running over her as she ducks out of the way. It's not as if she's dressed to stand out. She's plain, with a dull button-up and tan pants. Her black hair is straight and almost the same color as her shirt; she could use a makeover. At the very least, some color saturation. I hate to think it, but she could use a touch of Clarisse.

As she walks out of the park, Aden and I move from the sidewalk to the grass. There's a walking path around the park, and the elderly are there as always, training for their lengthy walk to Graceon. It's always peaceful to know they will soon head for their final destination for a well-earned rest.

We walk along a hedgerow that leads to the carousel. When we round the corner, small children jump for their turn on the unicorns, but everyone is polite as always. No one wants to invade another person's space. Every seat is full when the ride resumes, even the fire engines and benches.

The parents sit facing the carousel, and if I didn't know better, I might think their focus is on the children, but it's more likely they're using their visual optics to play a virtual game or watch funny clips. Everyone is having fun, as they should be.

Stopping by the carousel, Aden turns to face me. "I've got to get back to the farm, but I can walk you tomorrow, if you want."

"Oh, um. That sounds good!" My voice has jumped a whole octave, and I'm so giddy it's hard to hold still.

He blesses me with a broad, quirked-up smile that creates a huge dimple in his left cheek. "I'll see you tomorrow, then."

I nod, dumbstruck, and take him in, but he doesn't seem to notice. In fact, his sudden shrug indicates he might be as nervous as I am.

He walks away a few steps, and I bounce up and down silently until he turns back just before the corner. I freeze and wave awkwardly, waiting until he's gone before I squeal with delight.

My spring-loaded feet bounce as I walk home, daydreaming of what colors I'll choose tomorrow, and if he'll hold my hand.

Chapter 3

Everything smells fresher, cleaner, more alive, but it's any other perfect sunny day. Except during the heavy rain season, the weather here is always warm and the florals are always in bloom.

I come back down from my fantasy when I see my house and the small walkway leading to our white house. Passing the thick hedges and the porch overflowing with yellow florals, I sit on the swing and kick off my shoes, returning them to the short shelf outside the front door before entering the house.

Clarisse throws out her manicured hands to greet me with two soft kisses that don't quite reach each cheek. She finds the habit to be "*en vogue.*" Her words, not mine.

The pressure from the hug reminds me of the necklace, and I feel a little tug at my heart for keeping it from her. Especially since I don't know why Dad is keeping it a secret.

"Oh, I meant to tell you this morning." Clarisse slides fashion panels into her red leather portfolio. Her eyes canvas the room, making sure she's getting everything she needs. "My meeting will go a little long, but I threw something together for you and Elizeus to eat tonight. It's my turn to pitch for the upcoming fashion showcase, and I really believe I have a shot of winning this season. Won't that be exciting? Having Della model my work!"

I should respond with well-wishes, but after the hundredth time you've heard something, it's hard to work up any excitement. Clarisse is an overachiever. Instead, I grab a glass of water and a fudge cookie from the plate in the middle of the table and take a seat on the couch.

"That's fine. I'll warm it up in an hour or two when Dad gets home," I say between nibbles. Aden Cade has made my stomach too flip-floppy to eat.

"How did academy go today?"

She asks me every afternoon, and usually the news is uneventful. The test scheduling at the academy is flawless and the measurements well-calibrated. The only real duty I have is to be there before the bell rings, and everything else takes care of itself.

In a few months, they'll discharge me into the role that best suits me and my preferences. I'm curious which area they'll place me, but I'm also confident in the academy's ability to decide.

"It went well," I say, withholding the obvious information.

"Any art testing? The assessors look for people with a sense of style and utility. You would have some fashion flair if you'd apply yourself."

I ignore her question, setting aside the cookie and taking a long drink of water.

If Dad asks me what I did today, I'll tell him I was also assessed as a balancer, just like him. I did well with that. For most things, I have a sharp eye. But that won't impress Clarisse at all. She doesn't want me to follow in Dad's footsteps. She calls it maintenance work.

Really, Dad has one of the most trusted jobs in town. As a balancer, the whole community depends on him and his co-worker. He's well-regarded in the community, and everyone seems to know and love him. He says it's because he is so good-hearted. I like it when he says that.

My family is lucky, because Dad's position means we get the best upgrades first. Plus, PR keeps our lives content and fulfilled by enhancing our senses. Everyone has it, and it's free. It's officially a law to have the programming, but why you'd want to be without is a mystery to me.

When Clarisse returns to her bedroom, I run up the landing and hang my bag on the hook before I settle on my window seat and stare out onto the perfect day. The moon hangs beyond the yellow and white plumeria blossoms on the tree in front of my window. It seems so far away, but it also looks as if I could reach out and grab it in my hand.

The neighbor across the street, Mr. Devonshire, has just arrived home, but Dad won't return for another half hour. I've nothing to do between now and then, so I rifle through my closet to decide which colors I'll wear tomorrow for Aden.

When Dad makes his way down the street toward our house, I watch from the window as he grasps his briefcase with both hands and heaves a determined sigh before starting up the sidewalk. He does that every day. Clarisse says his work is tedious, and he sighs to put his day behind him. That makes sense to me, but it still makes me frown.

As usual, I don't rush down to greet him like I might have a few years ago. As I've gotten older, I'm more mindful of our personal space.

Plus, it'll feel odd to face both of my parents, knowing I'm holding two secrets from Clarisse. I'll also have Dad all to myself while Clarisse is at her meeting; and waiting gives her a chance to swoon over her husband for a bit.

I wait on the landing, listening to their muted voices while Clarisse mixes Dad a drink at the bar, until Clarisse calls up the steps.

"Everything is ready, Libby! You just need to turn the oven on. I'm off now."

"Okay, bye!" I call down the stairs just in time to see Clarisse pick up her keys and head out the door. Dad stands by the bar with a cocktail in a crystal glass.

"Dad?" I say, but he holds his finger to his lips as we listen to Clarisse's shoes clack down the garden path.

"We'll discuss it after dinner," he finally says.

I don't know why the delay, but his word is final. To punctuate it, he walks to the table and sits, pulling his paper up to his face and ending the discussion.

Again with the weirdness.

I turn the oven on before I copy him and take my place at the table. Clarisse made us individualized portions of a family favorite: Carne Espana, a rich stew recipe passed down from my grandmother, who I only barely remember. Like her mother, Clarisse is an excellent cook. We have something exotic on most nights, but this dish is a standby because everyone loves it so much.

Once the food is done, we eat quietly. I'm gulping mine down, but Dad barely touches his. In fact, I'm not certain he's eaten at all.

After I'm done, I bring up the necklace again, but Dad shakes his head and pushes food around his plate with his fork.

I would chide him about his shrinking portion sizes, as Clarisse often does, but I don't hold as much sway. It would be a waste of breath to complain about it. I'm not concerned, though; Dad looks healthy enough. Maybe his appetite is shifting with his age.

He doesn't look old, though, except for his graying temples. Clarisse says he doesn't do nearly enough to adjust his appearance. She hates that, but I think it makes him look unique.

By the time I take the dishes and put them back in the cabinet, Dad puts down his paper and watches me as I return the cookies to the table.

"How about a walk?" He smiles. "Is it a good evening for that?"

"When is it not?" I grin. "Let me get my shoes on, and I'll be ready to go in a minute."

Dad rises and steps into his study, closing the door. I make little of it as I return to the porch, pull on my shoes, and sit in the swing daydreaming about Aden until Dad joins me.

"Where are we going?" I ask, presuming we'll check out the more scenic walking trail that winds along the Voya river.

He slides on his shoes. "We need to get away from the house in case your mother returns. Tell you what, let's make our way downtown."

He's nervous. I can tell by the set of his jaw and the intensity of his eyes. And that makes me nervous too.

"I've got a lot to say," he says, "and I hope you can forgive me."

CHAPTER 4

His words hang in the air like a thick shroud on my shoulders. I swallow hard. He's caught me off guard, and I'm too stunned to ask him what he means, so I avert my eyes. Part of me wants to turn back to the house, and the other half is burning with a dangerous curiosity.

On the way through our residential area, we stop to look at the small garden with a fountain. The bright pink bulbs and the deep-coral florals are beautiful, but as always, the feature attraction is the butterflies. I would spend hours trying to catch them as a child but would always come up empty-handed.

"They used to be bigger, you know? They're different now," Dad says.

"The butterflies?"

"Before the virus came, they had wide wings. They were beautiful. They're not the same, I'm told. My grandfather told me about them when I was little."

I don't tell him I still think they're beautiful, because he's brought up the virus. No one talks about it or how we all got here. All I know is that it almost killed off the whole population nearly a hundred years ago. We're lucky to be among the survivors in this new world. In Sol Luna-Nueva, we don't dwell on the terrible past, but enjoy the present as best we can.

As the container ship blows its horn again, signaling its departure, Dad turns back toward the street, and though he looks as well-put-together as always, something is different about him. His movements are quick, and he seems to look for someone as he scans each face that comes our way.

"Are you all right?" I ask him, but he doesn't turn my way. Instead, he turns toward the road and grabs my hand.

It's such a foreign thing for him to do that I almost pull away. But when I look at him, he smiles and relaxes, so I keep my hand in his.

The moon comes into view as we continue our walk to the city center. Our house is close to the main thoroughfare. We are a short walk from most everything we need, while those who live farther out have to take their transports and bikes into town.

We own a transport though, tucked in the garage. Dad uses it during the rainy season when he goes to work on the other side of town. Sometimes he takes it on business trips across the river or when he takes Clarisse around on errands. Clarisse rarely drives, but when she does, it's terrifying.

Aden has a bike because he lives far away, yet he's willing to set it aside to walk with me. Just the thought of him brings goose pimples to my arms.

"What are you smiling at, Liberty?"

"Just... enjoying the day," I say lightly.

Looking around, I refocus on the houses. Our neighborhood is a nice one. Most of the houses are bigger, all with beautiful hedges and floral gardens.

Here, the houses are two stories, painted in shades of pastels. The interiors are all built similarly, from what I've been told, but I haven't been in any of the neighbor's houses to find out. Home is a sacred place for most people. Well, except for ours. Mother runs her business out of ours, so we host dinner parties and meetings on occasion.

No one is on the road, so we walk on the median lined with tall palms. The steel buildings of city center loom over the park as we pass through the trees. Children laugh near the carousel. We're almost there.

Truthfully, my nerves are on end as we get closer. I don't know what it is, but something's up. He's holding my hand on a walk when we could have stayed at home and talked over the table.

Dad tugs my hand across the street toward the park on the other side of the carousel, which is as full as it was earlier. I let my hand drop, worrying I look like a toddler holding his hand. He must understand because he doesn't pick it up again.

From a set of bushes along the path, a rustling sound catches my attention. A man jumps out of nowhere, making me jump back and catch my breath.

He's dressed nicely and is well-groomed, but there's something very foreign about him. He dresses nothing like the other park-goers. Instead of traditional pants and buttoned shirts, the man wears a thick, red, pinstripe suit that makes his legs look impossibly long.

He says to Dad, "Hey there, Captain! The crew saw the storm coming, but they've nestled in their beds. Why are you heading into the storm? Are you trying to make landfall?"

I have no idea what he is talking about, but Dad seems to know. He smiles and says, "There'll be no storm today, but there's something looming. Best make sure you batten down."

The man opens his mouth and reveals a toothy smile. He starts to say something but stops as his eyes fall on me. He purses his lips and nods.

"I'm at the ready, Captain."

"Good to know," Dad says and pulls me toward the benches.

"Is that man all right?" I ask. "He's speaking in riddles."

Dad shrugs. "Puck? He's not exactly right, but he's not off either. He's one of the smartest men in town, really, but not always as he seems." He points ahead to a bench that sits off in the shrubbery, and we walk toward it and take a seat.

"Tell me about your day." He sits facing me. "Was it good?"

"It was..." My thoughts return to Aden. I've never talked to Dad about a boy before. There hasn't really been anyone, as I'm usually more of a daydreamer. I want to tell him now, but part of me worries that saying something about it will change our relationship. It's bad enough for him that I'm no longer his little girl.

"Anything... unusual?"

I feel like he's trying to get to a point, and I'm anxious to find out what. "Dad, why are we here? Why couldn't we talk at home?"

"Well, we're out with it, then, are we?" He nods his head. "There's something I want to give you, but it comes at a high price, and I don't want your mother to know."

Again, with the warning! What can't Clarisse know?

"The necklace. It's a big responsibility, but I know you're ready, and I'm running out of time."

"Time? What do you mean, running out of time?" I reach out to him as if he may disappear. "You aren't sick, are you?"

There aren't many services for sick people in town. You're expected to take responsibility for your own health, so he has me worried.

"No, no. Not sick. But there's something more pressing." Once more, he looks around as if he's expecting someone, but there's no one there. "It's time you learned more about who you are and the choices you make every day. I don't want you to have to grow up in short order, but I'm afraid there's no choice. I'm hoping to give you a head start."

I shake my head, lost. "You're confusing me. A head start on what?"

"It'll be easier to show you than to explain. But I want you to know that I'm here for you, and I'll help you make the transition, just as I had to make my own."

I'm no less lost, but I do trust him. He's my dad.

"This necklace is our secret." He reaches for it and then pulls back. "And you are to keep it hidden until you are ready to take it off for good. The necklace is on loan to you until then."

"I'll take good care of it." I smile, but he's staring at me. "Is this a special occasion?"

"Yes, sit back and I'll explain."

I sit back against the bench, and he puts his hand on my knee as if to steady me, but the result has the opposite effect. This whole situation is awkward.

"You know about Personal Reality."

My face must show my perturbance, but I keep my voice even. "Everyone knows about it, Dad. We've had it all our lives."

"I know you're familiar with it, but I'm not sure you know to what extent you're exposed. Each person alters their own reality, after all, dialing their choices for sensory details. You see what you designed to see. How do you know what's real?"

"Okay, well, let's see... I know the games I play aren't real and that I sense everything in the most optimal way. It's why Sol Luna-Nueva is always at peace."

"Good. That's all you need to know right now. Now, you mentioned the window changing this morning..."

I nod. He told me it didn't change, though now I'm wondering if he saw it too. Does that mean he lied?

He looks into my eyes. "You can tell me."

"Well..." I start slowly, "for a moment, the window was cracked, and the light shining through was blinding. Rather than looking like it always does, it didn't look nice. It was..." I can't find the word.

"Dirty? Weathered? Old?"

"Yes, that's it. Did you see it too? I thought it was a trick of the light. But if you saw it, too, it must have been a PR glitch. Is that what you meant when you said nothing changed?

He nods. "Not exactly. I did see it, though. Everything looked dirty and unkempt, but I'm used to it. It's the way things always look to me."

Dad must be under enormous stress. That's the only thing I can think of to explain his behavior. "That doesn't make sense. It doesn't look that way. Is your PR broken? Surely they'll reinstall it if you ask."

"That's just it, Liberty. I don't want the programming, and I hope you'll soon feel the same."

"What are you talking about?" I'm keeping my voice calm, but nothing he's saying is making sense. "PR is designed to enhance our life in every way. You're the watchman, the balancer—you give us a way to live life optimally. That's your job. At the academy, they tell us Personal Reality is the great equalizer: everyone gets to see the world in the best possible light."

He shakes his head. "No. That's what we've been told, but somewhere we lost contact with reality. We see the optimized version, not the harsh environment we're living in. Instead of building us up, it has become a facade we hide behind. It's not even close to the real world."

I laugh and scuff my feet on the ground in front of the bench. "Dad, we're basing our enhancements on something *real*. That's the first rule of personal reality: you can't make something out of nothing. We're only enhancing things, not recreating them."

Dad squeezes my knee to keep me from fidgeting. It does the job perfectly.

He's back to shaking his head, but this time he closes his eyes as well. "It's not nothing, it's worse than nothing. The time is coming when we will have to face reality again. I need to prepare you for the changes."

I'm not liking the tone of his voice. "What changes?"

"It's easier to show you than to tell you, but you must trust me. Do you trust me?"

Normally, I wouldn't hesitate, but now I have to think about it. Do I trust what he's saying? The short answer is no. It goes against everything I know. On the other hand, he's the man who raised me, sat by my bedside, and read me stories. He's supported me and loved me. I'll listen even if I can't believe it. I owe him that.

"Yes." The word fumbles out of my mouth, forced.

"I wanted to give you a glimpse. What you saw this morning was unenhanced. What you saw in those few moments was reality. How you truly live."

I freeze. That can't be right. I've spent my whole life in our house. He must have gotten confused during the glitch, and it reversed his reality.

"Dad, it was just a glitch." I pat his hand. "There's no need for concern, but you do need to report the incident at work. Things will go back to normal."

"Liberty, you aren't listening to me." He looks around again as if someone might be listening in, but there's nothing but the shrieking laughter on the carousel. "What you saw *was* normal."

"No. I mean, how can you know that? It's a matter of perspective, isn't it?"

"It is. I know your perception has been long distorted, and I've wanted to tell you for so long, but your mother insisted on giving you a perfect childhood. I can't mislead you any longer: it's time you knew. I've been waiting for the opportunity to get you alone so your mother can't listen. I gave you the first glimpse this morning."

"*You* did that?" Why would he create such an awful sight? "How? And why wouldn't you show Clarisse if it's true?"

"Your mother is far too integrated into the system now. She believes every lie in a way that it would threaten her to learn more. I hope I'm not too late for you."

It's all so much to take in, and I'm concerned about his wellbeing and what it means for our family going forward. I know he's been tired, but this behavior is unexpected.

Dad is clearly unwell.

Only people don't get sick in Sol Luna-Nueva. And they especially don't go mad. Even a hint of instability could cause some serious problems.

The carousel stops and the children get off and run back to the front of the line again. I'm watching while I'm listening.

"Do you want to see it as it is?"

Here we go again. "What?"

"The carousel."

I don't answer for a reason I can't put my finger on. I need to sort this out before Clarisse gets home and starts hearing about this real world.

Answering as delicately as I can, I say, "I want to see what you think is happening and why you think it's happening. But you can't turn off PR parameters. No one has that power. Even you."

"That's true to an extent. I can't completely turn off PR for the whole town, at least not yet. I don't have the power, but I know there are people who have that power and choose to leave us living in a fantasy world."

I've read about these in my history passages—conspiracy theories designed to keep people afraid, oppressed, and distracted. It's exactly the kind of behavior PR prevents. I never thought I'd hear one of these theories from my dad.

He continues. "I can't turn it off, but I can disrupt the signals. That's what I did this morning. It was a momentary blocking of your PR, so you might see for yourself how the world is, but I didn't have time to give you a full look around. And I didn't want to mess up your testing today. I thought it best to get away from the house before I show you again... But, mostly, I wimped out."

He puts his hand over his mouth and closes his eyes. "It's hard to take what looks like perfection from someone you love."

It occurs to me to let him talk it through. Maybe it will help him see how crazy he sounds.

"Okay... How did you do it?" I ask.

"At home, I blocked the PR signals used to transfer information from accessing your receiver. I can do it again here. You'll be the only one to see the changes, and everything will look different. Are you ready to try?"

I nod, because I need to play this out to see how far he's gone.

He stands and takes me by the hand, pulling me out of my seat and walking me to where I can now see the entire carousel. He takes the necklace and pulls the pendant around my neck to the back.

I'm about to ask him exactly what he's doing when I realize I'm no longer surrounded by the plush grass but hard, cracked soil. The bushes aren't green; instead, they're black vines that wind around rotten wooden posts. The light is bright, blinding, and I try to blink it away, but it's too much. My arm acts as a shield as I look at the sky, which is not blue but hazy with dust and filled with floating debris. There is trash everywhere.

Then I see the carousel. It's transformed. It's still a carousel, but it's ancient. A bulkish circle of metal that pokes up like giant heaps as the children climb onto the broken unicorns, the rusty fire engines, the sketchy benches. The structure is not going around, but swaying precariously in the breeze. It can't be real. It's far too destitute.

A man in a sloppy red-and-white painted suit jumps in front of my vision and starts doing cartwheels. He waves his hands and says, "Welcome to the Realsies, girlie!" As he sings, he steps in a short march, and the closer he gets, the more I back up.

I turn to see the moon is no longer a full orb in the sky, but a small globe a few hundred meters over the river. None of this can be true.

When I face my father, who still has me by the necklace, it's not him. It's a much older man with leathery skin, a pointy nose, and a weak chin. He says, "This is real. No enhancements."

My head spins. This is not my reality. It can't be true.

Overwhelmed, I turn to run. I feel the pull from behind as the necklace breaks from my neck and all turns back to normal.

But I'm not normal. Not anymore.

I reach full speed, running toward the safety of my house. I don't stop until I get to the front door. Only then do I turn to see if anyone has followed me, but no one has.

I don't remember passing through the front door and jumping up the stairs. But in no time, I'm in bed with my covers over my head, trying to shut it all away.

It takes a while before my breathing calms and I peek out. I'm not certain I didn't fall asleep between crying jags. It's dark, but all is quiet, clean, normal. I wonder if I dreamed everything.

A loud knock comes from the front door, making me jump. I wait for someone to answer, but the knocking continues. so I fold back the covers and carefully make my way to the living room.

A police officer stands under the yellow porch light.

"Liberty Moore?" the tall man says.

I nod, but before I can ask what he wants, the police officer speaks again. "You need to come with me to the station for questioning. I have reason to believe you were involved in a disturbance at the park."

CHAPTER 5

"Excuse me." Clarisse appears from behind me with her most commanding voice. "Is there a problem?"

"Yes, someone reported a crime in the park, and this young lady—"

"This young lady is my daughter. Her name is Libby."

"Yes, ma'am, but—"

"Mrs. Moore. Clarisse Moore." Clarisse says this with her eyebrows high, and I know that means she's getting angry, which doesn't bode well for the man.

"Oh, yes, Mrs. Moore, I'm Lieutenant Yates." He flips his badge to show us. "Witnesses saw your daughter running from the area where there was a disturbance a little over an hour ago."

Clarisse crosses her arms. "What crime is she charged with?"

"Nothing yet. We're still assessing the situation, but I wouldn't rule out assault."

My knees wobble beneath me. Assault? But I didn't hurt anybody.

"Who was assaulted?" I ask. It could have been anyone, but I can't help but think about Dad. He didn't follow me home.

Yates exchanges a glance with my mother, but he doesn't answer my question.

"What did the person look like?" I urge.

He puts his badge back on his belt. "I'll need a statement before I can give you any information, Miss Moore."

Desperate, I turn to Clarisse. "Where's Dad? Did he make it home?"

"Elizeus commed a half hour ago that they needed him for an emergency, so he left. But if there's any doubt, I'm sure the officer will verify it."

"Well, who was it, then?" I ask Yates, but he doesn't answer until Clarisse glares at him.

"We don't know for sure. All we have is an anonymous tip that someone attacked a man in the park. The caller rang for help but did not identify themselves or the person attacked. Several witnesses from the park identified your daughter as running from that direction, and we are here to gather more information."

"Well, I've been home all evening. My daughter has been resting in her room. She would have told me if she saw an attack, and you don't have any evidence, so you have no right to question her if she doesn't wish to comply." Clarisse's tone becomes more stilted with every step closer to the door. I move back toward the couch to give her space to confront the police officer.

Clarisse must have come in while I was sleeping, but why would she say she's been here the whole time?

"There's no way you have grounds for her arrest, so will there be anything else?" she says as she reaches the threshold.

"I have a duty to keep our citizens safe," Yates says, puffing out his chest, though even he can't hide the beginnings of Clarisse-induced doubt in his eyes. "I'll return with a writ in the morning. Until then, I advise you to keep your daughter at home and out of trouble."

Clarisse takes a few steps toward him, backing him down the porch steps. "I think you'll find I'm well thought of at the precinct. If you're smart, you'll not return."

The lieutenant starts to speak, but Clarisse slams the door shut before he can.

Stunned, I'm frozen until Clarisse says, "Good thing I left my meeting early. Not to worry, I'll get it worked out in the morning."

I feel like I'm about to collapse. Dad wants me to keep his secret, but things have gotten way out of hand.

"I saw something—" I begin, but Clarisse shushes me.

"Libby, I don't need to know the details to know you wouldn't harm anyone."

I exhale and nod. That makes me feel better. "You're sure Dad is okay? He was in the park with me."

She pats my shoulder and shushes me. "Elizeus is fine. He's just gone to tend to a work emergency." She rests her hands on her hips. "Now, it sounds as if you've had a long day, and I'm up to my eyes with fashion panels. Go upstairs and get ready for bed, and I'll bring up a cup of cocoa in a few minutes."

As much as I hate to admit it, she's right. There's no sense in working myself up about Dad's safety. As for the rest of it, I don't know what happened. And at this point, I don't want to know. A brief rest of my eyes and this horrible evening will end.

Trudging up the stairs with the last of my dwindling energy, I rub my eyes as I enter my room. Opposite me is my vanity; my skin is flawless in the mirror. I tussle my hair and it bounces back into shape. Always perfect.

I turn off the vanity light and look around for dust or degradation. But I see only my room, illuminated by the brightly shining moonlight entering through the window and stretching over my bed.

I take a deep breath. If Clarisse is sure that everything is okay, then everything else must be a misunderstanding. It has to be.

As for the police officer, Clarisse will clear it up tomorrow. If anything, she's efficient.

A slight tap on my bedroom door signals Clarisse's arrival. Still dressed in her presentation dress, she has slipped off her shoes and come up the stairs unheard. She places the cocoa next to my bedside. The milky chocolate steams in the small mug.

"Libby," she begins, "I don't know what happened with you today, but I want you to know that I'm here for you no matter what. If there's anything you need to tell me, I want to understand. On the other hand, sometimes we have off days and things get confused and miscommunicated."

She takes her hand and pats the top of my head. I craved that attention when I was younger, but now I'm older, it's weird.

I feel my eyes close for the briefest moment as what she said sits with me. Things can get confused and miscommunicated. That must be it. Dad is stressed about work; I'm busy with testing. We both added to each other's delirium.

A break. That's what we both need.

After a few sips of cocoa, I slide down between the sheets. Clarisse smiles and tells me to sleep well, shutting the door behind her.

The weight of the day and the soft light from outside send me to sleep.

CHAPTER 6

Before dawn, a click at the door awakens me. I start from the bed and check my bedroom door. It's unlocked. Was it locked before? Did mother lock me in?

I chuckle to myself. Of course she didn't. Why would she?

But the idea of being locked up reminds me that the police officer is supposed to return today. I hope the lieutenant has everything worked out by now. Maybe then he'll be able to give me some answers.

The thought settles my nerves until I see the clothes I laid out for my walk with Aden this afternoon. I forgot about our plans. After everything else, it seems muted, far away.

After I rinse off in the sink, I put on my favorite skirt and hair ribbon. Today, I adjust the color saturation to soft green with a light-yellow cardigan. In the mirror, my eyes are bright and shining, though they feel agitated. I look cute, even if I don't feel it. But I'm hollow, unlike myself. My feet don't have the same lift. I give myself a fake smile; and that helps a bit.

Bounding down the stairs, I see mother sitting at the table with chocolate pancakes. She's wearing a bright smile and sitting in her usual seat, but Dad's chair is empty.

I stop.

Clarisse told me he left for a work emergency; he's not back yet? The brooding expands over my chest.

"Where exactly has Dad gone?" I ask casually.

She lowers her coffee mug with a sigh, the brightness in her smile flickering. "Libby, we discussed this last night. Elizeus had an emergency and stayed overnight to attend a conference taking place today."

A conference? Dad never mentioned a conference...

"I expect him to be back late this evening. You'll see him tomorrow morning."

"Have you contacted him?"

"No, and I don't intend to, darling. He's at work, and he won't appreciate being bothered. The police haven't commed this morning, either. Perhaps they've found who they were looking for."

That, or they're afraid of Clarisse.

"Now, let's talk about me." She smiles as if she's about to burst.

"Your favorite subject..." I mumble, causing her to laugh.

It's true that Clarisse is self-absorbed. We all are, but Clarisse is her own bastion of self-glorification. But that's precisely what makes her so successful. She works hard and sells hard, and she's good at what she does.

"I won!" The news pops out of her as she throws out her hands. "I sold my first set of design panels for spring. They'll be in stores tomorrow, and your mother's name will be famous. Della will even model my clothes for the vidshot."

Clarisse mentions Della often. As the foremost celebrity in town, Della is my mother's idol, though they're also friends. The rest of us commoners know her as Della LaClare, gossip star and renowned advice guru. She is the epitome of wisdom, having come from humble beginnings. Someone that all can aspire to. But I don't pay her much attention; Clarisse's constant name dropping ensures any novelty in knowing her has worn off.

"Are you listening to me?" Clarisse asks.

"Sorry," I say, coming out of my stupor and forking a pancake on my plate. I pour syrup on it and take a bite as my mother continues.

"Della will be here tonight, so I have a lot to do. She wants me to design a few specific panels for her so her seamstress can sew them."

"That's great," I say with little conviction. Clarisse climbs an impossible mountain each day, and after a while, it's hard to ramp up the enthusiasm.

"I'm glad you think so, and because there's so much to do, I thought maybe you would like to help?"

I raise an eyebrow at her from across the table. "Me? I know nothing about design."

Mom laughs as if that's the least of her problems. "I know you don't; consider this an introduction to the skill. If you can pick up my sense of style, it may spare you from the more mundane work placements."

"Like Dad's?"

"I didn't say that." She gives another wide smile. "But you won't want the assessors to stuff you in an office, even if I design it. You'll want creative license."

A tinkle in my ear lets me know I'm getting a com.

"Excuse me," I say and turn my focus to the receiver. Clarisse pulls another pancake off the pile and slathers it with syrup. It globs off as she takes it into her mouth.

"Liberty?" Aden says.

My heart palpitates. "Yes?"

"Mind if I swing by and walk you to the academy? I had to deliver some produce to the mall, so I'm close. Is that okay?"

Definitely not.

My nerves flare again. "Yeah, sure. Give me five minutes." I disconnect the com and jump into action.

"Do I look all right?" I ask Clarisse.

Her eyebrows shoot up. "Why do you ask?"

I really don't want to explain it to her, because she'll probably dress me up like her.

When I don't answer, Clarisse continues. "You really are a lovely girl, Libby. You only need a modicum of help."

Wow. That's as close to a compliment as I'll get from Clarisse. Sure, she loves me, but I can't say she's very good for my self-esteem.

That's okay, though. I really am more like Dad, anyway.

When Aden arrives, I quit worrying about my appearance. From his expression, I'm well put together. And my yellow hair ribbon must make the perfect finishing touch, because he reaches out for it.

We greet each other in soft voices, then walk down the front walk toward the city center. Aden is quiet, so I remain quiet. Instead, I focus on the beautiful florals that line the walk and feel the spring breeze wafting through the bushes.

The bushes.

Yesterday, I saw them differently. They were black vine and wood instead of glorious and green. I reach out to touch them and find they feel hard in my hand.

"Woah, don't touch them." Aden grabs my hand. "There are thorns."

He examines my hand for a moment, and though I can feel the sting of where I touched the branches, my palm is clean.

"Got lucky that time," he says and puts my arm down.

When I look up, Aden's standing in front of me, looking like he's gazing at the most beautiful creature he's ever seen. That's the power of saturation and vision enhancement. Not that I'm ugly—beauty is in the eye of the beholder—but PR isn't hurting anything.

Now that I think about it, I suppose he's enhanced too.

"What?" he asks.

I realize I'm gawking at him and avert my eyes. "Uhm..." How do I explain that away? I turn to the yellow florals by the walkway. "Look at these florals. Have you ever picked one?"

"You know I haven't."

"Okay, so have you ever seen one picked?"

"Not personally." He's looking at me funny now. "But sometimes women get them at the mall when the gardeners come. Otherwise, we can't pick them. You know the rules."

"I do." He's missing the point. "What do they smell like?"

"Florals, of course," he says as if that explains everything.

My eyebrows sink as I think of a better way to phrase my question. "And... what do florals smell like to you?"

"They're... distinctive. All the plants are, especially the ones on the farm. They're... um..." His brows furrow; he doesn't know how to respond. In the end, he shakes his head. "I can't describe it."

"Neither can I, but it smells familiar, doesn't it? I associate it with the water in the washbasin."

"It smells like you," he says.

Before I can react to his statement, the pinstriped-suit man from yesterday confronts me as we pass the carousel, and I jump again. I can't explain how he keeps showing up out of nowhere.

"You've seen it now, haven't you? You dad will have some time fixing it, you know. Personally, I'm not sure he can do it."

I turn away from his taunt and cross the path to where Aden watches the carousel. Good. I'm glad for the distraction. If possible, I want to look normal for Aden. There's no need for him to know that one way or the other, Dad and I are possibly delusional. Actually, we all might be.

As I turn back to see that the man in the pinstripe suit has disappeared once more, a man wearing black-rimmed glasses walks toward us. It's weird, because you rarely see glasses these days. When I meet his eyes, he turns away. He doesn't look familiar at all, but as we pass, he reminds me of the smell Dad has when he first comes from work, before mother's florals blend with the smells of our house.

The man with the glasses stops and looks in our direction. I look over my shoulder to see what has captivated him, but I see nothing remarkable. When I turn back to him, I feel like there's recognition in his eyes—like he knows me.

Aden, who has stopped beside me, gently puts his hand on my shoulder; so that I turn to face him.

"Hey, you seemed to be in another world then. Is something wrong?" He brushes my hair back, and I work hard to stifle a smile that I can't deny.

"No. No. Daydreamer, what can you do?" I say.

He raises his eyebrows and smiles, looking at me straight on. "Look, I know we haven't spoken much, but I've been watching you for a couple of months now. I don't want to sound vain, because I know I have my faults. My family lives a quiet life on the farm, so my conversational skills aren't the best. But I'm nice looking, and I'm smart. A lot of girls have tried to get my attention."

Wow. It's all true, but it comes out as a little too confident.

My reaction must show on my face, because he sighs. "I'm just saying. I want to spend some time with you, and you could do a lot worse than me."

Again, *wow*.

His cheeks flush red, and he squeezes my hand. "I want to try us. See if we're compatible. Maybe it'll grow into something more."

"Okay," I say, even though he's reminding me of Clarisse. Still, vain or not, I'm lucky to have his attention. Does that make me the vain one?

"Good, that's... great! I'm glad," he fumbles, but his crooked smile is adorable.

It's all I can do to nod, because he's making me a nervous wreck. I don't know what to do with myself, so I turn and start walking.

"Oh, you found a *lovely*, didn't you?" It's the pinstripe man again. He's ahead of us now, bouncing the balls of his feet against the sidewalk and blocking our way. Unfortunately, he's also caught Aden's attention.

"Isn't he a fine looker?" Puck whistles. "With perfect hair and skin and big build? Would you like to know what he really looks like? I could tell you."

Aden listens for a moment, but somewhere around the middle, he realizes he's being mocked.

"Excuse me, sir, do we have a problem here?" Aden's muscles flex under his shirt. "Because if not, you need to stand down."

Puck laughs like a joke has been told, but Aden remains silent, and Puck soon realizes that he's serious, perhaps even a threat. He steps aside and lets us pass.

As we do, he whispers over my shoulder, "Looks can deceive, and don't you forget it. Your dad would want you to remember."

A shiver runs up my spine, but I don't turn to him or reply. It would escalate the situation. Aden takes my hand again and walks me to campus.

Puck has set me to worrying about Dad again. I'll do everything I can to stay awake tonight for when he comes in. Nothing will cure this hollow feeling short of seeing him.

We walk silently, but a few times I catch Aden looking my way. My thoughts are deep, and I imagine I must look like the saddest girl in the world, but by the way he smiles, you'd think I radiated joy.

I should be overjoyed, but there's the feeling of something missing. A space that Aden can't fill. Only seeing my dad will do that.

CHAPTER 7

Academy was another battery of tests. Most of it's a colossal bore, but today I was grateful for the distraction. My nerves are more at ease than they were this morning.

Usually, I'm the first one out of the academy door. But today I had a second test as an assessor, finding flaws in a pattern of numbers. I think I did pretty well. We'll see. I just wish I could tell Dad about it.

I can't stop thinking about what Puck said. Dad would want me to remember. He wouldn't have said anything just to alarm me; he must have thought it was important. All I can think about is him getting home tonight, so I can ask him what's going on.

It's off-putting that Dad never mentioned this conference. I will ask him about that too. Perhaps preparing for that was the source of his stress, and he'll feel better once it's over.

When Aden commed earlier, I was excited to hear from him, but it turns out he has to work on the farm this afternoon. That leaves me to walk alone from the academy. That's too bad. It's great to have his attention, and I'd love for others to see us together. It'll make me very popular with my friends.

I take my time as I pass the flag pole and leave the gates. I don't want another run in with the pinstripe man downtown, but there's no way to get home without passing him.

When I get close to where I normally see him, I cross to the other side of the road, only to find him sitting on a bench in front of me. I grit my teeth; I can't cross back again because people might think me odd. But it's too late. He's already looking at me.

Truth is, I don't want him to know he gives me the creeps, so I continue toward him with my eyes forward, though I can feel his stare like a pressure on my cheeks.

As I get closer, I step into the street to give him a wide berth and hold my breath.

Just as I think he may ignore me, he says, "Dreaming about beautiful people? Yes! I believe you are, but now you've seen us, you'll never be sure. You don't even know your own skin. Tsk. Tsk."

I stop and turn to face him. "Leave me alone," I say, channeling Clarisse's command. "I've nothing to do with you."

"Not yet, you don't. But the word is the colors are fading and the people are becoming restless. Restless enough for the big shots to notice. We're not looking for a battle, but a war. Did you see the moon?"

My mouth opens to say something, anything really, but no sooner do the words come up my throat than I swallow them whole. The moon had looked different, but so had everything else.

I shake my head, realizing I can't outwit this man. That's fine. He's not my responsibility. Best to leave him for the next passerby. I turn to leave.

"Wait until you see the view. It's quite a picture."

On the way home, I don't stop, but can't shake his words. They haunt me. I don't want to give them credence, but I can't help but tie them to yesterday.

The larger concern is that he's suggesting that other world might be real and not a glitch at all. That makes at least three people who have seen that destitute existence. What if there are more?

The pictures of the plastic moon, black vines, the run-down carousel flash through my memory. Things had looked awfully different in those brief moments, and if things were that bad in those short minutes, I can't imagine how bad it would be to witness them as full reality.

Personal Reality would mask a lot of things, making everything look okay when it's clearly not. I can't imagine living in that world. No one belongs there, not even the pinstriped man.

I need someone to talk to, and my best bet is Clarisse. I need to figure things out and the way to do that is to sit down with her and see what she has to say on the matter.

By the time I reach home, I throw open the front door and call for Clarisse. No answer.

I charge across the kitchen and check in her bedroom. She isn't there. The bed is made, but her favorite shoes and handbag are missing.

I drop my bag off on the landing hook before slowly heading back downstairs. In the kitchen, I find the note.

Libby,

Meeting moved to Della's. Sorry for the late notice. Will make a big breakfast for you and Elizeus in the morning, but for tonight, I'm afraid it's leftovers.

C

I open the cold storage and find a perfectly portioned plate of Carne Espana, but I leave the plate there. I'm way too anxious to eat.

As I close the cold storage, my eyes land on Dad's study door, and I realize I have a unique opportunity—and a distinct reason to take it. With no one home, I can look through Dad's library and hopefully get some reassurance about his trip.

I tiptoe across the living area, though no one is home, and put my hand on the doorknob, expecting to find it locked.

Surprisingly, it turns. As I push the door aside, a giant pile of papers topples to the floor, fluttering under the desk and over the shelves. Obviously meant to catch a snooper, they were sitting just behind the door.

I scramble to pick them up. With no way to get them back in order, I have to do the best that I can, grabbing thirty or so at a time and shuffling them into a pile. It is probably not as neat as the first pile, but it's the best I can do and still have some hope of having a look around. I anchor it with the butterfly ball.

I do pause long enough to smell the sweet scent of Dad's work coat. The whole room has his earthy vibe, and for a moment, it feels like I'm a little girl again, being picked up to ride the carousel. For a moment, his presence feels so real. I glance around to make sure he isn't standing there watching me, but I'm alone.

Pictures of the moon adorn the walls, all taken over the river at night. Whoever took the photos got it from several angles. All of them are stunning. I can't help but wonder if Dad took them. If so, I had no idea he was a photographer.

On his desk is a family photo and a few files that he's left out. Stacked in a neat pile are lots of file folders, large envelopes, and a small leather-bound work diary. Maybe he recorded his trip there. It's the reassurance I'm looking for.

I stop reverently before sliding into his well-worn chair. When I open the diary and thumb through, I find that it's a two-year cycle calendar. It takes a bit to get to the current year, but as I do, I notice that this month and the next have been ripped out. All I can see is the top end of a letter written in the margin. Maybe an "S." The following months are all empty, so I flip backward instead to a page of scribbled meetings. The word "PREP" comes up a lot,

and I try to place it in our conversations over dinner. Didn't my
father mention it?

In the study, there are no windows, and I suddenly get the feeling of it being very dark outside. I glance at the clock on his desk;
I should have at least another couple of hours of sunlight. That
means it'll be awhile before Clarisse even thinks about coming
home.

I replace Dad's diary where I found it and swivel around in his
chair to face the back of the room. There's a filing cabinet in the
corner that's made of polished wood. I tug on the top drawer, but
it's locked. I could probably use an envelope file to break in, but
then Dad would know I'd been snooping.

On a wide shelf behind the desk are books primarily devoted to
software, Dad's specialization, but there are a few on biology and
quantum coding. Nothing to get excited about.

But then my eyes fall on an old book without a title on the spine.
It looks heavy, but when I pick it up, it's lightweight. I open the
cover and see that it's hollow. A single envelope lies in the space,
addressed "*Clarisse*."

CHAPTER 8

I snap the book shut before my curiosity gets the better of me and put it back on the shelf.

But I don't remove my hand.

It would be wrong to open an envelope not intended for me, and it might contain intimacies that would embarrass them both, and me, but...

I set the book on the desk and slide back into the seat. One look at the clock helps me decide that I have plenty of time. Opening the cover again, I examine the envelope; it looks crinkly, as if it's been in a pocket. The shape indicates there may be more than paper inside, because it stands off the base of the book.

"*Clarisse.*" It's definitely Dad's writing; I can tell that by the notes he's written on his calendar. Maybe it's a surprise, or some unknown anniversary, or a celebration present for Clarisse's recent success. Whatever it is, it isn't meant for my eyes. Still, I lift the envelope out of the box.

There's something inside. I can feel the weight, but it's not very heavy. It feels very familiar in my hand.

I shake my head as I admonish myself to put it down again, but it's no use. My curiosity burns. I put my finger in the gap of the envelope and carefully pull the flap, trying to keep from ripping it. I have it almost open when I hear the tear and stop.

There's no going back now.

I purse my lips and hold the envelope on its side; the contents shift. I pull from the other side of the adhesive, but in the end, I've already ripped it. The flap comes loose, and I tip the contents onto the desk.

A necklace—and not any necklace. It has a long, pink crystal pendant attached: a replica of what Dad slipped around my neck before the whole world withered in front of me. But how did it get here? The one he gave me was lost in the park when I ran.

Without knowing why, I slide the clear wire over my neck, wrap my hands around it, and close my eyes. Sitting there for a second, I'm half waiting for something and half scared to open them again. Though logic tells me there's more to it than this; after all, I wore the necklace for an entire day at the academy without incident.

And when at last I pry my lids open, logic prevails: Everything is the same.

I flip the necklace to examine the clasp that opens and closes it. Nothing happens, so I turn back to the pendant. At the top of the long crystal is a metal band. I turn it.

My heart quickens. The atmosphere in the room has become heavier, and there's a smell in the air beyond Dad's earthy musk. Slowly, I look up.

Except for the messy pile of paper that I knocked over upon opening the door, the room is immaculately clean. The furniture, however, has transformed. The big wooden desk is merely an old handmade table that could use a coat of color, and the pictures on the wall no longer show the moon over the river, but now show a large manmade sphere. The different angles make sense now.

And there's one picture in the corner I didn't see before. It's a glimpse of another place. It looks like a large municipality, much larger than the one I live in, and there are high-rise buildings that overlook crowded streets where people come and go in plain garb. There are transports everywhere, and on the corner is a small building labeled "Coffee" next to a cup with steam rising from it. No one has bright hair or vibrant clothing; everyone looks somehow... What's the word? *Together*. It's as if they might be one big family. The picture mesmerizes me, but I pull away.

On the desk sit the files from before, but I now spot that one of them is labeled "PREP." That same word keeps coming up. *Why?*.

A knock. It stops my heart. I put away the book, tidy the papers, and head to the study door, terrified of what the living area may look like, much less the person outside.

As I pass through the study door, I get my first glimpse. Our beautiful living room is gone—a beaten armchair and a crooked couch lean where the nice ones used to stand. The window is broken, and the stench is so terrible that somehow, when I breathe in, it's as if I'm taking a huge drink of the dilapidated room.

As a small insect scurries along the embattled floorboards, the person knocks again.

When I open the door, it almost falls off the hinges. I look out into the glaring light. In front of the door is a broad chested mountain of a boy about my age, but with a leathery complexion.

"Hey, I finished up early. You up for a walk to the carousel?"

I stare at his shaggy blond hair, freckled nose, and I know immediately who he is.

"Aden?"

He shrugs like it's a stupid question. And I guess, to him, it is. "You think your parents will let you go?"

My first instinct is to slam the door. "Um, I can't even... I mean, I can't. Not tonight."

"That's all right, but can I pick you up tomorrow afternoon?" he asks with a sheepish grin.

"Yes, that'll be fine. Sorry, I have to go."

His eyebrows sink. "Hey, are you o—"

I close the door and lean against it. That's Aden. The real Aden? He seems so different. Not in a bad way, but in a foreign way.

And this? This is my beautiful house? My hand goes up in horror as I feel my own face. If this is the real world, then what do I look like?

No. I can't worry about that now. Time seems to have sped up. I need to get that file and find out what Dad has been up to.

I go back to the study and realize now, though the furniture is not in good shape, it's probably the only clean room in the house. Dad must have known for a long time that we were surrounded by squalor, but he kept quiet. This room has always been his sanctuary, and now I understand why.

Grabbing the PREP folder, I sit at the desk. I'm about to open the file when I see that the family photo that sits on the desk has changed. In a chair at the front of the photograph is the same man who grabbed me in the park. He has short salt and pepper hair, a pointy nose, and a weak chin, but I know it's him: Dad.

In the picture, he looks like he's combed his hair in preparation for the photo. He tried to show me his real self, but I couldn't handle it. I wince. He watched me run away from him. I rejected him.

That must be me on the left. Who else would it be? Putting my hand to my face, I can see that the curls I'm so proud of are actually a wispy web of hair, poorly cut. My hair isn't red. Instead, the plain brown waves fall just above my shoulders. And my eyes aren't blue at all, they are brown like my father's. Also, like my dad and Aden, I have leathery-looking skin.

I'm kind of plain, but if I'm honest, not ugly. I have about fifteen fewer pounds on me than I thought, and despite being unkempt, I'm cute.

Clarisse is another story all together. It's not that her hair is copper instead of fire red. Or that her skin is deeply tanned and cracked. It's the layers and layers of pale paint beneath bright-pink cheeks. All different from the rich colors I'm accustomed to. She must know on some level things are not as they appear. Why else would she coat herself in paint?

She's wearing a sweater with a little knot that bulges out at the top. The necklace. She's worn it before.

Everyone must look different, and they have no idea of how dirty and inauthentic they really appear. Well, except for Dad. Why would he keep it from us? How could he face us day after day?

I gasp, realizing for the first time that the special sigh he does before walking up the sidewalk is not relief at being at home or shedding off a hard day at work. He is sighing because he's walking into the filth of our house and his disillusioned family. My heart sinks with shame. I have so much to ask him, so much to apologize for.

But for now, I need to focus my attention on the PREP folder. Perhaps it will have something to explain exactly what's going on. It might tell me when Dad will be back.

I pull open the file and read the description:

"PREP: the Personal Reality Elimination Plan is a program designed to bring the citizens of Sol Luna-Nueva back to reality by eliminating the signal from the biome. It is our hope that our people can adapt without Personal Reality.

It is our wish that the people can reverse some of the damage done to the environment during this time. It is with great—"

"What are you doing in here?"

I nearly jump out of the seat as I snap the file shut.

Chapter 9

"Elizeus doesn't want us in here, Libby, and you know that," Clarisse says, arms crossed in the doorway. "So, once again, what are you doing in here?"

Thinking fast, I scan the room, looking for a likely excuse, but she's caught me like a butterfly in a net. I won't be able to wiggle free, and I can't even focus because of Clarisse's hideous face and eyes. To see the makeup and hair in 3D is definitely too much to take in at once. I start to cry.

"Come here, child." Clarisse beckons me toward her, but I can't find my feet to move. I'm faintly aware that I might be going into shock—a term Clarisse uses to discuss small let downs is actually a real thing. A cold chill runs down my back even as my heart thumps loudly in my chest, but I can't regulate my breathing.

"Libby, are you all right?"

Clarisse comes around the desk and takes my sweaty hands. Up close, my mother no longer smells floral, but rancid. It does nothing to help my rising nausea, but I follow her out into the dirty living room and up what now is a rickety staircase. It creaks as I take the first step, but I'm in no hurry. I'm doing everything to keep myself from falling apart, and for now, that means slow and even steps. Clarisse opens the door and turns on the single bulb in the center of the room, pulls back a battered blanket, fluffs a flat pillow, and helps me lie down.

"No pajamas for tonight. I think you've had a shock, but Elizeus will be here in the morning, and we can talk about this."

His name pulls me out of my stupor. Dad will explain everything in the morning, and I want nothing more than to understand.

Clarisse quietly leaves, and I don't move for a long time, until I feel the necklace, heavy on my chest. The necklace got me into this mess, and now it would have to help me out of it. Closing my eyes, hoping it will work, I fumble with the top of the necklace, grasping it between my fingers and turning the band.

In that instant, I'm back in my bed, back to the familiar. I do everything I know to push the other images away, but I fall asleep before I can manage it.

• • • ● ● • ● ● • • ·

For a few hours, I sleep well, my body exhausted from the shock, but during the night a thud downstairs jolts me awake. I hate walking in the dark, but I'm hoping it's Dad. When I run down the stairs, I'm confronted by the front door, swinging lazily in the breeze funneling down our street.

Strange.

"Dad?" I call, but there's no answer.

I turn from the kitchen and see a light on in the study. "Dad?" I call again, more cautiously this time. For a moment, I think I hear somebody shuffling about, but then all falls silent.

I swallow hard and walk closer.

As I reach the study door, a bright light hits me in the face, and a large shadow jumps from the doorway. I freeze, blinded by the flashlight in the figure's hand. He rushes me, knocking me to the floor. When I sit up, the glint of the flashlight shines on the intruder's glasses as he runs toward the front lawn.

My heartbeat is on a fast track, and for a moment, it's like I'm glued to the floor. But when I realize the man might return, I get to my feet and look out the front door. The street is still, not a shadow moves.

Whoever the man in glasses was, he's as likely to have run down the street as to be lying in the bushes in wait.

I pull back inside, closing the door, then look out the wooden blinds, trying to catch sight of the late-night intruder.

What could he want? There's no call to steal when there's enough for everyone.

A loud crash makes me jolt away from the window, but it sounds like whatever it was is far down the street. I exhale slowly and turn to face our living room. There's not much light, but everything looks in place, aside from Dad's study door, left ajar. The dim light from inside illuminates the kitchen table.

Maybe I should wake Clarisse. An intruder is on the prowl. Or at least there was until I scared him, and he scurried off into the night.

On the one hand, the man could come back. On the other, she'll kill me if I interrupt her beauty sleep. And it's not as if Clarisse could stop him, and the police won't be able to do anything now the man is gone.

I look back at the study door. Dad will be home in a few hours. He'll know what to do.

If only there was a way to lock the door... Instead, I take a heavy vase and push it against the wood. Only the vase is lighter than it looks, and it makes no sense from its size and material.

I could turn the necklace, and see what's actually there, but no. I'm not going through that shock again unless Dad is by my side to explain what I'm seeing. I hadn't completely heard him out, and there is obviously much more to the story than I thought.

With my ears on high alert, I climb the steps and look out onto the street from my window seat. The intruder appears to be long gone, though I watch for a few minutes to be sure. When nothing happens, I slip off my clothes and pull my floral nightgown over my head. Sliding into the warmth of the bed, I pull the covers tight around my ears, as if that will give me an extra level of protection.

I drift off, imagining Dad's warm smile at breakfast in the morning. I rarely ask, but tomorrow I'll request a big hug. It'll be such a relief to see him.

CHAPTER 10

When I hear voices downstairs, I jump up and throw on my robe as fast as I can. My adrenaline is so high that I misbutton it and have to start again. Dad's home, and I can finally breathe easier.

I step onto the landing, but I stop there. My heart is about to beat out of my chest, and I realize that I'm scared. Is he going to look right to me? Will everything be normal? I want to see him, but I'm afraid of what news that may bring, what reality will unfold.

I listen.

"Would you like some more coffee, Elizeus?"

"No, thanks. There's a pot at work; I'll get some there."

She gives a broad smile. "You've eaten as big a breakfast as I've ever seen. Did they starve you at the conference?"

"No, no. There's just nothing like coming home. The road takes a lot out of a person."

I listen, comforted by my parents' morning routine. Clarisse's chair pulls out, and I hear the spoon in her coffee. I picture her how I know her, deeply burying the wispy memory of her caked in makeup. Now Dad is home, things can go back to normal.

As I hit the bottom of the landing, Clarisse is putting her cup back in the cabinet, and Dad is sitting in his usual spot, reading the morning paper. I freeze.

"So," my mother starts. "Tell me what the new PR enhancements are. Della will be dying to know."

"Unfortunately, we mostly worked on bugs and glitches. But the biggest thing on the agenda was possible beta testing for mutual holiday getaways. The prototype location is a beach with retreats by the seaside, but there are others being developed. All in planning. Speaking of which, I expect my day to look different today. We're doing some restructuring, so my job duties might change a little in the upcoming weeks."

He puts down his paper to grab his napkin and sees me standing there.

"There's my girl. Did you miss me?"

Before he can finish the sentence, I run to him and throw my arms around his shoulders. I hold tight until he pats me on the top of my head.

"Let go of your father, Libby. Sit down and eat something, so you'll be ready for testing this morning. Elizeus needs to go to work."

I let go, carrying the sweet earthy scent of his jacket to my side of the table. Clarisse loads my plate with scones and jelly and fried beef chips, but I'm far too excited to eat.

"I missed you, Dad. The police mentioned an assault in the park. Then we had an intruder last night, and I thought it was you. I'm so glad you're home."

"An intruder?" Dad asks.

"I never heard a thing," Clarisse says, shaking her head. "Libby has been letting her imagination run wild. It's caused a bit of trouble."

Clarisse gives me wide eyes, and I know she wants me to come clean before she has to tell on me. I put down my fork and clear my throat.

"Dad, I went into your study. I was looking for your diary to assure myself you were on a trip, and I'm sorry. It's just... after we spoke the other night, I had lots of questions, and you weren't around to answer them."

His lips tighten, but it doesn't diminish the smile in his brown eyes. "Well," he says, "did you find anything interesting?"

"Uhm..." What am I to say to that? If I mention the PREP folder, we'll have to talk about precisely the thing I'm trying to forget. I need to trust his judgment, to know he's got the situation under control. That way, I can let go of any responsibility. Go back to normal.

I know I'm taking too long to answer, so I pull out the only other thing I can remember. "No, only that your calendar has two months of data missing, and that there's a family photo I hadn't really seen before."

At this, he laughs. First, it's quiet, but eventually it's full and robust, and, to be frank, a little scary. But the smile never leaves his eyes.

"Sorry, I'm so boring. Afraid old Dad doesn't have much excitement." His face stills as he cocks his head and looks at me. "But we have a rule about that room, don't we?"

For a second, I think he's really asking me, but Clarisse nods her head, and he resumes. "It's my workspace, and you shouldn't tamper with it. The files may not look like much to you, but they're vital to my work. You're not to be in there without my permission. No exceptions, okay?"

"Yes. I'm sorry. I was just so worried. I promise it won't happen again."

"That's fine and well," he says, "but I think there should be some repercussions."

I nod. I can't really complain, after all.

Clarisse scoots back from her plate. "I have an idea, if it suits you, Elizeus. I have to go into town this morning, and I'd love to show you my new display. You can drive me and we'll let Libby put up the morning dishes."

"Yes, I can do that," I smile, knowing that I got off easy. "But I need to get dressed first."

Clarisse waves her hand. "Go on, then."

I push from my space at the table, disregarding my uneaten breakfast, and leave the kitchen.

Upstairs, I dress into my favorite blouse and summer sweater and run my hand over my red locks to make sure my hair is in place. For an instant, I remember my image in the picture. I run my fingers through my curls, smoothing them out. It's strange to know they are there, but I can't feel them.

I bring my hand down when I remember my hair isn't red at all, but brown. Forgetting isn't going to be as easy as I hoped.

I arrive at the foot of the stairs as Clarisse clicks her way across the house in high heels. "See you this afternoon, darling," she says as she exits the garage door.

Dad must be right behind her, because I hear him call, "Have a good day, Libby."

My lips form a goodbye, but no sound comes from my mouth. It's as if I have no air at all. Dad has never called me Libby as far back as I can remember. He doesn't do it because he loves the name he gave me. He only calls me Liberty.

It's such a small detail, but it brings with it a deep worry.

Something is off.

I remember the necklace and pull it out. I don't want to return to that horrible world, but I have to know.

Turning the top of the necklace, I watch the rich molding on the door become rough-hewn pieces of wood, and the door is once again old and ill-repaired. I rush outside, hoping to see my parents as they exit the garage, hoping to see Dad up close.

Squinting into the blinding light of the outdoors, I watch the rusted transport pulling from its port. I can't see Clarisse's side, but in the driver's seat is not the Dad I've grown up with, nor is it the man from the park and photo. This guy is hunched over the steering column with a younger face.

That's not Dad. So where is he? And who is this man impersonating him?

Watching this imposter and Clarisse drive down the street in a banged-up transport, I notice that the hedges are no more than thorny vines. The lawn is scorched, and the blue sky is an impenetrable haze that glows down like a supernova. The sweet florals are high weeds that look dry enough to catch fire. Can this all be real?

I walk to the street to get the first full picture of my house. It's so dilapidated that it looks like the second story is melting into the first. The windows are cracked, and the siding is a cheap, coarse wood, somewhat painted white. Two painted five-point stars, one in a bright yellow and the other red, flank my bedroom window.

I freeze, trying to make sense of all the lies as they stack up. It's more than I can take, but it isn't going away. I'm so confused by what I've seen and not seen, but mostly missing Dad and wondering what's happened to him.

As I stand there, my fists tighten and my shoulders tense. I can feel the fury creep up my arms and into my face. Not only do I live in squalor, but my whole life is a lie. I'm second-guessing everything I know. But more than that, much more than that, I must face the fact that the man sitting at the table this morning was not Dad. Someone has replaced him. The man who named me and tried to teach me the ways of this twisted world has disappeared.

A loud noise cracks as someone rips through the bushes and heads toward the next house. It's a big man wearing thick glasses and mismatching clothes. It's the man from the park. He's the intruder!

"Hey!" I shout.

I chase after him, but the slides flop off my feet, and the pavement is too hot.

"Who are you?" I yell as I watch him pass the fountain and turn out of sight.

It's the third time I've seen this man. That's no accident. Maybe he knows something about Dad's disappearance. I try to run again but find that between the crying and the frustration, I'm breathless. Still, I make it to the fountain, but the man is nowhere to be seen.

I plop down on the rock basin with tears in my eyes when a large black bug flies toward my face. I swat it, hitting its big leathery wing, and pull my hand back in disgust. A different one dive bombs my mouth, and I jump up and back away. They surround the sludgy fountain. They must have eaten... No, they must *be* the butterflies.

Everything is crazy, none of it familiar. More tears spill as I walk back home.

I don't have time to feel sorry for myself, but I don't have the strength to overcome it, either. How am I ever going to find Dad if I don't know what I'm up against?

I'll need help. Clarisse seems unaffected by Imposter, so it'll be hard to convince her otherwise. Unless I give her the necklace, which I promised Dad I wouldn't do.

I need the police; they're my best bet. But the only person I really want to see now is Dad—my real one. Tears roll down my cheeks and land on my blouse. When I look down at myself, my clothes are not what I thought I put on. I'm wearing a frayed skirt, a ripped blouse, and a pilled sweater, along with the big clunky shoes I found on the porch.

I need to do something, but what? I can't go inside. This is hardly my house anymore, and though that is a horrible feeling, my first response is a maniacal laugh.

Whoa, Liberty. You're losing it.

I bury my face into my leathery hands, feeling its roughness beneath my calloused fingertips, and take several deep, calming breaths. Though with each one, I only bring in more of the smoggy air. How have I been breathing this my entire life?

I've got to figure out what's going on, but first, I need an excuse note from the academy. That will give me a chance to work things out today.

I dust a little dirt from my skirt and start moving down the sidewalk.

At the farthest end of the street, the fountain is not much more than a container of water with a piece of wood in it. Black vines wrap around the stick and drape across the muddy water. Gnats hang in the air, swarming the stagnant water as large insects fly around in erratic circles.

I tell myself it's okay, but it's a lie, like everything else.

When I arrive at the carousel, it's as it was the night Dad disappeared. Desolate and littered, the park is no longer the same.

Ahead, the baked paint colors the buildings in the city center. The storefronts are covered in old letterings in unfamiliar languages, spray-painted graffiti, and a few more five-point stars in yellow, red, and blue. Before I realize it, I'm walking toward them.

Yesterday, the shops were sleek steel and mirrored glass, tall and pristine. But today, they look impossibly old, as if they're leaning on each other. Most of the buildings bear the mark of businesses past—probably before the virus came. Along the storefronts, there's a deli, a grocery, a watch shop, a bank.

A sun decorates the bank. Not a likeness of the blaring haze above me, but of a yellow sun with rays bursting from it. It's the sun of the charmed world I knew before the PR could turn off.

I run ahead to look into a window when a man moves onto the sidewalk from an alley. I know him as soon as I see him. Wearing his white suit with red lines painted on, Puck is still tall and slim, but his hair is a white mop on his head. There's no sense in hiding. He's seen me, as he always seems to.

At about ten meters away, he calls to me. "Ah, well, now you can see me for what I am, can't you? Isn't it lovely, girlie? All the trash and debris piled on from years of neglect?" He holds his hand out, like he's proud of this broken-down world.

"Who do you want, Puck?" I ask.

"I prefer the name Plucky, but since most people call me Puck, I'll let it slide." He smiles; his teeth are long and yellow. "I've got a secret. Do you want to hear it?"

I turn around to see if anyone is watching. I'd feel safer to know we're being watched by one of the park-goers.

"Most of them don't see me, girlie. But you still have your PR values on. They can still see you as before. Lucky, you don't blend into the background—not yet. The only reason anyone sees me is my signature suit." He runs his hands over his lapels.

He's right. No one seems to be paying us much attention. He taps me on the back and tightens his shoulders, giving a little shudder of excitement.

"You and I are now in the same situation. We aren't getting any younger or healthier, and the world is literally falling to pieces. Did your father tell you? We are almost out of time."

Dad. Puck knows him! "You know my dad. Have you seen him?"

"Not today, but I knew him for a long time; he brought me food now and again. It's so hard to keep that PR slop down, and the smell is terrible. Have you seen it yet?"

I don't know what he's talking about, but I'm very aware that he answered my question with the past tense.

"You said 'knew.'" My voice trembles. "Did... Did something happen to him?"

Puck clucks his tongue. "I saw him with you near the carousel. I don't like the noise, so I was closer to the other side of the park when I saw you together. He gave you the necklace."

"Yes! I lost it that night. Do you know what happened next?"

He laughs, slapping his leg like I'd told a hilarious joke. "He turned that pendant, and as soon as you saw him, you ran. It's been years since I've seen one of your kind in any great hurry! What a sight! He chased after you with his arms waving, and I was having a good laugh until he fell into the dirt. He lay there for a few minutes before I realized he had keeled over."

I know what *keeled over* means, but this eccentric man speaks differently to anyone else, so I hold out hope by asking, "What do you mean 'keeled over'?"

"He slapped dirt, bit the dust, leaned on the horizontal—"

My impatience flares. "What does that *mean*?"

"He fell over. Kaput."

Despite the sunlight, my vision fades to black as my balance leaves me.

Kaput. I know the word well from my vidclips. *Kaput* can mean dead, but I'm uncertain that's what Puck is saying.

I don't know how I make my way to the cracked concrete step and sit, because my breath is coming in heaves. I try to push it all away, every bit, but the thoughts won't stop bouncing around behind my eyes.

"What happened next?" I ask carefully, not sure if I can handle the answer.

"Next minute he was gone."

Gone. There's a vacuum around me. The air disappears, time stops. All I can think is that I pushed him away. I ran when I should have believed in him. I was reluctant to hand over my worldview, my comfort zone. Here I am in the gritty pollution, learning that this is what came between me saving Dad, or at least a chance to say goodbye.

"Do you mean gone as in *disappeared* or gone as in *dead*?"

He tilts his head to the side. "Oh, girlie, what's the difference, really?"

I huff as I throw my head back. He's not making sense, and I need answers.

"Why won't someone tell me what's going on! Where is he now? Did someone move him?"

Puck raises his eyebrows at me as if the answer is obvious. "The police, of course."

"Where did the police take him?" I plead, but the old man laughs.

"They headed to the suburbs toward the living quarters, but that's all I can say. Here one minute, forever gone."

As if demonstrating, he steps back and walks in the opposite direction.

"Wait!" I call, but he whistles as if he hasn't torn the ground from my world and left me in freefall.

He can't be right. The police would have told his family—us. I would know, wouldn't I? No. I need a more reliable source.

Clarisse. I could ask her, but she's with Imposter. There's no one to confide in.

I'm trembling all over by the time I reach the campus. Students are shuffling through the gate, past the flagpole, toward the building. Everyone looks vivid, almost electric, and I miss their carefree gaits and misinformed content.

I feel like weeping, but instead, I ball my fists and tighten my jaw. For every face, there's another lie, though they have no idea what's happening beyond the programmed view.

Overwhelmed, I scream, "Who are you people? Is everything a lie?!"

I continue to scream at the leathery-looking people who pass me by. They can't even see me anymore because I have become plain without my enhancements. I even grab one girl by the shoulders, but when I do, she says, "No, thank you," and bows her head before continuing her approach to the academy.

"Stop!" a voice shouts across the campus.

I turn a full circle, trying to figure out where it's coming from. I'm about to start the second turn when I hear it again.

"Stop drawing attention to yourself. It won't help anyone."

A girl stands at the base of the flagpole. She's sitting on the concrete block and looking straight at me.

CHAPTER 11

I t's the girl I saw at the carousel—the one who was watching me at my window. But I can see her better now than before; she's clearer and not as plain. With black hair and long legs, she's wearing clothes as old as everyone else's. But she's tucked her shirt in and has a metallic barrette pulling back her carefully combed hair.

"You... you can see me? The real me?" I ask.

"You're real enough." The girl hops off the block and walks my way. "I've watched you come in every day for a week, looking as raggedy as anyone here. You still don't look that hot, but you've detangled your hair, which indicates a level of self-awareness I've not seen before."

She holds out her hand, and I don't know what to do with it. After an awkward moment, she pulls it back and says, "My name's Byz."

"I saw you on my street." I tell her. "Do you live nearby?"

"I walk all over town," she snaps. "If I was near your house, it was a coincidence."

"Okay..." I murmur, uncertain why that made her so jumpy.

She studies me for a moment, her mouth pulled to the side. "Are you okay?"

I snort, but not in humor. "Well, everything is upside down, and a stranger told me my dad is gone. But I don't believe him. I don't know who to believe." I wipe my eyes, refusing to cry again. "Are we friends?"

"Not really." She folds her arms over her chest, taps her finger against her elbow. "Well, not anymore. You don't notice me anymore. I don't stick out like other people, because I don't belong in your world. To you, I'm too plain. Unenhanced. It used to hurt my feeling that people were that way, but over the years I've grown accustomed to it. I've learned to entertain myself."

"I've only known about this reality for a few days... When did you turn off your PR?"

She raises her brow. "Actually, I never had it. I don't technically exist in the other world. My parents kept my birth a secret so the authorities couldn't put in the programming. Your parents decided to go along with it—mainly because of your mother, I think."

"Wait, you know my parents?" I barely get the words out of my mouth when a boy runs into me. The girl grabs my arms and pulls me out of the way of another boy, who isn't paying any attention to where he's going.

She reaches out and steadies me. "You'll get used to that." She dodges out of the way as someone almost runs her over. "But yeah, I've known your parents my whole life. Met them many times when we played together as kids. Some of my best memories, really."

"We played together? Then you know my dad? Do you know where he is?" My voice is desperate, but I don't care. I've got to figure out what's going on.

Byz shakes her head and frowns.

"I'm sorry," I say lightly, hoping she won't snap again. "I don't remember you. Where is it we've met? Here?"

"No, not here." She takes a big breath. "We've talked. Many times, in fact. My dad and your dad work together." She rushes her words to correct herself. "Truman Lawson. Ring a bell?"

"Yes, of course it does. I've known him my whole life, but I haven't seen him since Dad stopped picking me up from the care center. Maybe he knows something about where my dad is?"

Her lips press together, but she nods. "We can ask him. He's my father. I'm Sage."

"No, you're not." I frown. "I've known Sage since I was a toddler, and she looks nothing... Oh." My eyes widen.

"You don't look the same either. You've grown, for one thing."

I feel like an idiot for not realizing immediately. Sage. Not a close friend like the ones I have at school, but we spent a lot of time together as kids while our dads were working on their projects. I remember her dark hair, but she's trimmer and more athletic than she was as a child. I wonder how different I must look from then.

Wait. She can claim to be anyone she wants. How would I know one way or the other? "How can I be sure you are who you say you are?" Remembering she introduced herself as Byz, I ask. "And for that matter, why are you going by a different name now?"

"We changed my name a few years ago when we had a run-in with another townsperson who found out my first name and threatened to turn me in." She shrugs. "After that, my parents started calling me by my nickname. I kind of prefer it. Sounds complex, out of the ordinary. Your name is not common, either. Dad said your father named you, and your mother liked the sound of it."

I cross my arms. "If you're who you say you are, why did you quit talking to me?"

"Hello?" She puts her hands on her hips. "You quit showing up with your father, and you stopped noticing me. *You* quit talking to *me*."

"Maybe... None of that proves who you are. Why should I believe you?"

"I was there when you fell off of the jungle gym by the river, although it was actually a mound of chicken wire. Your dad picked you up and kissed your arm to make it better while my mother put a bandage where you scratched yourself."

"Huh..." I say. It was a long time ago, but it hurt bad enough that I remember it well. "I guess you are who you say you are... I liked your mom; she always gave me gummy bots when I was little."

"Yeah, that sounds like my mom..." Her voice trails off, like she remembers them too.

I stare at her, trying to reconcile what she looks like now compared to the girl I remember. She's changed too much for me to see it.

I wave my hand toward the dilapidated academy building where I've been testing. "What's the use of testing if none of it is real. Will the academy do me any good now?"

She shakes her head.

"And... this is how the world's been your whole life?"

"Nah, not really. It gets worse every year, so it's always been bad, but never this bad. Our fathers keep the PR maintained and functioning, so the rest of you can get on with your delusional lifestyle."

Wow. Dad is responsible for this... How is that possible? "I know he works with programming, but that's all. I know he keeps things running. I just didn't realize that what's running is fake."

Byz's frown is sympathetic. "Our fathers make sure the PR runs as seamlessly as possible." Her face is expressionless except for the sadness in her eyes. She seems disappointed that I don't remember her.

"Why are you at the academy if no one knows you're alive? You don't need to take part."

Byz shrugs. "I may not get much interaction, but I need people. That, and my father is gathering information on PR enhancements, and I can slip into the assessors' conversations and overhear the latest features as they are introduced to general use. This week is lucid dreamscapes, but only the betas have them. Are you a beta?"

"I am. Was. I don't know anymore. I'm confused, angry, and doing what I can to push off a complete meltdown."

"It's a shift, a jarring change, but hardly a reason to have a meltdown." Byz turns back to the Academy's entrance. The crowd has thinned out. "You'll learn to live and adapt, just as everyone else has done. Lean on your family. They'll help you adjust."

"But I can't lean on my family. My mother is delusional and Dad is…" I can't say it; saying it will make it real. And that's the reality I can't take.

Byz nods her head solemnly. "Gone?"

CHAPTER 12

My heart leaps into denial. There's no body, but there's no sign of him either. The anonymous caller had called it an assault, not murder. But why replace him with a replica if he's alive and well?

I stop myself. If my dad was dead, I think I'd know. It would be like losing a limb. He must still be alive. I will not entertain another thought.

Bathed in the white light of the blazing sun, I look at Byz. "My dad is missing, and I can't get any answers." I'm numb.

"Here, I'm sure you have a lot of questions." She hands me a flyer for the spring panel show at the mall. Ironically, my mother is the featured stylist. "Meet me there in a few hours, and I'll help you understand."

I hold on to the paper as Byz walks away from the flagpole and out of the gate. I watch her until she is out of sight. Turning around, I look at the austere academy. I don't want to be here. I'm in no mood for testing for a fake future.

With no other game plan, I enter the academy building, trying to make sense of how dilapidated it looks compared to the sleek facility I'm used to. It looks like it could fall around me.

There's a hard lump in my throat. I feel absolutely alone, and I just watched the one person who knew what's going on walk away.

But it's more than that. I've lost track of the person who matters most to me. I lean my back against the corridor wall, trying to anchor myself, but I end up sliding to the floor as my heart cries out.

People pass by, not seeming to notice me as I tuck my head into my knees and cry until the hall is clear and the test coordinator comes down the hallway, nearly falling over me. She gives me an excuse pass and sends me home with a warning to return ready to work or face the consequences. No sympathy from anyone—except Byz. I need to meet her.

From the academy, I turn in the direction that Byz did; a direct course to the mall. But first, a stop: the police station. Puck has roused my suspicion of them. I want to figure out if they know any more. It's a little risky, but I have to try. Until I talk to Byz again, it's my only lead.

As I walk into the city center, I feel fortunate to not run into Puck before I reach the police station; a small building surrounded by dead bushes. It's an old storefront, because painted letters above the door read: GROCERY. Windows line the front of the building. Most are in disrepair. Above the windows are two Red Stars.

I open the door, step in, and a bell chimes. I jump, but before I back out, the door slams behind me. On the dirty tiles where the shelving used to be, there are now partitioned walls that go back pretty far. On the rear wall is a large shelving system that is no longer in use. I walk up to the one desk not in the chest high maze of partitions and wait.

A woman from several stalls back pokes her head over the wall; she's barely tall enough to see me.

"Be a second. Take a seat, and I'll get to you soon."

"Yes, ma'am." I answer, and as I sit down, I realize that her blond hair is neat. Maybe she sees me as I am, too. I run my hand through my hair, as if it will do any good.

The chair has a crack running down the seat, which pinches me. I take a newspaper from the windowsill and place a piece under me. The rest I pick up to read.

The date reads "July 4th, 2025"; that's almost ninety years ago. The headlines read about new discoveries in wet programming, virtual reality, and bioengineering. I'm about to read an article titled "Climate Peril" when the woman stands again and walks to the front.

"Sergeant Everson. How can I help you?" she asks.

Now that I get a closer look at her, she's wearing an old checkered suit with a red flower embroidered on the lapel. She looks to be outside PR. She must see me for who I am, though she says nothing about it.

I swallow and drop the newspaper. "There was an attack a few nights ago by the carousel, and I wonder if Lieutenant Yates found a body or has new leads in the case."

"Look, we haven't had a murder case in years, hon. People are too self-involved to concern themselves with anyone else." She picks up a pen and starts clicking the top.

"But the lieutenant said there was an assault, and my dad was near there. He's been missing ever since."

"What is your father's name?"

"Elizeus. Elizeus Moore."

"Oh, you must be Clarisse's daughter." She's suddenly looking at me with eyes half open, sneering down at me. Her expression is disappointed, as if I'm twelve and just ate the last cookie. "Yeah, we got a complaint about an assault in the park, but when the officer questioned the witnesses, they weren't very reliable. Let me see." She waddles toward the desk she had been sitting at before, and I hear her shuffling things around. "Here it is."

She's reading the file as she comes to the front. "Yeah, an anonymous com and a few witnesses that couldn't give any specifics, except for the vagrant that lives out near the city center. He said he saw something, but he isn't exactly reliable, either."

Puck. I'm instantly reassured that the woman thinks he's unreliable. But if he's wrong, where is Dad?

She clicks her pen again. "Lieutenant Yates followed up at the Moore home and was told that the suspect was resting at the time of the incident." She raises her eyebrows at me, then drops her gaze back to the paper. "Says here, Ms. Liberty Moore expressed concern for her father's welfare. The vagrant corroborated her concern. But then, Lieutenant Yates verified with the authorities that Mr. Moore had been called away for a work emergency and subsequently was to take part in a conference. It was determined that Mr. Moore would be home today in the early morning. With no victim and no suspect, the case was closed."

This is the point I need to make. "A man showed up, but he's not my dad. He's got everyone fooled, even my mother, but I know he's not the same man. Also, a man with glasses broke into our house last night. I saw him in the park yesterday morning, too. The two incidents must be connected."

The blank look on her face gives me pause. She takes in my hair and clothing, scanning me from top to bottom. "Is your PR operational?"

"Yes." It's not exactly a lie. Dad told me that the signal was only being disrupted.

"It's against policy to not use the required system software. Without it, the crime rates go up, the food sources deplete, and the public becomes restless." She sounds like she's reciting from a manual with her flat voice. "It's illegal to tamper with the software. It is there for your protection, but it also serves the greater good."

She's peering over her nose at me, as if asking me a question that she doesn't want to verbalize.

"Yes, ma'am. I'm aware of the benefits of PR, but at the moment, I'm more concerned about my dad. I'm worried someone might have hurt him."

"Why do you think that?" She stops clicking her pen and looks at me with dull eyes.

"A man at the park told me you..." I swallow hard. "I mean, the police took him, but I'm not certain I believe him. Then, there's the man who broke into my house. But mostly, it's that Dad's gone when he should be home."

"Tell you what... Lieutenant Yates is off duty, but the shift is changing in a couple of hours. I'll leave him a message and have him follow up with a home visit to make sure everything is on track at your house and that your dad is indeed who he says he is.

"In the meantime, I would advise you to be cautious about making unfounded accusations. They will disrupt the neighborhood and cause a great deal of attention to fall on your family, and on you, in particular. Do you understand me?"

I nod, but I can't find words to answer, not sure if she is threatening me on purpose or as a byproduct of concern. Either way, I'm not going to get any answers from her. I need to wait for Lieutenant Yates.

CHAPTER 13

With a couple of hours before the deputies are on duty, I strike out to find Byz at the mall. Hopefully, Imposter and Clarisse will have concluded their errands. They're probably already sitting in the coffee shop, where Clarisse will go on about her style panels.

It occurs to me that Imposter must know what happened to Dad. He must. It's something to explore if I ever get to see him close.

I walk to the back entrance of the mall for two reasons. The first is I don't want to risk accidentally being caught by Clarisse and Imposter. The other is that the front entrance looks like it's barely standing. When I get to the other side, I find Byz waiting on the curb, sucking on a lollipop.

She startles when she sees me and jumps up off the curb. "I wasn't expecting to see you so soon."

"So, why are you already here?"

She doesn't meet my eyes. "My dad was supposed to come pick me up, but he probably got caught up in his work. Here, have a lollipop. My mom made them."

"Thank you. But since we're at the mall, we should get some real food. Let's go into the food court and get a bite," I offer.

"No, that's a full pass." She throws her hands out as if she's distancing herself from the idea. "I've got something else." Then she drops her hands and cocks her head to the side. "Wait a minute, have you seen it since you lost your PR?"

"Seen what? Everything is different," I sigh.

Byz shakes her head. "No, the food. It's a nightmare."

"It can't be that bad."

"You'll regret saying that," she says. "C'mon. I'll show you."

As we approach the building, the glass door slides open, but no one has cleaned the glass in a long time. I'm not sure what the black stuff is in the far corner of the door frame, but it looks like something is growing there.

I barely get in the door when I smell the stench of something rotting. It's overwhelming, and I can't identify it. My hand shoots up to my nose and squeezes off my nostrils, but that makes me taste the foul air, so I let go.

Byz laughs. "It'll take a few minutes to adapt, always does."

"What is it?"

She shrugs. "If I had to guess, I'd say body odor, grease, and mold."

Right next to the entrance is a small eatery that I've been to hundreds of times. It's my favorite place to eat at the mall. Byz points to the sign: "EXOTIC DELIGHTS."

"Sounds good, if I can eat with the smell so oppressive."

Byz laughs as she walks ahead of me. "You just wait."

As I walk past the glass display, I look at the food. But I don't see food. Everything looks like brown or black sludge in the pans. My favorite here is the red noodles, but I don't see it. There are wads of unidentifiable food in the corner where the fruit and dessert should be.

I feel like I'm going to be sick, so I slide down into a seat at one of the small tables lining the front of the restaurant.

"You okay?" Byz asks as she sinks into the seat opposite me.

"Is that what I've been eating? No. Don't answer that." I feel like I'll puke as it is. "How could I not know it was slimy and nasty, regardless of the way it tasted?"

"You got your sensitivity turned up for the maximum experience?"

I nod.

She shakes her head. "Almost everyone does. It's the default. It filters the sensitivity of your senses."

There's bile in my throat. "Will you get me some water so I can get this rancid taste out of my mouth?"

Byz walks to the counter and orders the water as I place my head on the grimy table top. Gross. I put my arm between my face and the surface, trying to breathe in the clean scent of my clothing, but as I do so, I notice that the smell is mildewy. I readjust my nose by building a shield with my arms and shoulder and close my eyes, willing away the nausea.

Byz returns, but my stomach is swimming, and I can't look up, not even to get the water. She says, "I can't imagine having to take this all in at once."

That's enough for me to pull my head up. "You eat this stuff every day?"

Before she can answer, I get a look at the water, which has a yellow tint to it and is filled with floating particles. I put my hand over my mouth.

Byz folds her arms. "You remember where the restroom is?"

As soon as she says it, I take off down the short hallway where the restrooms are, and my vision tunnels in my desperation. I throw open the door, open a stall, and hurl.

I roll my head back and feel the sweat cool on my brow. The paneled ceiling is black. I right my head and take in the restroom. Black mold grows on every surface, and the smell is going to make me vomit again if I don't get out.

"You better?" Byz asks me as I stagger back to our little table.

"You could have warned me, you know." I'm so nauseated it feels like my eyes are crossed.

"I did! I told you it was a nightmare," she says. "Anyway, now that you've got a good look, I have a gift for you."

She pulls the small bag off her shoulder and rummages around in it, bringing out a tin of small muffins and placing them on the table. "It's real food. My mom baked them this morning, so they're fresh. But I've got to warn you, you'll have trouble digesting it. It's probably been a long time since you had any real food."

I take a tentative bite and recognize the nutty flavor at once. Dad used to sneak these to me all the time when I was little, but I quit eating them because they made me use the bathroom a lot. When I was older, I refused them, wanting other foods instead.

I put the muffin down. "I'm not that hungry," I say.

"You'll get hungry," Byz answers, then wraps the muffin up in a cloth and tells me to put it in my bag. "I have something else for you."

She reaches in her bag and hands me a thermos. I look at her sideways. I've had all the food surprises I can take today.

"Go on," she says. "You'll like this one."

I open it up; inside is a clear liquid. "Water?"

"Yes; it'll help cleanse the toxic stuff out of you and hydrate your skin. Drink it. It's good."

I do as I'm told, and it's the best water I've ever tasted. I want to swallow it all, but I only take a few drinks so I don't throw up again.

"Where'd you get this?" I ask. "Were you expecting me today?"

"No." Her answer is quick and assertive. "I carry water with me everywhere. It makes sense to have it on hand."

I'm not sure if she's being fully honest with me, but I can hardly tell up from down at the moment.

"As for the water, a friend of the family dug a well for us. It's the water we drink every day. If you come to my house someday, I'll make you some herbal tea from it. It's so much better for you than what you've been drinking."

I nod, and soon, a lull falls between us. There's a lot for me to take in, and it feels like she's waiting for me to say something, but I'm clueless as to what.

"I feel like my dad is still alive," I finally say, my voice quiet, broken. "But he wouldn't stay gone this long, and he'd never leave me behind." The rest falls out of my mouth faster than the food erupted. It's what I've been thinking since I spoke with Puck, but it's the first time I've said it aloud.

Another pause, and I realize I've dropped a huge bomb on her, but I need to tell someone. Maybe she'll be the one to believe me.

She finally replies, "Are the police involved?"

"I went by there today to tell them about the imposter who showed up this morning, claiming to be Dad." Choking on the lump in my throat, I manage to keep from crying. "I bought his act until he called me Libby on the way out of the door. Dad always calls me Liberty, without fail. Imposter has a younger face in reality, not like Dad's at all. But they both look identical in PR." I bury my face in my hands for what feels like the hundredth time today. "What a mess. Nothing is as it seems, and it appears to be getting worse."

"Did your dad give you that necklace?"

I peek through my fingers to see Byz pointing to the bump under my sweater. I cover my chest as if to guard it. How did she know it was there? I look at her with big eyes. Could she be in on it?

She must read my mind, because she shakes her head. "No, I knew because of the little bump it makes under your shirt. I've seen them before. My mom had one in her jewelry box for a few years, but it went missing."

"This is the second one I've had," I explain. "Dad tried to give me one the night he disappeared, but I panicked when I saw him and he looked different. I ran away and lost the necklace in the process. This one I found in Dad's study. He intended it for my mother. She might have tried it, but I'm not positive."

"If he gave it to her, she wouldn't be the first one to decline. A life of ease and delusion is hard to walk away from."

My hand is still covering the necklace, but I'm glad to talk about it. "He sealed the necklace in an envelope for her, but there was a picture of her in the study. It looked like she might be wearing it under her sweater, but I can't be sure. As for this necklace, I only turned it a few hours ago. I desperately want to go back to the way things were, but I have to know the truth to find my dad."

Byz purses her lips. "You're up against bad people, you know?"

"Okay, but which ones are the bad ones and which are the good? Puck? The police? Oh, and there's also a man who broke into my house; he's heavyset with glasses. I told the police about him, but the sergeant seemed unimpressed."

With her head down, Byz responds, "Probably a peep. I wouldn't worry about him." Then she lifts her head and looks into my eyes. "As for the police, they're more likely to arrest you than the perpetrator. No one higher up is really giving them oversight. They're pretty autonomous."

"When I went to the station, the woman was dressed a little old-fashioned, but she looked put together. Do they not run with PR?"

"I don't think so, but technically, I'm an illegal child, so I do my best to avoid them." She shrugs. "It's hard to blend in while they're about, but if they found out about me. Well... I don't know for sure what would happen, but I'm reluctant to find out. It would put many people in danger, specifically my parents."

Parents. If Dad's missing and Clarisse is fully in her virtual setting, I have no one but myself to rely on.

I'm new to all of this, and Byz is my only confidante. Well, there's Puck, but he's unreliable, and I can barely make sense of what he says, anyway.

I pick up the thermos and take a drink.

Byz closes her bag and puts it back over her shoulders. "Rest of that is yours, but use it wisely. I'll try to bring you more tomorrow. Can't promise, though."

I hear her, but the words slide through my mental sieve. I look up at her. "What am I going to do?"

"You'll either adapt or return to your PR programming, but even that illusion won't last long. I suggest you come to terms with this reality. It's the one you can really make a difference in. Now, you say you turned the necklace a few hours ago?"

I nod.

"And you've not turned it back off since?"

I shake my head, but I'm considering it right now.

"Was that the first time you turned it?"

"No, I saw my mother and my room and then panicked and turned it so I could sleep."

She nods and leans back in her chair. "The necklace is a signal blocker; it's usually good for a limited number of turns. And they won't last long. It's best if you don't turn it off again—for any reason. The only purpose PR serves is to distract you from what's really going on. That would be bad."

"But I have no idea what's really going on," I say, and it's the truth. I know everything is a lie, but I don't know the components of that lie. I'm like a newborn in a new world, taking it all in for the first time since... I'm not sure when. Maybe forever.

"Also, the necklace will have to charge soon, so you must decide which reality to live in when it comes time." She takes a deep breath. "I don't want to scare you too soon. Things are dire. But remember, there's a plan to fix it."

"Whose plan? Yours?" This is all too much.

"No, I can't do this alone." Byz takes a bite of one of the tinned muffins. "I'd rather not go into the specifics of that until you understand the problem."

She has my full attention. I'm eager to learn about this world, hidden in front of me for all these years.

"It'll take a while to tell you it all, but let's start with the most obvious problem, and I'll tell you more when I feel you can handle it better."

My lip quirks up on one side. I don't want to hear it, but she's making sense. This is a lot to take.

"The climate is failing. The sun has worked its way through the different layers of atmosphere; it's drying up the planet and causing extreme weather. We've known for over one hundred years that the planet couldn't sustain the damage we humans inflicted, but there was a ton of power associated with that information. Anyone who tried to warn us was discredited, disappeared, or lumped in with 'junk science.'"

She shrugs. "At the same time, people were looking more at social media sources for every part of their life, who their friends were, what they ate, read, and watched. It seemed like a never-ending utopia on the other side of the screen. People got sucked in, not wanting to deal with the chaos. The government saw an opportunity and marketed their own program: PR, Personal Reality. The people quickly became complacent about the state of the Earth and the fallout."

I shudder, hardly believing what she's saying. But after today, anything's possible. "So they just started embedding us all with the programming?"

"Yes, it was mandatory, but there was a great consequence as the infrastructure of farming, clean water, and sewage treatment grew out of hand. That's when they started enhancing the rotten food and treated the nutritious food with a PR resistant coating."

"What's that for?" I ask.

"It makes the good food look rotten and the rotten food look good. Anyway, I'm sure you know that in 2025 there was an outbreak of several viruses, fueled by antibiotic resistance. It's suggested that eighty percent of the population died. The resilient moved to smaller communities to continue their delusion. Our parents' generation was the first to be born fully into Personal Reality."

"Does it have anything to do with PREP?" I recall the acronym from Dad's calendar.

Byz smiles and opens her mouth to answer when she looks at something over my shoulder. I don't even get to turn around before I hear him.

"Libby? There's my girl. Why aren't you at academy?" says a man I recognize from our transport this morning.

"Elizeus?" There's no way I'm calling that man Dad.

Chapter 14

"**G**otta run," Byz whispers. She grabs her muffins and walks off before I can ask when I'll see her again. Imposter doesn't take any notice of her.

"Libby, what are you doing here? You're supposed to be at the academy." The man is even taller than he looked in the transport. He has sandy hair and is wearing an ugly plaid tracksuit.

"I have an excuse from one of the assessors. He sent me home." I reach into my pocket and hand him my note. He barely glances at it.

"Why?" he says as he lays the excuse on the table.

Because I found out an imposter is pretending to be my dad comes to mind, but I just say, "I felt sick."

"So you came to the mall? That doesn't make much sense."

No, it really doesn't. I'm hesitant to lie, because I've always been truthful to Dad, but this isn't him. I don't even know what my lie is until it comes out of my mouth. "I was hoping Mom might still be here running errands."

He scratches his head and takes Byz's empty seat. "You're in luck. Your mother is still in her hair appointment. Have you seen her panels yet? I'll take you; she's quite proud, and you might know better what to say. I'm hopeless at fashion." He attempts a cordial smile, but in the circumstances, I see it as mocking.

I must be staring too hard, because he adds, "You feeling all right? Anything wrong?"

I'm not all right, and of course, there's something wrong. I'm talking to someone pretending to be my dad. This man must know what's going on, too. He'll have had to come from somewhere and know that he's not Elizeus Moore. Or maybe he's as much under the delusion as anyone.

"Tell me about your conference," I ask him as I lift my bag onto my shoulder. "You didn't mention it before you left."

He waves his hand away. "Oh, lots of boring meetings; there's nothing to talk about, really. I had hoped there would be new developments for PR, but instead, they were tweaking existing programs. Truth be told, I wasn't much help at all. They should have left me at home with my family." He smiles, like he's the most natural thing in the world.

"I thought something happened to you. The police came about an assault in the park. Have you spoken to them yet?" I watch his face for any sign of recognition or indication of lying. "I told them I was concerned you were assaulted."

He laughs. "You worry too much, Libby. Yes, the authorities did check in with me while I was at the office, but here I am, alive and well, if that wasn't enough to convince you."

His lies come so naturally, I can't tell if he's playing a part or actually believes himself to be my dad. I'll have to continue watching him closely to see if he's more aware than he's letting on.

I need to trip him up. Especially in front of Clarisse.

He picks up the glass of water on the table—the nasty one Byz got from the food vendor—and takes a long gulp. That tells me what I need to know. No one who could see that water could drink it. There's no way, which means this guy is probably some dupe being used as a replacement. But he still has to know that he is not who he says he is.

Until I can figure out his game, I need to proceed with caution.

"Ready to see your mother's handiwork?" he asks, wiping the excess drink off of his lip. I suppress my shudder by nodding my head in agreement.

The mall is a long hall full of kiosks and displays where you can buy the latest fashions and have them tailored to your body. Of course, the wearer will be able to choose the colors and prints, but Clarisse's designs provide new foundational canvases to work with.

I'm in here fairly often. Clarisse brings me every Saturday and purchases me a new outfit. The outfit I got last Saturday had been a yellow sundress for the summer with ruffles all around and a matching headband for me to wear. It was Clarisse's design, and I knew she had made it with me in mind. Now I wonder what it really looks like.

The tall walls of fashion displays change as we pass. All the elegance that I used to see is gone. The fabrics are thick and outdated, and I'm sure they look nothing like that to the shoppers who ogle at them with admiration. The models are surprisingly plain, and their hair is a mess, but they're still above average women in appearance. Unfortunately, all of them look a little sickly and hungry.

We reach the place where my mother usually displays her panels and find it is being ignored by much of the onlookers. It takes me a minute to understand why. The panels of clothes are plain, but coordinated. Old-fashioned, but tasteful. The model is definitely more suited for the PR-induced population, but the clothing must be meant for people who can see. I gravitate toward the display when I see a guard with his eyes firmly on that kiosk. I can't help but wonder that if I go closer, it will mark me as a person of interest. I should take Byz's word and be careful about revealing my newfound sight.

Imposter doesn't even notice it as we pass by.

"Wasn't that Clarisse's display?" I ask.

"Where? Oh, back there. No. She's being featured on the Turn this week, and Della LaClare has used her image for the vidshot. You're going to love it."

The Turn is a staged area with holograms. If Della is the model, it will show a series of videos of her wearing Clarisse's clothes. There are six other kiosks in the display where shoppers can see themselves in the clothing and pretend to be Della. It's a manipulation, a very good one.

When we finally see the panels, I'm expecting to see the long-line skirts and kimonos that Clarisse showed me last week, but I find something very different instead. It's a shiny black dress that looks like an inside-out garbage liner. Around the model's shoulders is a wrap that looks as if it's made from the fabric of a centuries-old couch, and on the model's chest are two pencils tied together with a garbage tie as a broach of some sort. The shoes are much the same as the slides I'm wearing, except the front is cut out of them so they resemble an open-toed shoe.

I look at Imposter's face, and he is beaming. This is the worst display I've seen today, but there's a small group lined up to try the dresses on and look like Della.

It's more than I can take. I seat myself at a bench a bit farther down. There's so much to think through that my head is spinning. I look to the other wall, full of closed doors, and at the open skylights leading down the hallway. It's the first time I realize the mall must have been an old school, back when people needed almost two decades to become skilled enough for jobs.

"There you are. Elizeus told me you were excused from academy," Clarisse says. I look back to where she's standing by her stall, showing off her dangerously thin white-painted face, matted copper hair, and ridiculous makeup. She's dressed in her garbage bag dress and lackluster wrap. "I'm famished. Are you feeling well enough to eat?" she asks.

I don't answer. I'm struggling to remember what the two pencils are supposed to be, but I can't recall the panels she last showed me. There were so many to remember.

And that gives me an idea: this man pretending to be Dad wouldn't know any of it at all. I can't directly point out that this isn't Dad without giving myself away, but I can make him squirm by asking him questions that he should know the answer to. Maybe then Clarisse will realize something is off.

"Libby?" Clarisse speaks again; she's next to me now, looking down at me. Her outfit is even more hideous up close, and I realize the garbage bag is used, based on the smell emanating from it.

I let out a slow breath as nausea rolls through me once again.

"Yes, you are looking a little green..." Clarisse pats my head. "Let's go get something to eat and then we can take you home to rest."

Our family transport is a death trap of rusted metal in reality. I take my usual place in the back and watch Imposter kiss Clarisse's white-painted face before he starts the engine. This is my first chance to trip him up.

"You two are like newlyweds," I say. "I bet you remember everything about where the two of you met. Where was it?"

"Not far from here," he adds generically. "I saw your mother and was awed by her beauty."

"How far from here?" I ask.

Clarisse shakes her head, most of her attention drawn outside the transport window. "We had quite a time that day, didn't we, Elizeus?"

"A day unparalleled," he answers vaguely.

He hasn't a clue. "Where exactly?" I continue, being as subtle as I can manage.

"Liberty Hope Moore," Clarisse says, laughing. "You've heard this story a hundred times. You know we met at the carousel one night when we were vying for the same unicorn."

I don't need Clarisse to answer. I need Imposter to, so she can realize he's not Dad!

"That's right," I say. "And, Elizeus, do you remember where you proposed to mother?"

Imposter looks blank for a minute, as if he's trying to remember. Then he looks at me suspiciously through the rearview mirror. "Do you remember, Libby?"

Of course I do. I've heard the story thousands of times about how they rented a paddle boat on one of the creeks, and the water started leaking in. Dad had to stop the leak with the sole of his shoe and paddle at the same time. They barely made it to shore. As they watched the paddle boat go down, Elizeus told her they could have died, but he would still have been glad to be by her side.

He took her hand on the rocky shore and asked her to marry him.

I take so long to think about it that it's obvious I know the story. Imposter smiles at me, but it's not a sympathetic smile, more a victorious one. I don't know if it's a momentary victory for having beaten the challenge, or a much more sinister victory for having duped Clarisse and me. If he knows, he's not about to give himself away.

CHAPTER 15

Imposter pulls into the teahouse on the next block, which we could have easily walked. Both my parents order an oriental soup and a special Japanese tea, whereas I order the blueberry mint: my favorite. I watch the waitress as she writes our drink order, taking note of how her clothing matches and her hair doesn't stick out like everyone else's does. She must live in reality, too.

"What would you like to eat, Libby?" Clarisse asks.

Oh no. I forgot about that part. I turn my attention back to the menu in my hands, balking at the dishes, imagining how bad it's all going to be, and it turns me off food immediately.

"I've changed my mind. I don't think I'm hungry, after all. Don't bring me anything."

The waitress nods. "Just some water then?"

"No!" My answer is assertive, and everyone stops and looks at me.

But the woman smiles. "I recommend the cranberry salad."

It doesn't sound too appetizing, but Clarisse and Imposter are staring. In fact, several other tables are watching me, too. It's not often anyone raises their voice in public. There's never the need. I should order something.

"I think you'll find it fresh and colorful." She turns her head away from Clarisse and Imposter and winks at me. I have no idea what the signal means, but bow my head and let her know I'll try it.

The tea house is busy, as always. I can't help but gawk at the different outfits everyone is wearing, but a few are dressed plainly and appear more put together than the rest.

When our food comes out, I realize why the waitress was so insistent. She must have realized from my harsh reaction that my PR was off. My parent's soup is a strained brown liquid that smells like excrement, but my salad looks fully edible. Truth be told, I'm pretty hungry at this point, so I dive in. The taste is spectacular as I allow the berries to roll around in my mouth, mixed with the light dressing that is tart and sweet at the same time. I eat as if I haven't eaten in years and drink the tea, which is not the blueberry mint that I ordered, but a clear herbal blend that tastes clean on my palette.

Clarisse gets a good look at my food and turns her head up in horror. "That looks awful, Libby. I thought she said it was colorful. I can send it back if it's inedible."

So Byz was right. Food not enhanced by PR looks unappetizing to those in the program.

Clarisse shoves another brown lump in her mouth and strings of whatever it is stick to her lips. The sight makes me want to barf, so I focus on my plate and continue eating. I try to engage in the conversation, but I just can't watch them eat. My stomach rolls at the fact that with a quick turn of my necklace, I would be eating it as well.

"Absolutely no one has said a word about my new hairstyle. Do you like it?" Clarisse asks, half perturbed, half hopeful.

Imposter nods and takes a sip of tea. "You look beautiful as always, my dear. I'm afraid I get too lost in your eyes to notice your hair sometimes."

I don't want to take part in this conversation; there are many things I'm going to have to fake my way through if I'm going to stay with realism, but my mother's hair looks grotesque. The beauty shop has used something to make it stand high off her head, revealing her long spindly neck. It looks as if a sharp nod would totally behead her.

I focus instead on the white paint smeared toward her neck, the red circle around her lips, and her bruised-looking eyes. I've got nothing positive to say.

"Don't you like it?" Clarisse frowns.

"I think you are the most interesting looking woman in the room," I say. I kick my leg under the table and squeeze out a smile. Elizeus looks at me with his eyes narrowed.

The waitress takes the food from us before I finish and leaves us with our respective drinks. I start to tell her I'm not done, but I stay quiet. She probably knows something that I don't.

I finally realize she has done me a favor when all the raw vegetables and dressing hit my stomach like a brick. The following belch is unavoidable, as if my body doesn't quite know what to do with real food.

The conversation turns to Clarisse—not that it wasn't already there. She boasts about her panels and her quick rise up the influencer list.

"You know we are so lucky to know someone with such sway as Della," she says, dabbing her mouth with a napkin. "Excuse me."

Clarisse stands to go to the restroom, and Imposter immediately turns his attention to me. "Are you trying to get me in trouble with your mother, Libby?"

Obviously. "Uhm, no?"

"I think you were. And that concerns me, because I've not seen that malice in you before."

Before I can meter my words, I blurt, "Well, you've only known me since this morning."

He pulls his head back as if I have greatly wounded him, but there's something else there. It's not concern for me, but for himself.

I instantly regret what I've said. I'm going to be caught, when Byz was adamant I not draw attention to myself.

Imposter's face goes cold. "I don't know what game you're playing, but you will not screw this up for me. Do you understand? You'd be wise to avoid any more outbursts; I can make things very difficult for you."

My mouth hangs open. I manage, "Yes, sir," but I'm not sure it's audible.

"Good. Now, I'm going to take your mother home and let you think about things for a while. When you come through our front door, I don't want to hear any more second guessing or verbal attacks. Are we understood?"

This time, words fail me completely, but I manage to nod.

He sits back in his seat. "I'll make an excuse for you."

Needing no further prompting, I take off out of there as fast as my legs will move. I'm halfway across the transport park when I realize I didn't take the time to thank the waitress properly. At the very least, I won't spend the day starving.

I turn back toward the mall, hoping Byz may still be there, but I do two full laps before I give up on finding her. Inside, I pass by the restaurant Byz and I sat in and spot a mother and daughter sitting at a table, sharing a plate of some unidentified object.

They look so sweet sitting there that I feel like I have to warn them. I walk up to the table, and they both look up at me with black juice dripping from their chins.

"You need to stop eating. Your meal isn't what you think it is. It's not real." My voice comes out louder than I intended, and soon the Exotic Delight's attendant comes out from behind the bar and grabs me by the arm.

I don't fight him as he escorts me to the exit.

"Don't come back disturbing my diners!" he says as he closes the door behind me.

I quickly flee the area. I'm in trouble at home, at the academy, and even at the mall. I'm not navigating this world yet, and I really want to turn the necklace, head back to my perfect room, and get some much-needed rest.

But I can't rest, I can't pretend. I'm the only person who seems interested in the whereabouts of Dad. It's up to me to figure out what happened and get him back.

If I even can...

CHAPTER 16

I t's a long walk back to the carousel, but I'm convinced that if I
go back, I'll have a chance to remember something I may have
forgotten or overlooked. By the time I reach it, I'm damp with
sweat. The sun, or whatever that bright light is beyond the clouds,
and the haze are relentless. I tie my sweater around my waist and
undo a few buttons on my blouse.

Personal temperature regulation had made me oblivious to the
heat. My skin is so tanned that I feel like I'm in the wrong body.
Usually so pale, now it looks withered and old. Not as bad as
Clarisse's and Imposter's, but it's terrible, nonetheless.

At this time of day, there aren't many people on the carousel.
Most are at work or at the academy, not frolicking on the carousel.
The children, too, are all at Daydreams, the care center, where
they're given all the attention they need through virtual means.

That leaves me and a half dozen aimless people hanging around
the area. There's a woman and a newborn in the rattiest pram I've
ever seen. She stops and pulls out a protective cloth to put over
her shoulder. I'm about to lose it if she gives the baby that rotten
stuff, but thankfully, she makes a tent to breastfeed.

A police officer I don't recognize sits on the bench on the other
side of the carousel. Another passerby walks by in a hurry, as if

she has something important to get to, but it's all a facade. I shake my head.

An elderly lady is making her rounds in the park, as prescribed by custom. She'll need to have the strength for the long trip to Graceon, and judging from her age, I would say she's about to take that journey. Her form looks good, though. Both of her feet leave the ground, and her elbows pump. She should have a good shot at making it to Graceon. That makes me smile. She'll escape this horrible existence soon.

The other inhabitant of the park is Puck, wearing his pinstripe suit. He either has more than one or he wears the same one every day.

I'm confused enough as it is, and I'd like to avoid his riddled speech. I know he sees me, but he looks down at the pile of boxes around him as if he's looking for something. That's fine by me.

As I step around the black scrub of a bush, I see the bench where Dad and I sat, and tears threaten my eyes. I miss him. I miss everything.

He must have thought he was in trouble. Otherwise, why would he have chosen that moment to share reality with me? And in the park? He clearly wanted us away from the house. But why?

Maybe he knew he was in trouble, and he thought I could help him somehow, get him to safety. I might have been able to change things. Instead, I got scared and ran.

Given the circumstances, it's not surprising I panicked. But in the process, I missed the opportunity to tell Dad I loved him. I still love him. I always will, and there's no one who can replace him in my heart, no matter the resemblance or programming.

The police officer looks my way. He's probably wondering why I'm not in testing, training, or at home. I have the excuse from the assessor, but that won't explain why I'm in the park in the middle of the day. I need to be quick or I'm going to have some explaining to do.

Let's see... Dad gave me the necklace, and I stood up and faced the carousel so he could turn the top of the necklace. When I turned to ask him about the changes, I expected to see him there, instead of the short man with his pointed nose and weak chin.

I ran away while I was wearing the necklace, but I must have lost it, because things turned back to normal.

If that's the case, the necklace might be here, assuming no one has taken it.

I turn and look at the carousel from where I think I was that night and spin around abruptly. I took only one step before I recall the necklace being ripped from my throat, then I broke into a full run.

Bending down, I look at the dead lawn that's not quite grass, but some sort of scruffy yellow plants spaced intermittently around the dry, cracked ground. On my hands and knees, I start looking under every plant, hoping to find what I'm searching for.

Nothing is there.

I sit back on my heels. I'm so frustrated that the tears push at my eyes again, but I'm interrupted by a noise on the other side of the black shrubbery. The tops of the plants part, and through them, I see Puck's white shock of hair and his weather-beaten face.

"Looking for something, girlie?" he says.

"Not right now," I tell him. I have enough going on. I won't trust anything he says, anyway, and I'm seriously time-crunched with the officer looking my way.

"Alrighty, then. I thought you might want to find the necklace, but if you are dead set against it, I understand."

Stopping, I look up. "You know where it is?"

"Come and see," he gestures me toward the city center.

The black vines close over again, and he's gone. The police officer is standing now, walking in my direction. I hasten out of the brush and back onto the footpath and watch Puck go through a large wooden door on the other side of the road, leading to what looks like an old watch shop from the drawings above the graffitied stars. On the windows, the faded wording is barely legible: "THE CLOCKERY." White paint on the inside of the glass prevents anyone from seeing inside.

I glance back at the police officer. His eyes are definitely on me, and he raises a hand in greeting. I do the same, feigning a smile, and before he can catch up with me, I cross the street and go to the door Puck disappeared through.

I almost chicken out when I reach it, but knowing the police officer intends to question me if he finds me, I pull open the door and enter the darkness, keeping my hand on the door handle, in case I've made a poor decision.

My heart is making a serious attempt to beat out of my chest. I can hear its random beats.

Going forward will take me to Puck, while turning back will mean confronting the police officer. I don't trust either, but if I duck in for just a moment, maybe I can get away from both of them.

"Turn on the light." I recognize Puck's voice and place him a little in front of me, but not in range to grab me.

"You turn on the light!" I reply, much braver than I feel.

"As you wish. We'll sit in the dark," he says. "Suits me fine."

Ticking noises fill the dark room, and I realize it's not my heartbeat but something else. It's making me nervous, and I know I'm either going to leave or do as I'm told. I feel around either side of the door for the switch.

"No, no," he says. "There's a lamp on the table to your right."

I don't have any trouble finding the lamp, but I'm suddenly more afraid of what's waiting in the light than what I can't see in the dark.

He must hear me hesitate, because he says, "Be brave, Liberty Moore."

I turn on the light and look around. On every surface, time pieces tick-tock back and forth. There are clocks everywhere. It's rather dark, but the place is also kind of homey except for the wall painted with a mural of clowns. I glance from one face to the next; there's a reminder of my mother's thick makeup in each one.

Puck sits in an easy chair and motions me to the sofa. Neither piece of furniture is in the best repair, but they look clean and comfortable.

"Sit," he says.

"How did you know my name? I never told it to you. And what about the necklace? Where is it?"

"Why is everyone always in a rush? The planet is literally dying in front of us, and everybody wants to speed up time. Seems silly to me." He stares at me long enough that I feel his eyes boring into me.

I consider leaving, but then I might as well hear what he has to say. Even the best lies have an element of truth, and I desperately want answers. If I leave, I won't find out what he knows—or what he *thinks* he knows. This time I have to be brave, if not for me, then for Dad.

I take a seat as far away as I can get from him on the sofa. The cushions are the type that envelop you when you sit. I feel my frame sink into the cloth and pillows come up around me. Were I not scared out of my mind; this would be a perfect place to take a nap. But I'm scared, so I scoot up to sit on the edge of the seat.

"I must make you nervous, Liberty, but you'll get used to me yet."

"Seriously, how do you know my name?"

"All in time, girlie, all in time."

I grit my teeth. "Look, you might have all the time in the world, but I'm looking for my dad." I push myself off the cushions to stand, but find myself suctioned in the chair. It takes me a moment, but I manage it. "If you can't or won't tell me anything, then—"

"Wait," he says, and I know I've got his attention. "I know your name because your dad talked about you from time to time."

"Yes, you knew Dad. But why have we not spoken before all of this? Why am I only meeting you now?"

"That's a long story." He motions me back to the seat. "Sit, and I'll tell you."

I hesitate, not anxious to return to the chair after the difficulty I had getting out, but I want answers more than anything, so I do.

"The short answer is it that us Realsies do our best not to draw attention to one another. Though I'm gifted with words and eccentricity, most people tune me out."

"Realsies? That sounds like something a child would come up with. I don't have time for games, Puck."

He shakes his head. "No, I assure you, this is all as it seems. Realsies is a child's name. We used to be the Realists, but your dad introduced the name from a game you used to play when you were little. Do you remember?"

I'm in the midst of rolling my eyes when I remember a game that Dad would play with me a lot when I was younger. It might have been Realsies or something like that. He would show me weird scenes where he would have me look at opposite items and tell me they were the same.

Puck must see the recognition in my eyes, because he nods. "That's right. Only you came up with the name after you mispronounced 'What we really see' as 'What we Realsies.' The name got shortened. Your dad wanted you to know what kind of world we live in, but he couldn't take the chance of endangering you to do it. He loved you very much."

I clench my jaw to keep my chin from wobbling. This is not the time or place to have a breakdown.

"Okay..." I breathe, steadying myself. "I see it now, and it's grotesque. None of that tells me what happened to Dad, though."

"What you call grotesque is the real world. We call seeing it clearly 'Clarity.'" He lifts his eyebrows. "And I can't tell you what the police did with your father, but I know about the necklace you're looking for."

He reaches into his pocket and pulls it out. It's like the one around my neck, only the plastic cord hangs broken. "This is a tool. We use these to bring people we need into the PREP program. Most don't want to bother with us until we show them the devastation. There are six of these necklaces in existence. You happened to have access to two of them in a short period of time."

I put my hand to my chest, over to where the necklace lies. "Where are the others? Who's using them?"

"Oh, now, don't stretch too far, little Moore. There are many things that even I don't know. I don't have full clearance, because I tend to get a little playful with the information. But I would guess it's either in storage or being used to convince someone in the sciences to join your father's cause."

"That doesn't make sense. I don't have any specific scientific knowledge."

"Maybe, maybe not. But I suspect your dad went against protocol to get these to you and your mother. He wanted you to be part of the solution. You have to understand that it's hard to watch someone you love be so unsanitary. He wanted to protect you from your own fantasy world. As to why he chose now, I'm not sure, but I feel in my bones he felt rushed. He must have known someone was out to get him. He didn't have enough time."

"Do you have any idea who—" I ask, but before I can finish my thought, there is a rap on the front door.

Puck tuts. "Here, I'll show you the back door. The alleyway is crowded and largely unsupervised, so I suggest you tread carefully."

He leads me past a small desk to a big metal door.

"There are messages in the graffiti. Seek out the rest of your answers there." He opens the door, gives me a slight nudge, and promptly exits behind me. He takes off down the alleyway, leaving me in the dark.

When another pound comes from the front of the building, I hurry after him down the alleyway.

CHAPTER 17

Something squeaks by my feet, and I squeal, uncertain what the animal could be in this horrid new world. But it's not new—it's what's always been around me.

I don't want to look at the creature, so I close my eyes and scurry away from the sound. When I open them again, I see only darkness. The only light is a strip of sky overhead where the buildings don't meet.

With no time to waste, I hurry along. It's likely the person at the door was the police officer, and it won't take long for him to realize I've used the backdoor. It keeps me at a steady pace, and I follow in Puck's direction. Just as well, too. It's the path of least resistance. At least I know it's passable.

All kinds of debris block the alley. Not that I can see it. But each time I take a step, I bump into something. It takes me a few minutes before I can see a gate at the end of the alley, still open from Puck's exit. I keep my focus forward, though I'm tempted to turn the necklace so I can ease through without realizing the terrible stench and the mounds of garbage.

I hold my breath to keep out the smell, and it makes me light-headed. I have to put my hand on the grimy wall to steady myself, and the unexpected sliminess of the bricks makes my hair stand on end. The gateway is close.

Something touches my ankle, and I shriek much louder than before, then quickly clamp my hand over my mouth.

"Hey, what do you mean, waking me up?" It's a man sleeping on the alley floor.

I can't get a good look at him as I jerk my leg from his grasp, though that's probably for the best.

I push through the gate and emerge on the sidewalk a block away from the carousel. I feel flustered, my breathing rapid and my eyes wide, but I turn on my heel and continue down the street at the same leisurely pace as everyone else.

What do I do now? I got information from the police, Puck, Byz, and even a little from Imposter, but I feel like I'm no closer to figuring out what happened to Dad.

I'm not cut out for this, but who else cares enough? At least there's Byz. She'll tell me more if I can find her. That's the trick, though—finding her.

Before I know it, I'm at the academy gate as testing is letting out. I search for Byz among the throngs of students, but I can't find her anywhere. But I do spot a boy walking alone as he exits the academy. While everyone else keeps to their individual cliques, he seems content by himself.

What's more, his clothes match and his face is clean of dirt. He must be living outside of PR.

I follow him. It's a long shot, but perhaps most of the Realsies, to use Puck's term, live in a specific area. If so, maybe I'll find Byz there.

I follow almost an entire street behind the boy; I don't want him to notice me and report me for stalking. After a few blocks, the sidewalks thin of people, and I feel safe enough to open my bag and pull out Byz's thermos.

The water is warm on my dusty throat, and I have to remind myself not to drink it all. I carefully close the cap, and by the time I look up, I'm at an intersection, and the boy is gone.

I look left and right, but it's impossible to know where he went. With a sigh, I take a minute to rest on a bench by a grand, old building labeled "LIBRARY." I try to remember what the building looks like in PR, but I'm too turned around to know exactly where I am.

Graffiti covers the base entirely, but there are lots of books painted all along the side. The pictures show a cowboy at the rear of the building and a little white boy and black man on a raft. On the front wall, someone has written "BIG BROTHER" above a single eye. It's very well done. I wish I could see beyond the spray paint to make out the bottom of the mural, but wishing it won't make it so—at least not anymore.

The library has two columns holding up the porch. Two rocking chairs look like the perfect place to sit and daydream or sketch the landscape of the city. That is, if there were time for that. According to Puck and Byz, we may not have much time left at all.

Above the door, two giant blue stars are painted. I step up to the porch.

Sitting in one of the old wooden rocking chairs, I have the perfect view of a crooked white house across the street. It's also covered in graffiti, but I can read at the top where someone has painted "Follow the Stars," underlined in yellow spray paint. Yellow stars cover the building.

I place my feet firmly on the floor and lean forward to see down the street. A building further along also has a yellow star.

Inspired and curious, I follow it to one house and then another and then another until I've gone a few blocks. The buildings are all abandoned, but I can see they used to be storefronts. As I reach another intersection, I notice a red-washed house with another bright yellow star. The walls are covered in yet more graffiti, but this is different. The writing is small and detailed, not the large, colorful tags I've become accustomed to seeing.

I read the old writing on the exterior wall, and it's a sad affair. It was clearly written when people knew the world was in peril.

"Beware" and "The End is Coming" appear multiple times. These are the words of a fearful people. Lots of memorials and what I'm guessing are death dates, though they may be birth dates. Most of them are in the mid 2020s.

That must be around the PR program became mandatory, or even before it began. These people are all dead or under the influence of PR. If any of what Puck says is true, some of them must have survived long enough to have families of their own. It's the only explanation for the Realsies. *Realists*, rather.

I look around at the adjacent buildings; there are more and more quotes, a few even include the birth and death dates. I wonder about the panic of the survivors. They must have buried their dead under a cloud of smog.

Just as I think about turning back home, there's another yellow star on a building not far down the street. I pick up my feet and hurry toward it. It's a path, a marker for where I need to go to find... what will I find? It doesn't matter; I have so much to learn, so I follow from one house to another until I reach an old church with a large cross on the front eave and two yellow stars beneath it. From there, I look around and see nothing. No more stars, but the church can't be anything special. It looks abandoned.

I go a block each way, seeing if I missed a star, but every way I go leads me back toward the library or the church.

Someone has chained the church doors to keep people out, so I walk around the building's perimeter. There's one other door on the side, but I can't move the handle; the intention is clear enough. This door isn't meant for easy entry.

If the stars lead here, then I must be here on the wrong hour or day, because not much is happening. So much for following the stars; I've done nothing but reach a dead end.

I climb to the top step of the small staircase that leads to the chained double doors and sit down. I look back at the neighborhood, struggling to figure out what to do next. The houses here are also covered in graffiti, but the yards look somewhat maintained. They don't have sweeping lawns, but there's no trash, either. Someone has taken the time to remove most of it.

Is this where the Realsies live?

If so, how do I know which house to go to for answers? I don't. I could knock on any of these doors and find answers, but it could also be a setup, meant to lure me in and identify that I've turned off my PR.

Examining the houses one by one, I'm saved when a girl comes out of the front door of her house and starts picking up tiny pieces of trash on her front lawn. She has long, black hair pulled up in a barrette, and I know instantly. It's Byz.

CHAPTER 18

I'm about to call her name when a woman follows out behind her. I watch them as the woman hands Byz a trash liner to pick up the stray paper.

This must be Mrs. Lawson. It's been years, but she's still nothing like I remember. She and Byz are laughing at a joke that I can't hear from the church, and I instantly feel a pit of longing in my stomach and chest. It's the kind of relationship I'd like to have with Clarisse if she weren't so involved in her other projects. And it's a hint of the connection that would have grown between me and Dad had I been able to share this world with him.

Byz goes back to picking up paper, and her mother puts her hands on her slim hips and looks around the yard. She turns as if she is going in, then she sees me watching them. She grabs Byz's hand and leads her inside.

I feel shunned, like I've seen something I shouldn't have, like I don't deserve the richness of humanity. But I don't let it stop me from walking down the street toward the house. I'm determined to knock on that door and get answers, and they might give me a clue about how to find out what's happened to Dad.

I'm almost to the drive when Byz comes out and waves me to her backyard. She ducks behind the fence as I approach. I trust

Byz so far, but I'm as hesitant here as I was at Puck's. I don't really know much about Byz's family, not really. It's been so long ago.

There's an old chain-link fence around the backyard, and as I pass the gate, I notice that the neighboring houses have a good vantage point of me. I can only hope no one reports me to the police as I walk behind the house to a small enclosed porch. Byz is sitting on a chair swing, waiting for me as I open the metal screen door.

I stare around the room. In the corner is a stack of boxes, but there are flowers everywhere and fabrics in a rich floral design. There's a glass tabletop, and a bright sun framed on the wall. This looks more like the world I'm used to. It looks like home in PR.

"You follow the stars?" Byz asks.

"What?" I shake my head and focus on her. "Oh, yeah. I followed the stars."

"It's pretty cool, isn't it? It's our haven. Here, have a seat."

As soon as I do, I feel a peace that I haven't had in days. This is an oasis between the exaggerated PR and the terrible reality. Beyond the two extremes, Byz and her family have made a safe place, a home.

"Do you want something to drink? We've got herbal tea and water."

"Oh, I have the water you gave me earlier," I say, digging through my bag and pulling out the thermos. I take off the lid and down it like there will always be more.

Byz laughs and grabs the thermos. "I'll fill that up for you. Have you tried the muffin?"

I truly hadn't thought about it. The salad I ate in the teahouse had more than sated me for a while, but I feel more open now to giving it a bite after seeing all the fake food available. "I'll try it now."

"Okay. Be right back with more water."

As Byz leaves, I pull the muffin out of my bag and unwrap the surrounding cloth. It looks dense, but now that I'm where the smell is minimal, it smells good. It's got a sharp aroma that makes my nose tingle. I pinch off a bite to eat, and it crumbles into the napkin. When I put one of the pieces in my mouth, it melts on my tongue.

After a minute, Byz returns with the water. I take a huge gulp, and it rehydrates the muffin in my mouth, allowing the flavor to wash over my tongue. I eat all the crumbs and follow it with a long drink of water.

"You must be starving."

"I shouldn't be; I ate a couple of hours ago."

Byz looks a bit surprised and maybe a little concerned. "Where?"

"The tea house by the mall. I had a cranberry salad. It was good, but it took my stomach a while to settle."

"Oh, Theron must have been your server. It's good she helped you, but not so great that it was obvious you needed help. Either way, you better take it easy. Your stomach hasn't had good food in no telling how long. It's going to take a lot to digest, and it might make you a little sick, and it will *definitely* make you poop."

"Ew," I say.

Byz puffs out a short laugh. "Yeah, but it's good for you. Now, how did you go from the teahouse to ending up here?"

I clear my throat as if I've anticipated answering this question, but in truth, my mind is still busy taking it all in. "I'm looking for information about my dad. Puck, the pinstripe man, told me to read the graffiti, and I saw a message that said to follow the stars, so I started looking for them, and they led me here." I shrug. "Puck also told me that being out of PR is called Clarity."

Byz leans in. "I know who you're talking about, and I don't think you should trust him. I don't know him well, but I know my dad avoids him."

"Do you know why?" He *is* kind of weird, but he got me here, after all.

"No, just an instinct." She leans back into her seat, having made her warning clear.

I nod, but my mind is on other things. "I've seen a lot that PR has hidden from me today, but I can't get distracted. I've got to find more information about Dad, and I can't help but think it relates to Clarity and the program that our dads were working on."

"Well, I'm not the one to ask about your father, but I know someone you can talk to. I know a little more about the crisis, but it's pretty bad news, and you've had a hard day already. Are you up for it?"

I nod. From the sounds of it, I never want to hear it, but that makes me as oblivious as the others, and I no longer have that option. "Let's hear it."

"Well, the planet is becoming uninhabitable." She pauses, giving me the chance to absorb the severity of what she said. "The people who could do something about it aren't here. They took off to somewhere else." Byz rocks the chair swing once, then anchors to the ground with her feet.

I grasp the handles of my chair. "Who are they? Where are they now?"

Byz looks around, like someone might be listening, before resuming. "The military leaders, the government, and others with influence took off to the biome. We call them the Watchers. We don't know exactly where they are, but we know they aren't big enough to contain the remaining population. We are the unfortunates left to collapse with the panic."

She rolls her eyes back and flutters her eyelashes. "But it's not all bad. We have PR to make it easier until another health crisis rips through or the sun becomes too hot to maintain life here, or, as you've seen from our food, we die of malnutrition."

Great. Lucky us.

"I'm being facetious, of course. We've essentially been left behind by the wealthy and powerful. They left no contingency plan for us."

I'm speechless, and Byz continues. "In my case, my great-grand-father left us behind because we refused to overlook mass casualties and go into hiding." Her face is still with determination and a touch of anger sits on her brow. "His son, my grandfather, believed we could keep the planet sustainable with a lot of work and sacrifices. He was working on repairing the ozone layers and reducing pollutants to keep the air and water clean, cutting emissions so that the sea levels and ocean temperatures stabilized for healthy life."

That may be the first good news I've heard in Clarity. "That sounds great. Is it working?"

"He *was* working on those things, but the rich and powerful were reluctant to give up their ways and profits, so they put all their energies in building a safe refuge—the biome—so they can be the first generation to inhabit the Earth when it begins to restore itself."

I puff up my cheeks as I try to figure out what she's saying. "What exactly is a biome?"

She gestures a dome with her hands. "It's a self-contained living space with its own atmosphere and protection from worldly disease. They should have their own food source, but they are stealing ours, so something must have gone awry.

She waits for a reaction, but I'm still working out what she's saying. Finally, she continues: "Anyway, my grandfather ended up joining them there, though there are many people who say his father tricked him. But my father refused to go."

"So the rest of us were abandoned here to die? We can't let that happen. There's no way we can let them do that to us!" My voice is loud, rushed, and incredulous, but it's a lot to take in. A strong reaction is warranted.

"How do you suggest we change it?" She waits for my answer like I have one.

I shrug. "We could sabotage the biome; giving the Watchers the same odds as us would make them help. They would be more interested if their extinction were on the line."

"We could do that. It's not that we haven't thought about it, but we'd have to find them. All we know for sure is that the biome is south of here. At least, that's where the ship goes. It's been said that it'd take a month or more by boat, but the only boat is the container ship."

"Yes, that's the big ship that docks here every few days. We hear the horn sometimes."

Byz nods. "It's heavily guarded because it's where they ship our best supplies to the biome. We'd take it, but we don't even know if there's a longer trek after the river and haven't been able to find out by ourselves. We need more people in Clarity to make that happen."

She stops to let my brain catch up, but I watch her intently. Her eyes stay on mine. I don't think she's making any of this up, but I'm a little low on trust from the past few days. It's hard to have confidence in anything when you find out your whole life has been a lie.

Continuing, she says, "The Watchers have taken some care to keep us from finding them. I don't know of any communities like this elsewhere, but there has to be more. The virus that killed off most of the population didn't affect everyone, so we believe there are a few more communities like ours, but we have no idea where. It's not easy to gather an invisible army to fight a hidden enemy."

I nod my head but realize I'm missing information. "Wait. How are they watching us?"

"Some through programming data, but I'm sure you've noticed the eye by now."

"The eye?"

"Yeah, the eye over the river. In PR, it's the moon."

My eyes widen. I knew it looked different. But it's a surveillance device? Everything is turning into a nightmare, and I shudder to think they've been keeping tabs on me all along.

"Dad must have known all of this, but why didn't he tell me? Or perhaps, that's what he was going to do—tell me."

"It's probable," she shrugs, "but I can't say for sure, of course."

I let out a low groan and rub my eyes with closed fists. "Look... I would love to help, but my first priority is finding Dad. If we can save the planet at the same time, that's awesome. But you need to know that's my main objective."

Byz smiles sadly. "I understand."

I take a drink of water. I'm about to swallow when Mrs. Lawson comes out of the door bearing a plate of cookies. They're still steaming hot. I'm about to thank her when a man follows her out that I instantly recognize. A man wearing thick-framed glasses.

CHAPTER 19

T he water spurts out of my mouth before I can stop it. I jump out of the chair, leaving the thermos behind, and yanking the screen door open. I flee toward the front yard, forgoing the gate by hopping over it.

"Wait!" I hear, but I'm not turning back. That man is dangerous, and I have no intention of sitting down for snacks with him. Why is he at Byz's house?

I slow, putting two and two together. That's got to be her father, Mr. Lawson. He's the one who worked with Dad, though that doesn't explain why he broke into my house.

I'm unsure whether I should turn and confront him or run and get help. But I know I can't do this alone, so I run again, but the strain on my lungs keeps me from reaching top speed. By this time, Byz is catching up with me. She calls after me; but she doesn't even sound winded.

"Why are you running?"

"Your dad is the man who broke into my house. He may have something to do with my dad's disappearance," I reply breathlessly, stopping to get some air. I turn to see that it is Byz behind me and not the man, so I lean over and put my hands on my knees. The air is sharp, like there's not enough oxygen in it.

She steps forward, but I hold my hand out, gesturing for her to stay back.

"My dad couldn't have hurt your dad," she says. "I mean, he wouldn't have. He's not capable of anything like that."

"Is he how we ran into each other?" I heave another sharp breath, but the accusation is full of venom. "Did he send you to scout me?"

"No. It's not like that at all."

I manage to stand again. "How is it, then?"

Byz opens her mouth to answer when a police transport squeals around the corner, barely missing me. It rumbles to the end of the street, then turns around, heading straight for me. This time, I dodge into the vines, but the transport comes to a halt at the corner.

"Liberty Moore, I've been looking for you for hours," Yates says.

I turn to Byz, but she's disappeared. I swing my head back. That's right, she doesn't exist to the police.

The lieutenant steps out of the transport and opens the back door. "You filed a report this morning about unusual activity in your home. The sergeant worried you might be unstable, and I think the same thing. I'm here to give you a ride home."

"You almost ran me over; I think I should walk," I say, taking the first step toward home.

He clears his throat. "You've misunderstood. It's not a suggestion. I'm here to take you home, assuming you're prepared to go there. Otherwise, we can take you in for a mental health examination."

I don't move, standing in the road with my mouth open. I don't want that. People who go for mental health examinations don't come back.

He comes and takes me by the shoulder and pushes me in the direction of the transport. There are few options. I mean, I could run for it and maybe lose him among the houses, but it's not like they don't know where I live. They'll find me that way. Reluctantly, I duck into the backseat.

Yates slams the door and gets behind the wheel. "Buckle up," he says. "It's the law."

I laugh. No, really laugh, like my head's going to fall off laugh. Whether it's the strain of the day or the ridiculousness of the statement, it strikes me as hilarious. I'm not doing much to keep myself out of that mental health examination.

I take a few deep breaths to calm myself. This can't be happening. It's too much at once, and I'm not accustomed to this much stress. My nerves are frazzled. I feel my veins constrict, and it becomes very difficult to breathe all of a sudden. My head feels inflated, floating on my shoulders.

When he sees me through the driver's mirror, he turns. "You're having a panic attack. Sit still, and it will pass."

Yes, panic. Today has been too much, and I'm overloaded. It takes me at least fifteen minutes to calm down and breathe properly. To his credit, Yates waits until I nod for him to go on.

"Panic attacks are not very common with people using PR," he says. "That worries me, Miss Moore."

His words do nothing to calm me. I'm well aware that I don't have the upper hand in this situation.

"I'm going to take a couple of turns around the block. We need a little talk before I take you home."

He turns his eyes toward the mirror, and a shudder runs up my spine. His greasy hair is back with some kind of gel, and his features are sharp, but it's the sneer I find most frightening.

"PR is a luxury, Miss Moore. I need to know a few things, such as how yours is turned off, why it's turned off, and how we're going to deal with that. I'd like to give you the simplest solution to resolve this problem, but I'll need to know what you have learned first. Are you listening to me?"

I realize I'm staring out the window, and he wants my full attention. I turn to face him again.

He's given me a lot of questions to answer, but he looks at me and waits. The truth is, I don't know how much information is safe to share with him. The police haven't been the most endearing people, and that's not looking to change soon. What's clear enough is that they would prefer it if I were under the illusion we are living in wonderland.

Even if I were to turn on the program now, there would be no way for me to unknow what I've learned, so the only other solution would be to get rid of me or get rid of those memories.

One thing is for certain; I'm not giving up on Byz—at least, not yet. I need to find more information about her. She may not be aware of her dad's weird activities, but I am. I can get around all that if she gives me the information to find Dad.

He clears his throat. "Let me be more direct. Is your PR turned on?"

I want to lie, but it's apparent that I've gone off track today. Instead, I decide not to answer, since he's got to know already. The lieutenant smiles. "I know you have turned it off. What I don't know is how?"

I'm definitely not giving that information up. If I do, they'll take my necklace away, and I'll go back to the disillusioned. I can't let that happen, but I need to throw him something so he doesn't take me for the examination he's threatened.

"My PR glitched the other morning, and I know things aren't always how they appear. What I don't know is why or how? I'm trying to figure out the purpose and what it has to do with Dad."

"Your father has been accounted for, though according to your statement today, you don't believe the man who returned this morning to be him. What makes you think so?"

"Libby. He called me Libby, and my dad would never call me that." I stop there. I can't tell him Imposter looks completely different to Dad. That sounds insane and would out me immediately.

"And that's the big reason you think he's not your father—because he started calling you by a nickname?" There's a victory in his eyes that makes my fists clench and my jaw grind.

"Yes, sir." Maybe it's enough, maybe not, but it's all I'm giving.

"I advise you, Miss Moore, to stay close to home for a few days. Let your parents keep a good watch over you."

"Yes, sir," I repeat, because it's working, but there's something I have to know.

"Do you have PR?"

"Officers don't use PR. Having it removed is required for the force. If I could have it and get my job done, then I would. It's a marvelous invention that lets you live your life to the fullest. I would advise you to forget the glitch and move on from here." He taps the seat in front of me. "Let's get you home."

Yates turns the transport back onto the main thoroughfare, and we head back toward the city center, past the library, to the stop sign nearest the carousel.

There, I see Puck. He smiles ridiculously as we pass and puts his finger over his mouth, issuing a "Shhh..." from the distance. I look up to see if Yates notices him but am pleased to find Puck overlooked.

Puck knows more, and I'm going to have to find a way to get the information from him, but first I'm going to have to do some time at home to satisfy the police. Maybe I'll speak with him on the way to testing in the morning.

My stomach rolls over queasily. The muffin and my meal from the teahouse are ready to evacuate. On the second cramp, I double over, clenching my stomach tight.

By the time we pull into the drive of my house, I'm acutely aware of Imposter watching from the porch. I have to take deep breaths in order to not say anything that might incriminate me further. It's hard to go home to a stranger.

As for him, he looks nervous, his eyes darting from the transport to me to the neighbor's house.

Clarisse is nowhere to be found.

I'm afraid to get out of the transport, worried one wrong move will cause my stomach to upend itself. To add to that, I'm going from one nightmare to another. It's when Yates opens the door and offers a hand that I realize I have little choice in the matter.

"Is there a problem, officer?" Imposter touches his temple where a pool of sweat is forming.

"It's lieutenant. Sir, I've reason to believe your daughter is not making the most of PR. That, and she's showing signs of mental instability. I'm sure you'll keep a good eye on her and make sure she gets the attention she needs. We won't have any more issues, will we, Mr. Moore?"

A third roll of my stomach, much further down than the last. I might have to make a break for it.

"No, sir. And thank you, lieutenant," Imposter says. "I'm so very sorry for the bother. I know you have other duties to attend to. Libby, your mother and I have been worried sick. I'm glad to have you back home, but we really need to discuss your obligations to your family."

Yates nods before returning to his transport. I watch him drive away with a growing sense of dread. As soon as he rounds the corner, Imposter grabs me by the wrist, but I pull away.

"Now look here, Libby. You're going to drop this. No more police reports. I don't want to back up his assessment of your mental stability. Are we understood?"

I want to argue with him, but I really need to use the restroom. I say nothing, so he eventually opens the front door and disappears into Dad's study.

Dropping my shoes by the door, I make a beeline for the bathroom, making it just in time. I'll have to be more careful about how I acclimate my stomach to real food.

The bathroom is indescribable. It's dark and dank and smells terrible. I wash my hands at the basin in yellowish water and close the door behind me to stifle the smell.

Deep breaths. At the top of the landing, I notice that Clarisse has come to the table to work on her panels.

I know my mother loves me in her own way. If nothing else, she loves that I'm a reflection of her. She also loves Dad. They may be opposites, but they're a team. How she's not realized Imposter isn't her husband is beyond me, but she can't possibly know and go on like everything is normal. Maybe she's been too busy with her fashion panels to notice. If so, my parent's marriage is much more superficial than I would have ever imagined.

I descend the stairs as she pores over panels, and now that I get a look at the materials she's working with, I can't imagine a single outfit she's shown me over the years. They must have all been atrocities as far as I'm concerned.

"Hello, dear," she says, glancing up for a second and then focusing back on her work. "You didn't do the dishes this morning."

Dishes? That's her main concern? "Oh, I completely forgot."

"It's okay, you can do them tomorrow," she says with a sigh. "Your father and I missed you this afternoon. Did you enjoy your walk?"

"It was fine." If I ever get out of this, I'm never telling a lie again. It's very taxing.

"Oh, that's good," she answers absent-mindedly. "It was a beautiful day for it."

She doesn't look up from her panels. So much for the concern. I don't know why I'm surprised. She's always been self-centered, but it bothers me more now. Probably because I could use a real ally about now.

"Have you noticed anything unusual since Elizeus came back?" I attempt to wedge some reality in.

"Just that you've been acting strange. You need to be careful, Libby. Rumors of instability can cause dire consequences. I want what's best for you, no matter what that is."

Another veiled threat about a mental health examination. This time it's wrapped in an effort to look concerned, but the damage is done. Even my own mother would let them take me if I seem off.

CHAPTER 20

I'm eager to get to my room and get a proper look at my space to see how it compares to what I'm used to, but I'm only to the landing when my com rings. It's Aden.

With everything that's happened today, I stood him up for our afternoon walk. It was the one thing that was going right, and now it's ruined, too.

But now I see things as they really are, the butterflies don't appear. I mean, he's a little arrogant, but he's still sweet. I had put him on a pedestal, and it's not fair that my feelings have changed, but I can't help it at the moment.

I answer the call.

"Hey, Liberty. I commed to check on you. The main office at the academy said you got an excuse for home today. I wanted to check on you and make sure you're okay? I didn't do anything to put you off, did I?"

"No, no. It's nothing to do with you," I say as I twist my doorhandle.

"Oh, good. I didn't think so, but you never know," he says. "I have an early delivery tomorrow. Can I walk you to academy?

"Sure—Oh my word!" I say as I get the first real glance at my room. "This is awful!"

"You can always say no..."

"No, Aden, it's not you. It's something else. I'll explain tomorrow morning. Got to run." I close the com.

The golden-rod walls of my bedroom are now bleached yellow. The glass on the window is cloudy, and dust flies through the air—but that's better than the rest of the room.

The bed I sleep on is an old, stained mattress, and the covers look to be half-eaten. One of the legs at the foot of the bed is missing, propped up on a pile of wood.

My instinct is to throw myself on it and cry, but the idea of that cloth touching me is too much. It's going to be a very long night if I'm expected to sleep there.

The dresser holding my clothes is old, but it's covered in black char. I don't bother to open the drawers.

In the closet, tatters and rags hang, including the front hanger that holds the dress Clarisse bought for me on Saturday. It's awful. Everything is, except for one thing. In the very back of the closet is a gift from Dad. He brought it home for me one day last summer.

It's a floral dress, that I remember my mother had rolled her eyes at it: it was too plain. I guess it didn't stand out from the PR enhanced items. I hadn't cared for it at the time, because Clarisse had scoffed. I only wore it once, and that was to a training function with Dad, if only just to please him. But now I see it for what it is: it's beautiful. I take it out and run my hand down the skirt. It's sleek and flowy and so much better than anything I own. But best of all, it's a present from Dad.

I walk toward my mirror, but I'm too scared to see my reflection now. I slide off my pilled sweater and throw it over the glass, unwilling to see my leathery skin.

I drop my threadbare blouse and tattered skirt on the floor to see that even my underwear is worn and stained. I slip off the bottoms; I can do without them, but I'm well past the age where a bra is negotiable. It'll have to do.

Sliding the dress over my head, I twirl around, feeling beautiful—a feeling I've taken for granted every day of my life. Dancing to the window seat, I throw off the ratty cushion and lie up against the worn wall.

I must fall asleep, because the next thing I know, Imposter calls my name. "Dinner, Libby!"

Normally, I would help Clarisse prepare dinner, but I've missed all that. It's probably for the best, since I don't want to look at the food, anyway.

My stomach drops further than it did after the muffin. They're going to expect me to eat that muck!

I take my time going down the stairs, wondering if I can stomach the offered food or whether I can sweetly decline. I'm hoping for the latter.

"There she is," Clarisse winks. "I missed my helper in the kitchen today."

"I think I fell asleep," I say, just now getting around to rubbing my eyes.

Clarisse laughs. "There's no doubt about it. I came up to ask if you wanted to help and you were on your window seat fast asleep. I almost woke you to get in the bed, but you looked so peaceful. I didn't want to wake you."

"Thanks," I say, but I'm too concerned about the food to consider it further. Imposter sits down and folds his napkin on his lap as if he's about to dine on fine cuisine.

Mother has set out the glasses, so I pour, starting with Imposter. What comes out is much thicker than what they drank at the coffee shop this morning, and I feel my gag reflex triggering. Unfortunately, I don't stop in time, and I deposit what I had kept down on the floor next to Imposter.

I stare at my vomit on the floor and wait for some sympathy, but neither of them reacts as expected.

"A little spill," says Clarisse and puts the napkins on the floor over it and presses down with her foot. I'm afraid I'm going to repeat my expulsion, so I get in my seat and steady my stomach by staring at the ceiling.

Clarisse pulls the lid off the plate she has placed in the middle of the table, and I pluck up the courage to look down. It's a large hunk of something. I'm not sure whether it was alive at any point, but Clarisse's face shines brightly with pride.

I must turn green, because my stomach does another flip as Imposter carves himself a piece. The black glob turns out to be somewhat gelatinous, wiggling on the plate as he saws at it. And then the smell hits me. It must have been released when he made the first cut, but it's indescribable, like nothing I've ever smelled before, though it looks like the waste I've seen in the restroom.

"I need to be excused," I announce. But Imposter isn't having it. He slams down his fork and knife. "You will sit and eat with your family. No excuses."

I bite my tongue. I can sit, but there's no way I'm eating that food. Imposter goes back to carving another glob and piles some on Clarisse's plate.

He clears his throat and looks at the platter and then my empty plate, indicating that I'll need to eat some as well. The nausea wells up again as I try to think of a way around it but come up with nothing. Carving my own glob and releasing more of the dreadful smell, I plop it on my plate, splattering my arm with chunky gravy.

I can't eat this. I just can't. But maybe I don't have to. If Clarisse and Imposter are so delusional that they can't smell and see vomit, it'll be hard for them to keep up with the blob.

Sorting the glob on my plate, I spread it around with my fork. The smell is unbearable, but the other option is inconceivable. There's no way I can put it in my mouth.

I scoot some off in my napkin, and then some more, until it looks like I've eaten half. It's going as well as it can, given the circumstances.

Imposter looks over the table at my plate and nods. "So where did you end up going today, Libby?" My name sounds like poison from his tongue; I'll loathe that nickname forevermore.

"I just walked around and enjoyed the day."

"Oh," Clarisse says, "Anything of note?"

I play with another forkful of the glob. "The florals are striking at this time of year." Striking, as in nightmarish. "It was good to get some fresh air after having felt so rotten this morning."

Imposter nods. He approves, but he takes another look at my food and tilts his head to the side. "You don't have anything to drink. Here, hand me your glass."

Darn. I hand him the glass, and he fills it up to the brim with the nasty concoction that I'm supposed to drink. No. Can. Do.

He hands the glass across to me with eyebrows raised. It's a dare, and I'm on the losing end. I set the glass by my plate and resume moving the food around, managing to drop a few bits on the floor, before he glares at me again.

It's then I do the only thing that I can think of.

"Could you pass the salt?" I ask, reaching my arm toward my mother. As I do, I knock the glass of muck with my elbow, sending the contents over my plate and the table. I feign a gasp, but Clarisse is already on it.

"Not to worry," she says. "A few towels to soak that up."

For the first time in a long time, I feel a tenderness toward Clarisse that I've been missing. She's my ticket out of this situation.

"I'm really sorry. I've not been feeling well all day, and I think the food was a little much. May I be excused so I can get some fresh air?"

Imposter is about to intervene, when mother laughs. "Of course, you can, darling. This isn't a prison. Get yourself some air, and I'll put you a plate aside in case you want to eat something later."

He interrupts, "Actually, Libby has roamed around all day. I'd prefer it if she spent time at home. If not with us, then up in her room. I don't want her in any more trouble, and she needs to get some rest so she can get back to the academy in the morning."

Every part of me wants to roll my eyes, but instead I trudge up the staircase without a backward glance. In my room, I crawl up on the old window seat and close my eyes.

How did Dad do this every day? Did he turn it on and off to cope? Should I?

Part of me wants to twist the necklace and have PR return. The world is in horrible shape, and I'm too small to make a big difference. What would the harm be?

But I know the harm would be that nothing would change, and I'd never find out what happened to Dad. More than anything, though, my deepest fear is that he'll be forgotten. My dad. The one who played with me dared to free me. The most important person in my life wouldn't even be a memory. I would learn to accept Imposter in some form, maybe even grow fond of him if I played along. That can't happen. I'll figure this out. I need to keep gathering information.

What I really want is to curl up and go to bed, but there's absolutely no way I'm sleeping on that mattress. Zero chance. Instead, I grab the ratty blanket, pull it around me, and rest against the wall next to the window—it's the cleanest place in my room.

For a second, I think I see something move. A shadow between the dry shrubs. I focus there, but the darkness is still. I remind myself I'm on the second floor, but that doesn't help my racing pulse. Why do I feel like I'm being watched?

I look down the street, but it's quiet, then I look up toward the moon. A face moves close to my window.

CHAPTER 21

I let out a loud wail. If I had anything left in my system, I would have lost it then. But as I realize who it is, I hear Imposter call up to my room.

"What's going on up there?" he bellows.

I put my hand to my lips, warning my intruder to be quiet, then rush to the door and yell. "I'm okay. I stubbed my toe on the corner of the bed."

His voice sounds like gravel when he calls up again. "Keep it down up there. I've got work to do."

"Yes, sir."

I close the door again and run to the window. The main picture window doesn't open, but the two windows that flank it do. I open one and whisper out, "What are you doing here?"

Byz shrugs her shoulders. "I didn't finish what I had to tell you earlier, and time is running out. I don't want to call any attention to myself, but I had to let you know what was going on."

"Why didn't you com?"

Byz looks both ways out of what used to the be a healthy plumeria tree, but now resembles a half-dead vine growing near the house. She looks terrified. "Because I don't exist in PR; I can only use my mobile com for an absolute emergency. I've already used it, so I'm waiting for a new device."

"Fine, come in." I say, scooting back.

"You think you can come out instead? Not now, but in a second. For now, get out of sight. The patrol transport should come around any minute."

I certainly don't want another run-in with Yates, so I back away from the window as the blue lights flash into view. The patrol transport slowly makes its way up my street. I don't know where Byz is. She must have dropped back into the vines, but whatever she used to climb up must still be there.

When the transport finally makes its way past, I poke my head out of the window to see Byz huddled behind a big, black tangle of weeds in front of my house. There's a narrow corridor where she can move.

"They're gone," I say as she looks up at me. "How am I supposed to get down there?"

"Climb the lattice woodwork against the building. Put your head out farther; you can see it."

Just as she said, there's wood crisscrossing the side of the building. I don't know what it's for, and I'm kind of weirded out that I haven't seen it before, but the truth is that the whole world is new to me. Why should this be any different?

"Is it sturdy enough? I've got to get back in without being detected. Why don't you want to come in?"

"Honestly?" she says. "I need to be able to run at a moment's notice. I'm unregistered, so I'm taking a big risk by being here. Plus, if the rest of the world is any indication, your room sucks, and it probably doesn't smell so hot."

"Got me there," I say. I pull myself out from where I'm sitting on the sill and grab the wooden lattice to climb down. I misjudge how far up I am and try to jump the rest of the way, but when my feet hit the hard ground, I realize I was farther away than I thought. My bottom hits the dirt, soiling my pretty dress. Not that anyone but Byz will ever notice.

"Is your father here too?" I peek over the bushes, but she pulls me down.

"No. He said I could explain."

"Good, because he's highly suspicious." In truth, this whole situation is making me angry. I give her a dead stare. "Both of you are. For the record, if you do anything weird, I'm willing to scream my head off if necessary."

Fear flashes over her face, giving me a hint of how much she's risking to be here. "That won't be necessary. Promise," she says.

"Okay." I brush excess dirt from my bottom. "Explain."

She puts her hands on her hips and shifts her weight to that side. "I don't need you to believe in me right at this minute, but I need you to listen as I explain what's going to happen tomorrow. It's important you know so you can easily get to safety."

"I'm listening."

She blows out her cheeks and blurts, "Okay... so... PREP, the group you asked me about... Tomorrow they make their first run. It's the first step to Clarity: a return to the real world for our citizens. For a little while, all will be pandemonium. You'll need to be in a safe place."

I frown and hold out my hands. "Whoa, slow down a bit. I have no idea what you're talking about. First run?"

She takes a deep breath, slowing down, only to ramp up again. "You need to find a safe space. You're welcome to join me and my family at the meeting. I think your dad might have liked that. But first and foremost, you'll want to avoid being out in the midst of everything. If you choose not to come to us, I suggest your bedroom or a similar quiet place. There's no telling how everyone will react. My family will be—"

"Wait. What exactly is going on tomorrow? What do I need to be safe against?"

She giggles nervously and circles her head back and forth, presumably as she tries to figure out where to start. "Sorry, I get ahead of myself. PREP will block PR in the morning—for everyone. It's going to be a mess."

I press my lips together tightly, trying to imagine everyone waking up to Clarity at once. I don't need to think far to understand Byz's warning.

"There's so much more, so I need you to listen for a minute," she continues. "Your dad's disappearance has worried a lot of people; PREP's entire timeline has been moved up."

"Wait, what?" I ask, suddenly frantic. "You mean there are more who know about my dad? Why didn't you mention this before? Do any of them know where he is?"

All this time, I thought I was alone. Finding out there is a community of people who all care about my father is game changing. I look at Byz with wide eyes, pleading with her without words.

But she shakes her head, and my excitement shrivels. "I'm sorry, but that's not why I'm here. I didn't mention it because my dad only told me after I spoke with you in the mall. There might be someone out there who knows more, but right now, we have other priorities."

This makes me frown. "I told you what my priorities are. My dad is missing, and I intend to find him."

Byz grimaces. "I didn't mean it like that. Please, just listen."

Her expression changes as she glances over the shrubs again. I'm reminded of the stakes surrounding her just visiting me here. And if Byz is caught, my one link to this community of realists would go with her. Reluctantly, I purse my lips and nod for her to continue.

She exhales slowly. "By this time next week, there'll be new programmers, and my dad will have to train them until they know the ins and outs of the software and hardware. But here's the thing..." She looks at me dead-eyed. "Our dads were trained by two predecessors who hacked into the biome's systems and programmed a message to display on the electronics there. The day after that happened, both disappeared and PR-free police were put in place. They've also heavily monitored our dads to make sure the unrest went no further."

"So they didn't have a choice?"

Her brows raise high as she registers my complaint. "That's right. Our dads were trained to hate PR by their predecessors, but they couldn't just turn it off. The most they could get away with were small acts of rebellion. My dad went off the grid first and took his family with him. Your dad was also off the grid, but for some reason, he allowed you and your mother to stay in PR."

That is strange. Why would he lead us wrong? That's what he was apologizing for the other night. But as soon as I ask myself, I know. Clarisse. There's no way she'd give up her life in PR.

Byz snaps her fingers in front of my eyes. "You with me so far? Because there's more."

I nod, not sure I can juggle any more information, but I'm willing to pick up whatever I can.

"Good. To make a long story short, our dads have spent our whole lives working on the PREP program. It was designed to bring us all into Clarity."

"It didn't happen though," I say, catching on. "Dad disappeared and PR is still very much active."

"That's true." She holds up her finger. "But his program is alive and well. The idea was to switch everything over before their successors arrived—they would be the final PR balancers. But it kept being put off because of the danger. But now, the next successors are being chosen."

I feel my heart sink. "So you really think my dad is gone?"

She shakes her head. "I can't say anything for sure, but he knew he was being watched. In fact, the police are paying pretty close attention to you, too. They must be worried about you. Same with my dad."

She huffs. "Anyway, I'm getting off the point. They're doing the first trial tomorrow. They've planned it for a while now—"

"Trial? Does that mean it won't be permanent?"

"Not tomorrow, no." She looks at me and breathes deeply. "There'll be a fifteen-minute window at noon and another at six. The next day, it will be longer. And then they'll block the signal for good."

"And all of this is taking place at the office? They'll come and arrest your father."

"No. He won't be there." She quirks her mouth proudly. "No one will be. The interrupter is in the church closest to my house. It's where we'll spend the next few days."

She pulls me down as the police transport rounds the corner again, putting her hand to my head like I'm going to jump out on the lawn and wave my hands for them. When it's gone, she stands. "Me, my mom, and dad will recognize you, but that's okay. We're here to help you. But you'll still be in a great deal of danger."

Danger, huh? From whom? "Who'll recognize me?"

"The police. And maybe the guy pretending to be your father." Byz nods and looks down the road again. "I'm out of time. It's almost curfew, and I have a long way to get home without being seen."

"I guess you could stay here?"

This time it's a genuine laugh. "No offense, but I got a look at your room, and I much prefer my own."

I would laugh too, but it's still a little painful. "That's fair."

"Well, it's true." Byz spreads her hands wide and shrugs.

"Anyway, I've got to go." She looks at me with urgency. "I wanted to give you a heads up so you don't get caught in the middle of everything. Promise me you won't tell anyone else, though. Both of our dads have worked hard on this project, and there won't be a second chance if it's exposed. I'm kind of putting all our lives on the line by telling you."

"Why tell me, then?"

She looks at me like it's the stupidest question she's ever heard. "My whole life, you've been the best friend I've ever had, Libs—even if we didn't speak for a while. Other than a few neighbor girls, you're the only one my age that I really know. Sure, the PREP people know me, but you're my peer. Look, I don't want anything to happen to either of us. I've been waiting for a real friend for a long time, and you're it."

I smile at that, despite the circumstances. "Okay. I can't promise anything, but I'll try."

"Then, stay at home with your mother. You can act as surprised as she is when reality goes live."

"I'll try."

"Good, I've got about ten minutes to get home before lights out. Wish me luck." She pulls me into an embrace, and I stiffen up like a board. I'm not used to having a close friend. I could get used to it, but it's going to take some adjustment.

CHAPTER 22

I wake up with a neck ache from where I leaned crooked against the windowpane. At some time in the night, I'd grabbed my ratty old coat out of the closet to create a buffer between me and the wood seating. And the tattered gold blanket wadded in a ball on my shoulder was too thin to provide much cushioning for my head.

The window has a foggy spot where I've been breathing on it. I wipe off the fog and look at the street below. No one is up and going yet, so it must be early. I look down at the bushes, somewhat hoping that Ryz might be waiting for me, but I can't really see where we were unless I open the window.

I need to figure out a way to get mother home by noon so she won't be in the frenzy when Clarity strikes, which is easier said than done. My mother is a force. When she's working, she's all in, and she tunes the rest of us out. I'll be catching her at lunchtime, which tends to conclude in the coffee house downtown.

Then there is Imposter to consider. I don't care if he gets disoriented. He's not my problem, but he's been staying awfully close to Clarisse, and he'll be suspicious if I change plans. It'll be a dead giveaway. I don't have a clue how to manage it.

From the landing, the smell of something being charred wafts up the staircase. I'm starving, but there's no way I'm going to eat whatever Clarisse is serving.

I don't bother changing from my dress—it's not like I have anything else—and head downstairs to see my parents scooping something from a hard rind; it looks putrid. That's a hard pass.

I slump onto the crooked couch and avoid the table all together.

Clarisse calls after me. "Are you not eating, Liberty?"

"No, I'm a little shaky from yesterday. Must have eaten something that didn't sit well with me at the tea house."

Clarisse nods. "I thought your food looked kind of strange."

"I think you should eat," Imposter says with command, but thankfully, Clarisse is on my side again.

"Leave her alone, Elizeus. There's no use in pushing it. She's a little queasy, that's all. It'll resolve itself soon enough, but until then, you can never be too thin."

She laughs, and I let out a nervous giggle. Clarisse is definitely too thin in Clarity. Maybe I can keep her from that, at least.

Imposter folds his paper shut and pushes his chair away from the table. "I suggest you get it resolved by this evening." Then he stands and puts on Dad's jacket by the door. "I've got to go to a meeting for a few hours, and it's likely they'll run through lunch today. I'm going to find out my new post. It's always good to get a change of pace. My new job will have less work hours if I can get the position I want."

Clarisse walks over and gives him a kiss on his cheek. Gross. "Good luck, honey," she says to him fondly, then looks at me, waiting for me to reinforce the sentiment.

"Yeah, good luck," I say, trying to pull some measure of excitement out of myself. What I do find is enthusiasm for him not being at lunch today.

"Good luck, *Dad*," he says. It's a challenge. He's laying the groundwork for the power structure. He stares at me and waits for me to comply.

"*Dad*," I say, but I can't hide the sharpness of my voice, because calling him that is a mark on Dad's name.

He kisses Clarisse, walks back through the kitchen, and disappears behind the garage door. As soon as the transport starts and the garage opens, Clarisse smiles at me.

"At noon, I want you to come straight home. I want to talk to you about some feminine things, and your dad won't want to hear about them."

"Uhm... Sure. I'll be here by noon."

That was a fortunate turn of events. But I'm at a loss as to what she wants to talk about. I mean, I'm seventeen. It's a bit late to talk about puberty and menstruation, but if it will get her here safely, I'll listen to anything she wants to say.

"Good, now, you need to get off to testing. You can't afford to miss another day, or they may hold you back to next year, or worse, put you in a loathsome job. Put on a good face. That'll solve most problems."

Out on the porch, I realize my feet are covered with dirt from the shrubbery last night. I wipe them off the best I can on an old WELCOME mat at the front door before I slide them into my ugly shoes. At least the shoes are comfortable.

As I walk, I scrutinize my street once again. The dilapidated old houses all seem to lean in different directions, a few so close in proximity that they're leaning on one another. In the yards are the same black bushes that a few days ago held bright colors. At least, that's what I thought. Now there is trash in most of the yards, and the ground is untrimmed.

I don't focus my energy on those yards, though. Instead, I'm looking at the neat yards and wondering about the inhabitants. Are they all off the grid? Are they friend or foe as far as the PREP community goes? Do they want Clarity?

CHAPTER 23

I'm almost to the carousel when Aden catches up to me. He's breathless, but wears a bright smile.

"I thought I was going to miss you all together. The chain on my bike came off. I had to ditch it in a friend's garage and run the rest of the way here."

"Sorry about your bike, but you don't have to walk with me every morning. I can make it there and back on my own." It comes out wrong, but I'm preoccupied with what to do about Dad.

He looks at me, and the light in his eyes dims, as if he's disappointed I've even considered the possibility of him not being there. "I know, but I'm glad to do it. It's a good break for me. That, and we look good together."

I smile, but it's short-lived.

"That's an unusual dress you're wearing. You might want to dial up the saturation a bit. It washes your skin out. I almost didn't recognize you."

Sounds like something Clarisse would say. I wish I knew how he saw me, because then I'd know how far off my real self looks from my PR self. He probably won't be so interested if he sees me as I am. I have a few days to prepare him for the real me when Clarity comes. Then it'll be out in the open. I shake my head; I can't worry about that now.

"Are you working today?" I ask.

"Yes, but I'll be in the warehouse taking inventory, so it'll be a quiet day. Extra people are being called in. Shouldn't take us long, I don't think."

"When do you get off?"

He looks up as he calculates his response. "Probably four or five o'clock, assuming everything goes as planned. Hey, how about lunch? We get a break from eleven to twelve. I could take you out."

"I can't. I have plans with my mother." My relief must seem obvious in my deep exhale, but if he notices it, he doesn't say anything.

A voice comes from behind. "Another day of the same, but there is a buzz of excitement!"

I jump. Puck is standing only inches behind me, giggling over my shoulder. He continues, dancing a half-circle around Aden and me until he comes to a stop on the path in front of me. "I don't know what it is, but something is going to change, and I'll be ready. I won't let anyone overlook me when the world is clear. People will call my name and know my face everywhere."

I maintain a pleasant smile; I don't want Aden getting angry again. "Have a good day today," I say to Puck.

It's enough to stop him cold. "Today is the day?"

I nod, and he nearly falls over his own feet, heading back to the Clockery. I don't know if he's going to prepare for the fallout or if he's going to hide.

Aden looks at me strangely, and asks what that was about, but I laugh it off. "He's weird. Don't worry about it."

When we get to the campus, Aden says, "Like I said, we look good together, Libby. Both of us are attractive and smart. Have you noticed how others smile at us, as if we're a perfect match?"

I shake my head. I've been far too distracted to notice other people, but even if I had, I don't know that I would have come to his conclusion. To be so caring, he can be kind of superficial.

"Want to take a walk later this evening?" he asks.

"Maybe," I say, remembering the six o'clock trial. "I think we're doing something at my house tonight, and I'm not sure my mother will allow it. We can talk about it later."

He smiles and waves goodbye as I head past the academy gate, but I don't get any farther than the flagpole.

I mostly stop because that's where I met Byz just yesterday, but I'm also intrigued by the flag. I thought it was checkered my whole childhood, but it turns out it consists of tiny flags from different places. There are over fifty, and I wonder which one represents where my grandparents come from. So many cultures are represented here, but PR gives them all a commonality.

I take the place where Byz sat yesterday and watch the students filter toward the building. If I weren't in crisis, I would find it comical. Hair gelled into odd shapes. The hand-me-down clothes, threadbare and mismatched. I look down at my outfit; I'm wearing the dress I put on yesterday. To them, it must look plain among the eclectic combinations.

There are exceptions, though. I count four people who look groomed in reality—hair in place with solid colors and plain pants. One has a hood over his head, and I look at him, confused. He must see me, because he points to the sky.

The sun is dangerous, he says with that small gesture, and I don't need to look at myself to know it's true. My once pale skin wears like leather on my arms. I haven't even looked at my face other than in the picture on Dad's desk. I reach up to touch my cheek and wonder.

The crowd dwindles, and I know I should go inside, but no part of me wants to test for a job that I can't pursue—at least, not as is.

I jump off the block and head past the academy toward the library that I passed yesterday. I look at the same murals again, smiling at the artistry. From the pictures, it seems as if the building must be full of books like the ones Dad has in his office. Most books are digital now, so I can see why the building is now obsolete. Hardly anyone reads anymore, games and vidclips being much more entertaining.

I stand in front of the library for a few minutes before someone comes out. It's a short, balding man with glasses on the top of his head. He yells from the front porch. "Are you lost?"

"No, sir." I say. "Just stopping to rest for a minute." I turn and walk toward the tall building with the star that I know I'll find ahead.

I follow it until I'm at the church where a few people are gathered near the backdoor. They're all Realists. I can tell by their choice in clothing and the way they're groomed.

I wonder if I blend in with them. Probably, but I'm not sure they're ready for me, and I don't want to hunker down just yet. I need to get more info on Dad. Maybe I can ask Truman.

Looking over to Byz's house, I notice the neat lawns and stable-looking homes. There must be several in the community who build and keep these areas up. We need someone fixing things around my house, before my bedroom makes it to the bottom floor.

Crossing their small lawn, I rap on their front door and watch the activity near the church while I wait. These people are like Dad. They're permanently aware. I feel sorry for those caught up in the PR, but I'm also a little jealous. Ignorance has its own bliss, and I'm not ashamed of how long I partook, but I am concerned with the damage done while I moved around, thinking life was idyllic—maybe even a little boringly predictable. It's not a delusion I can afford much longer if the glaring sun is any indication.

No one ever answers the door, and I wonder if they're already in the church, but I'm afraid if I go in, they won't let me out to return to help Clarisse or gather evidence about Dad.

Soon, I'm standing on the street in full view of the plastic-looking orb. It's no longer the moon, but an eyesore. It's hard to comprehend how the Watchers are monitoring us. The eye probably knows exactly what happened to Dad, but it's not like I can ask it.

I probably should keep moving as to not draw attention, so I turn around. It's too late to go back to the academy. They'll want a formal excuse for an arrival this late, and the fact that I was out yesterday will toughen up my consequences, rather than make everything better.

I also can't go home. If I do, I risk mother having her discussion early and leaving before noon. I'm also no closer to finding out what happened to Dad, though the reason he was in danger is clearer. Maybe Puck can clear some of the details up.

As I pass the library, the same bald man who asked me if I was lost sits on the porch in one of the rocking chairs. He's got a book in his lap, though his head is leaned back on the seat. I'm sure he's sleeping, but I keep my eyes on him just the same. He cracks one of his eyes open and spots me standing there.

"You again? Sure you're not lost?"

"No, sir. Sorry, I'll be on my way."

"Woah, hold on, now." He sits up, pulls on his glasses, and leans in for a closer look. "You're not Elizeus's daughter, are you?"

I hesitate, not knowing if he's a friend or an enemy, but he smiles. "I thought I recognized you. You're just a year under my granddaughter, Faith. I worked with your dad some. I used to be an astronomer at the observatory, but now I'm a researcher. Name is Shuyler, but people call me Shy."

I return his smile cautiously. "I'm Liberty."

"Yes, you look like your dad, but I saw you and your mother at the tea house yesterday. I heard about your father. I'm sorry they replaced him so soon."

He has my full attention now. "You knew that wasn't my dad?"

"Yes, anyone in Clarity could see that. Elizeus was a good man. Well-liked. Important."

"Yes, he was. *Is*. Do you know what happened to him?" I climb onto the porch, and he offers me the other chair. I sit.

"I don't know exactly what happened, no." He gives me a sympathetic smile, but I still slump back on the rocker, sending it swaying back and forth. "There are many people who won't benefit from Clarity. They're like gnats on a festering body. They feed on the delusion."

I frown. "But the only reason the others are that way is because of Personal Reality. They don't know how they're truly living." I say this, though Clarisse is a perfect example of somebody who rejected Clarity knowingly.

"That may be so for some." His eyebrow hitches. "How much do you know about the biome?"

"The people there, the Watchers, steal our food," I say, "And they have protection from the climate. They ran off and left us."

He nods. "You know quite a bit, then. Elizeus was a threat to their way of life. Same with the Red Stars. Lots of people are threatened by Clarity, and your father was making that a reality."

I tilt my head at him. "Red Stars?"

"I'm sure you've noticed the stars around the city center," he provides.

I pull my mouth to the side. "I've seen them around and noticed the different colors, but I don't know what they mean."

"Well, this is the Blue Star headquarters." He gestures around the porch and to the building behind him. "For years we've been collecting data and doing research. Our aim was to record everything but try not to influence the outcome. That was short-sighted. Now we are leaning more toward saving the planet, and we've slowly come to realize that such a feat is impossible while living under the delusion of PR. For the last year, we've been working with the Yellow Stars—primarily your dad and Truman Lawson. Although, the Red Stars are attempting to team up with the Yellow Stars, too."

I'm reminded of the yellow and red stars on my house: Dad and Clarisse. Does that mean they were working together? If so, I've seriously misjudged her, and in this case, that's a good thing.

"Personally," he continues. "I don't trust the Red Stars, and neither should you."

Oh. "Why don't you trust them?"

"I think most of the Red Stars want to sabotage Clarity, but I can't prove it. Not yet."

"But why would anyone want to do that?"

Shy shrugs. "They appreciate the power PR gives them over others."

I remain silent. If that's true, Clarisse must be a Red Star. She seems perfectly at home in PR, so it makes sense for her to be against Clarity. She also always strives for success, and it's difficult to think of her worried about anyone other than herself.

"Yes, yes..." He rocks his chair. "These are dangerous times. Speaking of which, you need to get where you're going by noon. The trial starts then, and everything will be in chaos for a bit. Run along and get somewhere safe. Unless you'd like to stay here."

Shaking my head, I stand and jump off the porch. "I need to go, but I'll drop by again if I get a chance."

"That would be nice, but I'll be very busy the next few days, so I might not be in. Lots of work to do before Clarity is permanent."

I nod and walk away. When I turn back, the man already looks like he's back to sleep.

CHAPTER 24

I move back down through the neighborhoods with a little more speed, but still trying to not look out of place. If I were a couple of years older, it would be a bigger problem. Working citizens don't generally roam the streets, but sometimes teens and children do. The rules allow a certain amount of freedom when we aren't in testing. Then there's the elderly who are preparing for Graceon; they need lots of exercise. Otherwise, adults are sparse. Travel tends to be direct and utilitarian, and police encourage people not to roam.

I can see the end of the carousel and a blue police transport. The officer will be nearby, and I hope it's not the sergeant from the station or Lieutenant Yates. I really don't need to run into either of them.

With my body aligned with the bushes, I look around for Puck, but see no sign of him.

I'm going to have to take a leap of faith here and knock on his door. If he's got more information on Dad or his disappearance, I can find out this way. Whatever I do, I need to hurry in such a way that I'm not seen and I can make it safely to my house by noon.

Rapping my knuckles on the door of the Clockery, I try to peek in but can't see anything for the glare on the glass and the white paint behind it. I check back for any sign of the police officer, but he's still not visible.

There's no answer. I know what I'm going to have to do, though I'm already dreading it. I cross the store fronts to an alleyway. There, I see the gate that will lead me to the back door.

I don't get to go through it, because Puck is already coming out of it.

"Are you running from me?" I ask.

He nearly jumps out of his shoes at seeing me standing there.

"You'll leave if you know better, girlie. Someone has found my hideout, and neither of us is safe." He tries to move around me, but I block his way. "Move! It won't take them too long to look for a back entrance."

"What makes you think they found your hideout?"

He puts his hands on my shoulders, and I cringe. "Someone knocked on the door a minute ago."

"That was me. I need to speak with you about my dad."

"We are in imminent danger." He squeezes by, too thin to block. "I confirmed it with Truman."

"I know about the trial, but I still need answers," I insist, though he shakes his head violently. Everything about him has become more animated, and it's starting to set me on edge.

He calls over his shoulder, "Coffee house. Meet you there in ten minutes. It'll take me a bit to get there, because I don't want to draw attention. I think we can talk there. The day barista is one of us, so she won't say anything. She'll let us talk in peace as long as no one else is in there."

Clarisse. She loves her coffee. "What if my mother is in there?"

Puck stops and turns. "If she's there, come back here."

"That works for me, but know that I need to be back to my house by noon. No matter what."

He nods hard. "That's the time, then. Yes, we really must work quickly. Scurry on, and I'll see you there soon." I barely catch his last words as he turns and scuttles away.

I passed the coffee shop on the way here, and I recall it looked busy at the time. I'm hoping there'll be a lull before the lunch rush. I've nothing to lose in finding out.

By the time I get there, one older woman is outside, drinking her coffee next to the window and enjoying what she probably considers good weather. When I enter the building, there's a loud clang from the bell on the door. I step into a tidy seating area, and the two inhabitants turn to look at me.

"Oh, hi, again," the customer behind the register says. I recognize her. It's the server from the teahouse. "I'm Theron."

"Liberty. Thank you so much for your help yesterday. It was the only proper meal I had."

Theron smiles. "We've got a new one, Myrna. Take good care of her."

The barista eyes me and smiles.

"Look at the time," says Theron. "Got to scurry. It's a big day, you know."

Before the door closes behind Theron, Myrna says, "You look like you could go for an iced latte with full milk. Probably wouldn't hurt to get some food in you, too. Your skin looks awful. Don't guess you've had much to eat?"

I want to tell her I've only known about this reality for two and a half days and haven't had the chance to navigate healthy eating habits, but I know she's being kind, so I suppress the desire.

"Tell you what, I made coconut salad this morning. Let me get you some of that, some clean water, and then we'll see about the coffee."

"Thank you so much." I mean it. I could use all the allies I can get at the moment.

"Glad to help. The washroom is around the corner. It'll be a good place for you to clean yourself up."

Clean myself up? I must be filthy, because in this fresh room, I can smell myself, musty and mildewy.

Doing as she says, I wash my hands once, realizing that some of the darkness is caked in dirt. I wash a second time, but short of a stiff brush, I'm going to have to accept some dirt for now. I also run the paper towels around my nooks and crannies, taking care to leave my face as is, in case someone like the police or Clarisse notice the difference.

When I come back, I find a coconut shell filled with greenery and a cream-based mixture. Sprinkled on top is coconut and another herb I don't instantly recognize. Beside that is a glass of water, with another pitcher of water beside it for refills.

I don't realize how thirsty I am until I've drunk a full glass of water before trying the salad. When I finally get to the salad, it tastes light and refreshing on my tongue. I allow the sharp flavor to melt in my mouth, bite by bite.

While I eat, I keep my eyes open for Puck and Clarisse. It's been well over ten minutes. Perhaps I should go find him.

But as soon as I push back the shell, the lady arrives with a to-go cup covered with froth and caramel. I take a drink, getting the milk on my nose while inhaling the rich aroma. It's sharp and cold with the lightest taste of the tan syrup.

"Good?" Myrna asks.

"It's the best! Thank you so much; I didn't realize I needed it."

"You're quite welcome." She takes the coconut shell. "I can bring more if you want?"

"No, this is quite enough; it'll make me sick if I eat too much. What you gave me was just right." I pat my stomach. "I'm waiting for Puck."

"Oh." She looks doubtful. "You won't be able to talk here. It's almost eleven, and you should probably go before the lunch rush. We're quite busy then."

Taking the hint, I push my chair back. I hope I haven't tarnished some sort of budding relationship by mentioning my meeting with Puck.

"Thank you so much for the food," I say as I stand. "It's Myrna, right?"

"Yep. You come back if you need me."

As I leave the coffee shop, I keep an eye out for Puck, but instead, I see Clarisse heading straight toward me.

I quickly pivot, stepping beside the palm tree that anchors the crooked sidewalk, and turn the other way, keeping my head bowed and pretending to look through my bag. That's when a breathy whisper hits my ear.

"Fancy meeting you here," Puck says in a timbered voice, but I don't respond.

Puck will have to wait a minute; right now, I need to be quiet and not draw any attention.

When I hear the door to the coffee shop bang, I'm sure that's where Clarisse went. I step onto the roadside and continue to the other side of the building.

"Hey, I'm sorry I'm late, but there's no reason to ignore me!" he calls after me.

I turn when I'm well down the path; Puck is standing where I left him. With a wave of an arm, I summon him to me.

"Sorry, I couldn't let my mother see me back there. I absolutely can't be caught out today. Already happened yesterday. We need a safe place to chat, but I don't really have the time. I'm to meet mother in less than thirty minutes, so she'll likely be coming this way any minute now."

"Here, follow me." he says, and I watch his skinny legs pump up and down as he slips into the bushes in the park; the spot right in front of his building, and most importantly, the last place I saw Dad.

"Where have you been?" I ask as I flump down on the old bench.

"I had things. We all have things, you know."

I'm so confused. Before I realize it, I blurt out the obvious question: "Do you know what happened to my dad?"

He stands up straight, the wide red lines lengthening in front of me. "I don't." His face is grave, so I don't know what to think about his answer.

"But you were a witness to some extent, right? If you didn't see it, then I'm left to assume you had something to do with it."

"That's a big assumption, girlie. But I know a few things that you don't know. And one is the most important."

"Go on, then. I'm listening."

"I'm not going to just tell you. I've given you enough about Clarity. Information is capital in the real world, and you'll have to pay a price."

I'm taken aback, but I stand my ground. "Well, I knocked on your door to give you some information, so I have that to exchange." If he wants to barter, I'll barter.

He laughs like I've told a quaint joke. "I don't want information. I have lots of that."

"What do you want?" I ask, folding my arms.

He smiles, and each pencil-thin tooth shows. "The necklace you're wearing."

He reaches out to take it, but I pull back, throwing my latte in his face. When he reaches a second time, I push him and make a run for it.

Tears push at my eyes, but I hold them back with gritted teeth. I don't know if they're from sadness, confusion, or frustration, but it feels like every emotion has decided to assault my senses at this moment. I run blindly until I get to my street and realize a police transport is parked in front of my house, and Lieutenant Yates stands on the porch.

I skid to a halt and throw myself into a row of black bushes. But the action makes such a racket, he turns in my direction. There's no use running from him, and if I stay where I am, I'll look more suspicious than ever. So I quickly push myself up and mutter a few faux "Silly me's" under my breath as I brush myself down.

Yates speaks into his com as I edge up the driveway, then he turns to watch me.

"Liberty Moore, I've been looking for you everywhere."

Well, this is getting old.

CHAPTER 25

I walk toward my porch as if I'm heading toward a slow death. I have no idea what to expect, but it can't be too good if Yates is standing on my front porch for the third time in three days. Stopping in the middle of the yard, I dare not get too close.

"Where have you been the past few hours, Miss Moore?"

"It's a testing day." I say.

He draws his brow down. "Yes, I know, and I also know you didn't attend your sessions. I've already been to the campus."

I heave what I hope passes as a regretful and tired sigh. "Honestly, I couldn't bring myself to go into the building this morning, so I took a long walk and ended up in the coffee shop to get a bite to eat and drink a latte."

Yates busily writes everything down, then looks up as if he's soaking me in like a sponge. "There was an incident on the south side of the city. We have witnesses that saw a girl your age."

"Surely there are a lot of girls my age."

His eyes bore through me. "There are, but all of them were present in testing."

Except for Byz; she wouldn't be in training, and she may not be the only unregistered child. Probably isn't, now I think about it.

Yates remains silent, and I realize he's expecting me to defend myself, which I'm not sure how to do yet. So instead, I buy myself some thinking time.

"I walked around, but I'm not sure of the area you're talking about. You need to be more specific."

"Were you on the south side of town in the last hour?"

"Yes." I purse my lips, willing myself to give short answers.

He gives me a look that tells me he's waiting for more, but I keep his eyes and don't move my mouth. Eventually, he elaborates. "There's a building there—not far from the academy, but it stands out among the houses. Do you know the one I'm talking about?"

He must be talking about the library. It's settled in with a lot of houses, but there's been no break-in; I was just there with Shy. Still, I can't tell him that, because I'm pretending to be in PR.

"I do." I clench my muscles, waiting for the inevitable follow-up.

"Something was stolen, and you're a person of interest. We're looking for an item that was taken." Yates gives me a moment to let his words soak in. "I think it's best you come to the station and answer a few questions in an official capacity."

I take a step back, holding up my hands. "I didn't break in anywhere. You're welcome to check my bag. You'll see I have nothing on me."

He doesn't miss the invitation. Yates takes my bag and spreads it on the wooden floor slats of the porch. I watch my lip balm fall through the cracks and settle below the porch, but there's nothing of interest there. Some pens and pencils, the lollipop Byz gave me, the cloth from the muffin I ate, my wallet, and a hairbrush I stashed there this morning.

"You're clean," Yates announces, and I think he's going to put away my things, but instead, he throws the bag down. He glances behind me and hesitates.

Clarisse is coming down the road holding a cradle of coffee. She has her hair pulled up and gelled, so it comes to a point. Her mismatched outfit makes her wobble when she walks, as it is too tight in the hips. She is such a spectacle that both of us watch.

"What's the problem, officer?" She's put out. I can tell, because her voice is sharp.

"Lieutenant, ma'am. I'm investigating a robbery, and your daughter was in the vicinity when the crime took place. She's a person of interest."

"Weren't you at..." I know where she's going, but I wasn't on campus like I should have been. I should have gone to the academy for all I'd gotten this morning, but the fact remains that I didn't.

"Lieutenant, we have a misunderstanding. We've had some confusion, and Libby has been under a lot of strain since you scared her into thinking someone assaulted her father. I think I've got a handle on the problem, so unless you can arrest her for a crime, I'd like some time with my daughter—*alone.*"

Yates's eyebrows rise high on his face. This is the second time this woman has taken command in his presence. It doesn't take an academic to realize he's unaccustomed to it.

"Mrs. Moore, I'm sure you're quite influential in your home, and I've heard your name before, so I know you hold some sway with the community, but as far as police procedure, you have little say."

"Are you going to arrest her?"

"No, ma'am," he says. "We just need to ask her some questions."

"Have you asked them?"

"Yes, ma'am—" he starts.

"Well, now, you can either arrest her with no evidence or you can turn and go have yourself a nice, long lunch. My daughter and I will be inside doing the same thing, and I would like to get to it, if you don't mind."

Yates's eyebrows are just as high, but they've morphed into squiggly lines that seem to be trying to make sense of Clarisse Moore. He shakes his head and looks down at his scuffed shoes. "We're still gathering facts, ma'am. I might be back for further questioning."

"That's fine, but from this point forward, you'll not question my daughter without an adult present. That is non-negotiable."

Yates jerks his body forward while reaching into his suit jacket to retrieve his keys. "I'll come back if I need to."

Clarisse doesn't wait for him to get in his transport and leave but walks up the crooked steps and enters the front door. I follow her, because she's in control.

She sets her cardboard carrier on the table and pulls out two drinks. Both look equally vile. She then excuses herself to use the restroom.

While she's gone, I check the two cups and realize the one that says "skinny" on it must be hers, so I look into the one that's mine. It's foul. How could it come from the coffee shop I just left? But I know that it's differing perceptions. I'm certain I would consider the drink to be perfect were my PR active.

I pour it down the kitchen sink, using a fork to push the more solid chunks through the holes in the drain. This must be what I used to think was ice. *Yuck.*

As I slip the cap back onto the drink, I notice the clock. It's twenty seconds to twelve. My heart jolts in my chest. I take deep breaths to slow my pulse and sit at the table to watch a woman who must be Mrs. Belden, our next-door neighbor, water the black bush on her lawn. Everyone is due for a rude awakening in... I look at the clock... 5, 4, 3, 2, 1.

Clarity.

Everything looks the same to me.

A loud bang echoes from the bathroom as I watch Mrs. Belden drop the water hose and examine the plant closer. She turns her head back and forth, not sure what her eyes are seeing.

Beyond the bathroom door, Clarisse is whimpering quietly.

"Mother, what's going on in there? Are you all right?"

"It's very important that you stay where you are for the time being, Liberty," she says, her voice muffled and high-pitched. "I've been through this before, and it always passes. It's only a matter of time."

"Come out and speak to me," I say.

"No, no. Close your eyes, darling. This will pass."

CHAPTER 26

Through the front window, I watch people come out of their houses, gawking at the scenery, while Mrs. Belden has walked around toward the front of her house. I feel sorry for them all, especially those who have just sat down to enjoy their lunch, those who were staring lovingly in their partner's eyes, and those now struggling to find their way home. It's a rude awakening and enough to scare just about anyone.

The door shuts behind my mother. She navigates the room with her eyes closed. Fumbling from one thing to another, she manages to make her way to the table and sit down.

"Do you see it?" she asks.

"Yes, it's all different than it was." I'm curious why her eyes are closed, but then it's perfectly clear. Clarisse is playing the game of a child. She's pretending that if she doesn't see it, it doesn't exist. "Mother, do you see me?"

"No, the trick is to stay quiet. It always comes back on if you wait it out. It's never not returned. You have to be patient."

Her fragility takes me off guard. This woman who just talked down a police officer and owns the fashion world has turned into a child in front of me. I'm seeing her in a new way, and I don't like it.

I wonder what she sees of me. To her, I probably look plain.

"Can you tell me what I look like?" I ask her.

She smiles but doesn't open her eyes. She says, "Your eyes are blue, and your hair is red. You have the cutest nose. You get that from me. And you have your father's eyes. The clothing you have on today is unfashionable. I can help you if you'd like."

"Do you want to know what *you* look like?"

She shakes her head, but it comes across as more of a tremor. "I know what I look like; I don't need you or anyone to tell me. This is a trick. A trick. You'll see. Give it a few minutes and things will be exactly the way they were. There's no need to be afraid."

I remember the bump under her sweater in the picture. She must have been through this with the necklace. Dad must have tried to show her, but instead of accepting it, she withdrew, becoming immune to the images she was seeing.

Dad must have tried to get her to understand, but her stubbornness, her assertiveness, is tied to her mental wellbeing. She can't see it, because she can't handle it.

"I think this was the world Dad lived in; I think it's where he hoped we'd join him."

"Ridiculous. He's at work, and he lives in the same world we do. It's not possible for us to live in two different worlds at the same time."

"Do you remember him ever talking to you about it? Another reality, I mean."

She sighs and puts her fingers on her wedding ring, spinning it around. "I've never told you, but Elizeus is an alarmist. He believes in the worst-case scenario for everything. One sunny day, he tried to convince me that the planet was dying and that we were being held prisoners... Don't get me wrong, I love him, but sometimes he's difficult to be around."

"Dad disappeared, Clarisse. He's not here, and I don't know what's become of him."

She purses her lips together and shakes her head. "He's only gone to work, Libby. There's no need to be dramatic."

My worries about Clarisse being a Red Star disappear at that moment. She's completely out of touch.

A quick glance out the window tells me Clarisse isn't alone in her denial, either. Across the street, in front of the Devonshires' house, a woman runs after a man who is in nothing but his underwear. The Devonshires.

Mrs. Devonshire swings what looks to be a broom handle, but he's too fast. He grabs the handle and breaks it in two, using the weight of his foot. He pulls the shorter stick back, like he may hit her, but she runs around to the other side of the house before he gets the chance.

Mrs. Belden paces around in the street as if she's looking for her house, and Mr. Devonshire walks up to join her. He hands her the other side of the stick, and they turn in a circle, back to back, like they're both about to be attacked at any minute.

If it's this bad here, there's no telling how bad it is in the middle of town. For one thing, all those poor people are looking at the disgusting slops of food they've been eating. Their loved ones are strangers.

I push that out of my mind. Right now, my concern is Clarisse. She's going to need to acclimate to this world, and it'll be a difficult task.

"Why don't you want to see?" I ask her. "Are you afraid?"

"Yes," she nods, "and you should be too. This delusion is dangerous. The term is 'gaslighting,' and somebody is trying to drive us crazy by showing us worst-case scenarios.

"I know what I look like; I don't need you to tell me. I know our house well. I designed every piece of furniture, upholstery, art. All of it. I know exactly what it looks like, because I have sold those same patterns to customers who paid dearly to come by them. This is a lie, Libby. Don't believe it."

We sit in silence until the fifteen minutes are up, and PR resumes. With a glance out the window, I see Mr. Devonshire drop the broom handle and pull one hand over his chest and another to his underpants. I smile to myself as he turns around, sees his house, and dashes at full speed inside, leaving Mrs. Belden on the roadside. Coming from behind the house, Mrs. Devonshire is probably looking for the man in his underwear that accosted her. I can't hear her, but she's yelling something.

Ironically, she's probably calling for her husband.

Mrs. Belden looks over her left shoulder to where her house is and walks that way. She turns off the water hose, wipes her head, and goes inside.

I stand up and push in my chair, but Clarisse still has her eyes closed.

"It's all right, Clarisse. It's over."

She opens her wrinkled eyes and sighs softly. "You just have to wait it out, honey. That's all."

I don't know what to say to that. "I think I'm going out for a while."

Before I can make a move for the door, she stops me.

"Wait, sit down. I'll make us some soup." She resumes as normal, picking up her coffee cup to drink. It's enough to give me whiplash. "I've been wanting to talk to you. As you well know, I have lots of friends around town, and they like to keep me up with the latest news. I've heard lots of reports of you walking around with a boy. That's fine and well until I find out you're skipping testing and going missing for long stretches of time. I know you know a little about your body, but we've never really had the talk. And with a new boyfriend, especially one you've been sneaking around with, I want you to make good decisions, so I need to be upfront with you now."

Oh. My. Stars. She just hid from the whole entire world, and now she wants to have the talk. My mind can't even go there.

"We just met! Aden and I only started walking together a few days ago. It's no big deal!"

"You've missed a lot of testing while you were 'walking around.' I'm concerned you having a slightly older boyfriend is impacting your focus."

I stare at her, dead-eyed. Is there an accusation in there?

She shrugs. "You can never be too careful, Libby. The real world has some pitfalls, and I'd like to avoid you falling into them. There are years and years left to think about boys. You've a lot to learn yet."

There's no way to respond. She wouldn't even know if the real world came up and slapped her. So I pick up my bag, slide my shoes on from the porch, as Clarisse natters through the doorway. I step out into the glaring sun. I don't know where I'm going, but I'm not staying here.

• • • ● • ● ● • • •

As I walk through town, people are back to their normal schedules, but they're jumpy too, as if something is about to reach out and grab them. There are several old men by the carousel. They're sitting on benches when they should be walking. They look too flabbergasted to speak. The disturbed looks on their faces show that their wisdom doesn't encompass today's glitch. Or worse, they know the dark world is real. They may be old enough to remember the world pre-PR.

Today could have been some bitter homecoming for them.

I look for Puck, but I don't see him. *Good.* I don't want to deal with him any further. Instead, I make my way toward the library to follow the stars. I'm headed to the church to talk to Mr. Lawson. It's time for someone to tell me about Dad.

CHAPTER 27

On the way to the south side of the town, I want to stop and talk to Shy, but no one answers. I'm not surprised. He told me he'd be busy. So instead, I find myself in front of the church. It's locked tight. And when I knock, nobody answers.

I'm fairly close to Mr. Lawson's and Dad's office building here. I might go there, if for no other reason than to sit in his reality. I want to curl up in his chair and look through his desk. After all, there's a whole different part of him I don't really know.

He used to bring me to work when I was smaller, but that was years ago. I wonder why he shut me out of his world. I want back in. It's almost like I feel he's out there watching me, but if so, he'd have reached out by now. My head tells me he would be home if he could. My heart, however, holds on to hope. He's got to be alive.

I need to find Byz and her dad. I walk over and knock on her front door, but I'm too nervous to stand still, balancing from one foot to the other. I've experienced an overload of truths these past few days, and I'm suddenly resistant to more. This is my chance to get answers, though. I want to find a way back to some sense of normal.

I peek through the window into what looks like the kitchen. There are boxes spread out everywhere. It looks like they're moving, but there's no one there to pack. I walk around and look at the living room and find the same: stacks and stacks of boxes. No sign of people. I try the front door, but no luck.

"Hey, there!" A man yells from a yard over. "What are you doing?"

My heart thumps against my chest. I back away from the door to see a man who's clearly living the PR life in full. He has flashy pink pants on and a blue paisley shirt with an extra-wide collar. His hair is a brilliant red on one side, white on the other. He has a sneer on his face. It's safe to say he's not glad to see me.

"I'm looking for a friend of mine. She lives here."

"Yeah, what's your friend's name?"

I realize by his tone that he doesn't realize that a girl lives here at all. Byz is unrecorded, so the neighbors might not even realize she exists, and I don't want to alert him otherwise.

"The man who lives here is Mr. Lawson. Truman, I believe. He worked with my father, and I'm here to talk to him."

The multi-colored man squares his shoulder, and his angry eyebrows press on his eyelids. "You Elizeus's daughter?"

I don't know how to answer. Well, I do, but I don't necessarily want to give my name.

"Yes, Elizeus is my father."

"I haven't seen him in the past few days, but he stirred up a lot of trouble in our neighborhood. They think nobody knows what they're doing, but I notice. Your dad created some half-invisible cult that wears plain clothes and wears their hair down. They don't look right at all, and I don't want them hanging around my house." He strokes his hair. "Elizeus went missing from what I heard. Is he dead?"

Pain pierces my heart. "I don't know. Maybe." The word sours on my tongue.

"No offense to you, sweetheart, but *good*. Your father wasn't good for this community; he wanted to eliminate all the progress we've made over the years. None of the people I know listen, except for maybe the Lawsons. Where your dad is persistent, Truman is persuasive. Together, they have a lot of people confused. Your father's death can serve as a powerful reminder to those who go against the system."

My fists ball, but I also realize how much danger I'm in. The man could break me in two with little effort, and I seem to be sinking deeper by the minute. I have to decide what to do, but first things first.

"My father is an honorable man. I'm sorry you couldn't get to know him better."

The man gives a dismissive wave. "Lawsons moved out early this morning. New couple stepped in about noon. I would have introduced myself to them, but I wasn't feeling myself." He looks me up and down in a way that I know he suffered through the trial. He isn't sure I am what I say I am.

"Thank you," I manage. "I'll try to find them."

"Well, if you do, make sure to tell them to stay away. No one wants to hear doom and gloom all the time. People should leave well-enough alone. It's a beautiful life we live, and if someone can't find joy in that, then they need to leave the community before someone removes them altogether."

A threat. And it isn't particularly veiled. He's telling me to mind my business and avoid the PREP call, though I'm not sure if he knows what that means. And even if he has an inkling, there's probably a lot of information missing.

It reminds me of the fight I saw outside the Devonshire's and how confused they were. The upheaval that's coming tonight will be monumental.

I turn away from the house and can feel his eyes on me until I'm in the street. I walk back in the direction I came from and don't breathe freely until I hear the man's door shut. Looking back, I see I'm alone again.

That leaves the church; it's the only lead I have, short of finding father's work. And it's a bad idea to go there. There'll probably be an official inquiry because of the trial at noon, and I doubt things are going to go well. I suspect that might be why Byz and her family moved. Maybe I should have done more to warn Clarisse, but it's not like she would listen.

The church looks empty, and I can't hear any noise coming from it, but someone a house over stealthily makes her way toward the church's side entrance. She's wearing a bag like mine. Only hers is stuffed so full that she looks like she has a turtle shell on her back.

I really have nothing to lose at this point. I'm already disconnected from Byz's family and my own, and she sure doesn't look like a police officer.

I walk toward the church, timing it so we should both meet at the door. But she's going slowly, and I can't go any slower without being obvious, so instead of meeting her at the door, I meet her directly.

"Hey, you need any help?" I ask, acting as if our interaction is perfectly normal.

"Who are you? And where's your stuff?" Her face is cold, uncertain.

Another gamble, I say, "Byz didn't say I needed to bring anything, so I didn't."

Her face softens at Byz's name, but she wags her finger at me. "Well, there's no telling how long we'll be in there. You ought to have brought something. Byz doesn't always think long term. What do you have in the bag?"

"Nothing but school supplies and a hair brush."

The small woman sighs. "Well, I brought an extra blanket. You can use that tonight, but you're going to have to venture back or come up with a spare set of clothing somehow."

"Are you sure you don't want me to carry anything?"

"No, but you can get the door. Let's move. We've got to get inside before anyone sees us." I run ahead, but the door is locked, so I knock. Nothing happens. I knock again. Same.

"There's a secret knock. Byz didn't show you?" She eyes me dubiously again, and I swallow. "What's your name exactly?"

"Liberty."

The name is out of my mouth before I can even think that an alias may serve me better here, but what can I say? I'm not a girl accustomed to intrigue. Most of my life, the truth has been sufficient—or at least, I thought it had.

"Liberty?" There's recognition in her voice. "You're Elizeus's daughter?"

"Yes, ma'am."

"Oh, honey!" She pulls her hands up and raps on the door. Three strong knocks and three soft ones. "We've missed your father. He was very important to our community, and I'll tell you what, he loved you dearly. Pictures of you everywhere in his office. Until yesterday, of course. Truman took them all down so that the police wouldn't connect you or your mother to the PR outage."

Another woman opens the door, and I recognize her from the coffee shop: Myrna. "Penelope!" she says, too distracted to notice me behind Penelope.

Myrna ushers us in, closes the door, and secures the locks one by one.

We're in a small, cramped room off the side door. People are everywhere, coming and going from the sanctuary. It's like being inside an anthill, and I immediately feel claustrophobic by the lack of sunlight.

"Myrna," Penelope grabs my attention, "meet Elizeus's daughter, Liberty Moore."

When Myrna turns around and sees me, she throws her hands around my neck. I freeze up at first, unused to the attention and desperate for space. But she smells of earthy spices. Clean. The woman is large and warm, but she squeezes the perfect amount until I relent and hug her back. No one has ever hugged me like that except for Dad, and even he stopped as I got older. I had no idea how hungry I was for a hug. We stand there until I realize she's no longer hugging me, but I'm holding her. I pull away, embarrassed.

"I take it you know one another?" Penelope asks, putting her pack on a rack by some others.

Myrna pats my shoulder. "We're old friends by now. She's a great fan of my coconut salad, but why didn't you tell me who you were?"

I shrug. "Truth is, I'm starting to wonder who I am."

Myrna laughs, but then her face grows serious. "Your father is going to be known as a great liberator, and his beautiful daughter is going to carry out his legacy."

I pull my curls out of my eyes. I don't know how to carry out his legacy, and I certainly don't feel beautiful.

"You don't even know, do you, child? I forget. Come here and get a look at yourself."

She ushers me into the main sanctuary. The pews are not exactly full, but there's got to be fifty or more people here. Still, it's not as claustrophobic with the tall ceiling and the stage for the pulpit.

Myrna pulls me to an area behind the stage and stands in front of a mirror, pointing to her reflection. She looks the same.

"That's right. This is the real me, what I look like to people in Clarity. Are you up for seeing what you look like? You know what you look like in PR, but have you seen who you really are?"

I freeze. I avoided that at my house, so I haven't had a good look.

Am I up to it? I'm not sure. I've always felt attractive, and no one has ever told me differently, so it's not been a huge issue. Rather, much of my concern was on how I dressed myself, and Clarisse had a lot to do with that, so I guess I've been sheltered. I've never had reason to feel self-conscious. Not until Clarity.

"Are you sure this is a good idea?" I stall.

Smiling sweetly, Myrna says, "It's up to you, but the opportunity is here."

She says this, but as she does, she pulls me in front of the mirror and my image appears before me.

I'm not ready, so I close my eyes tightly. But if I don't look, I'm no better than Clarisse. Like it or not, I'm going to have to face reality. I open my right eye, then my left, and take in the image.

Instead of my gorgeous red mane, I have brown hair that falls in waves around my shoulders. My skin is so leathery that I look ancient, but the biggest thing I notice is my deep-set eyes. They're Dad's eyes; the same ones that had stared at me from the picture in his office. The thought makes me smile, and I see that I also have his smile. I'm not as beautiful as before, but I am beautiful.

I look at Myrna. "Thank you. I look like him."

Someone else says, "Yes, you've always favored him. The sun has damaged your skin, but you're a pretty girl, Libs."

"Libs?" I'm so enthralled with my reflection that it takes me a second to recognize the voice as Byz's. She comes and stands by me and looks at me through the reflection.

"This is the girl I want to see, not the one who has no investment in the future. You radiate power, my friend. We'll show them how it's done. No one can stop us now."

She smiles, tapping the man beside her. He turns, and I see the thick glasses.

"Dad, meet Liberty Moore."

CHAPTER 28

M r. Lawson steps up and smiles. "It was your dad's dream for you to know of our work, and I think he would be so proud for you to be here beside us."

"Thanks." There's so much to ask him, but the moment is awkward, and my mind goes blank. "Why'd you break into my house?"

"Yes, I'm sorry I scared you." He grimaces. "You startled me, and I didn't handle it well. I was trying to find the PREP folder before it got into the wrong hands. I knew Elizeus planned to talk to you about Clarity, and when he didn't come into work the next day, I suspected something had gone wrong."

That makes sense, I guess. But before I can ask him another question, he raises both hands until he has everyone's attention.

"The preliminary Clarity reports of this afternoon mostly involved a lot of confusion, though there were a few brawls. If PR is doing its job, it is now lulling the people back into their safe spaces in the darkness. We hope we have given them a brief introduction to their new truth, because tonight we will unveil the second awakening."

A few people clap, Myrna and Mrs. Lawson among them, but the quiet ones nod in approval, giving the room an overall feeling of determination—a need to set things right, no matter the cost.

That's good. They'll need that passion to get through to someone like Clarisse.

"There are new people among us today. Those who have chosen to take this journey with us. They've braved the confused masses and armed themselves with the fundamental truth of our existence. This planet is suffering deeply from the population's ignorance. The founders thought they might put a hold on the new reality, but all they've really done is keep us from realizing the problem."

He's as persuasive as the man with the pink pants said. If so, maybe he's got us all fooled. I'm considering that possibility when I look to Byz, who beams at her dad. I trust her. And if she believes him, then I'll try to do the same.

He continues. "Today, we face the truth together. Those who have bound us in this technology do not have our best interests at heart. While we struggle with enough oxygen to breathe, the Watchers have created their own safe space in the biome. They're not returning for us. We have essentially been left behind.

"Now comes the time for us to join together and challenge those powers that have abandoned us here. We have tried to work alone, but it is time for help to come. We can no longer save the population by ourselves. We have to help them save themselves.

Mr. Lawson puts his fist up as a sign of strength, holding it out to his fellow soldiers. They, in turn, raise their own hands, fists pumped with power, faces full of hope. For the first time since Dad disappeared, I feel anger rise in me. This is the burden Dad carried, and he passed it on to me. It's now time to do my part. Personal Reality is over. I raise my fist with them.

"To our newest people and those of you have begun the transition with a head start, we have called on you because our cause needs you. The time has come to make change."

A lady in a lavender dress pats me on the shoulder and smiles, while the man next to her shakes my hand.

"A new era of PREP has arrived." Mr. Lawson says. "It's time for Clarity. Elizeus and I have worked very hard for this moment. Unfortunately, Elizeus is not here with us. I see this as a sign to speed up the PREP objectives before others are lost."

A woman in the corner cries out, "We must be safe!"

"Yes, we will make our own safety," Mr. Lawson continues. "However, there is another mitigating factor. The interns will soon come to learn the job that Elizeus and I have held so long. Once that time comes, we lose our ability to fight back. It's taken most of our adult years to build an interrupter for the PR signal. We cannot let newcomers undo our life's work and sabotage the people from knowing who they are and why we must fight. We must find Clarity. We must find peace in our reality so we may work toward a brighter future."

Myrna chuckles. "We're going to have to keep them from fighting each other first, if we want any peace."

"That's true," Truman says. "But we must unite against the others and infiltrate the safety zones they have put up for themselves. We must mutiny, and we must start today."

He breaks for a second and whispers come over the small gathering. I look around for familiar faces. Aside from Byz, her mom, and Myrna, I also see Theron and the boy in the hoodie from the academy.

The crowd swells forward. I can't see what's happening, but the crowd moves, and I move with it. It's not until he reaches the front that I realize who's caused the commotion. It's Puck.

He steps in front of Truman and speaks. "Well said. I would like to welcome you to your first leg of progress. We cannot move forward with lies, and we can't fight the enemy if we make him invisible. I volunteer my services as a soldier in this war, and I think I'd make an excellent leader in that force. I'm trained and ready to defend the lives of the colony, and I'm merciless to those who have left us to die."

Whispers surface again as Puck has his say and steps back into the crowd. A man comes forward.

"We won't be able to control the riot that comes with Clarity. There aren't enough of us, unless the police force can mobilize on our behalf."

Truman takes back control. "That's not likely to happen, so I'm afraid we'll have to wait for the riots to diminish before we can work with the public. From that pool, we'll form a proper security force. Any questions?"

I look around; everyone is nodding, so I know this plan has been in operation for quite some time. There are only a handful who look as confused as me. Of those people, most hold hands with someone who is in on it. If things would have gone to plan, I would be standing here with Dad. That had been his intention, to let me know what was going on so we would be safe and prepared for the transition. I missed that opportunity, and if I hadn't handled the situation so poorly, he'd probably be with me today. My family intact.

Someone grabs my hand. It's Byz, and she's smiling at me like a proper friend. Maybe the only one I've ever had. The look of acceptance in her eyes tells me that Clarity is where I've always belonged and bids me welcome to the new normal.

Some of the newcomers stand in line at the mirrors to see the Clarity images of themselves, while Byz pulls me back to the corner of the room. It's quieter here and less crowded.

Byz asks, "Did you have any trouble with your mom? Is she coming?"

"I tried, I really did, but she tuned it all out, refusing to even acknowledge it. Her sanity may depend on PR. She wouldn't listen to me. She's going to have to learn the hard way."

Byz shakes her head. "I can't imagine having to switch realities. I've never had to worry about it, as I've always seen things as they are. I must admit, though, I've been jealous of them for periods of my life. What I would give to turn reality off and fall into a fantasy world... And when that happens, I remember what you eat!"

Laughter bursts from my throat. The humor, mixed with the tension of the situation, makes me embarrassingly giggly.

"You've got to admit; it isn't very appetizing," she says

Gathering myself, I have to ask. "Is it even nutritional—"

Truman interrupts her, putting his hand on my shoulder. "Byz, I need to talk to your friend for a minute."

Friend. We are friends. This is the truest relationship I've ever had. Byz must feel somewhat similar, because she grins at me as she leaves.

He walks me into what must be the pastor's office and tells me to sit down in front of the desk as he walks behind it and takes a chair.

"I'm sorry I frightened you. I don't normally skulk around people's houses, but I was desperate to get in touch with your father. Like I said, he told me he planned to speak to you."

His eyes are distant, remembering. He continues. "I knew something had gone wrong, but at the time, I had no idea it was so serious. When I came to your house, I hoped to catch sight of your father to make sure he was okay, but I never saw him, either that evening or since."

Swallowing the lump in my throat, I give him a sympathetic smile; I miss Dad too.

"Then I got the com call that he had been moved to a secondary office," he says. "There is no secondary office that I know of, so I couldn't make sense of it. You have no idea how saddened I am that he's not here. Your father was a great man, and I think you know he loved you very much."

A tear tracks its way down my cheeks. The mere fact that someone else remembers Dad the way he really was is reassuring, but bittersweet, because I only ever really knew him as someone else.

At the same time, I know that's not entirely true. I know he loved me and my mother. He held the burden all those years alone and loved us, though we were superficial and ignorant of the world around us. We must have been like coming home to a broken-down doll's house, playing our perfect parts as the house fell in disrepair around us.

"You don't know who was after him or where he might have gone?" I ask.

Mr. Lawson grimaces. "I know this: there's no way your dad would have left your family or this project. It was everything to him. You were."

It's the same thing my head has been telling me since he disappeared.

"There are bad people out there, Liberty. Most of them are away in a biome, but there are bad people here, too. I guess Byz told you that your dad and I were to be replaced soon. Whoever your dad came up against... Well, it could literally be anyone. Red stars, spies—I'm as clueless as you, and I wish I knew. My family is in danger, too."

I heave a deep breath. I'm no closer to finding out what happened, and Truman was my last hope.

"I'm sorry," he says. "Elizeus was my best friend."

I close my eyes, trying to find some peace with the situation, but it won't come. No matter how hard I try.

"*Is*. Is your best friend. I'll never give up hope."

"I know this is a hard time for you, but I'm afraid there's more." I open my eyes, and he gestures to the shelf behind him. "See that box? Those were the personal objects your dad left in the office. I know he'd want you to have it now, so I'm going to leave you a while to look through the box in private. Take your time."

He goes to the door, closing it behind him, as I stare at the box with uncertainty. It's been a tough few days. And given today's events, I really need to keep my wits about me. I can't afford to fall into the darkness while trying to liberate the rest of the population from disillusionment.

I also need every clue I can gather, since I'm no closer to the truth than when I started.

Pulling off the lid, I bite my lip to keep from crying again. On top is a picture of me, taken at six or seven years old, because my front tooth is out. Underneath that, I find a stack of PREP flyers—calls to actions that never had the opportunity to be seen. There's an envelope with Killer USB on it, whatever that is. Just under that, I find a small picture of Clarisse and she looks terrible there, but I bypass it pretty quickly. I just saw her at noon and have no desire to think about how that went.

Underneath the photo are legal pads. The first one says, *"Dear Liberty, There is..."*

Curious, I look at the second page, and the letter starts again. *"Dear Liberty, It's hard to imagine..."*

The third and the fourth pages are similar. A quick flick through the book shows some variation of the beginning of a letter to me.

A few of the pages have been torn off, and I wonder what they said and if they could give more insight into what he was thinking.

The second pad is a level of schematics that I'm hopeless to read until the last page, where he wrote about some apps from beta testing.

Underneath that is a pile of letters addressed to many people, and I scroll through them, recognizing most of the names, even if I won't recognize their features in Clarity. They'll be strangers to me now.

I sort through them until I come to one that will go to Clarisse. I put it in my pocket to give to her later. And then I see a letter with my name on it. It looks like he finished the letter after all. I open it up to look inside.

Dear Liberty,

I started this letter a thousand times, because I can't find the words to explain how I failed you. I should have raised you off PR, but your mother was so adamant that you live life with other children and families in our community. But she is not to blame; I am. It was my responsibility not to let anything sway me from my parental duties. In that way, I have failed you, and I'm sorry.

If you're reading this, then PREP time is near and you're coming into Clarity for the first time. I want you to know that while you feel alone; I know you. Really know you. You have not been alone all this time. My love for you and my pride for you never failed.

I tried to be a dad you could be proud of, and I wanted you to have the privilege of growing up as a normal kid, a benefit that I remember well. I let myself be complacent about your reality, because I really hoped that there would be changes and things would get better. At least, I thought that might happen. Now I know these were excuses. I was protecting you to a degree, but I should have been protecting your future.

If all goes well, you won't see this letter, but if it doesn't, please know that I helped create the mess to begin with. I can't go on with all the story, but I can get to the heart of the matter.

Those of you left behind must fight the disillusionment, must fight the PR program and make your way to the Watchers to take the biome built from our labor, and you must do it before the sun gets too hot to sustain life. My partner, Truman, will help you if he can, but if not, find Alaina Lawson and their daughter, Ryz. They know you and will always help you.

Other than those three, be very careful of who you trust. There are people who would sabotage our program. They're afraid of life in Clarity, but we cannot let them hide any longer.

I conclude with the most important information I have to give, and it's simply that since I first held you in my arms as a baby, I have loved you fully and as you are. You make me proud, and I know you will grow up to fight hard for others and for yourself.

You deserve any happiness you can find. Enjoy it, because the battle will be long.

Love, Dad.

My heart is melting into my chest, drying up like a squeezed sponge, and the tears threaten but don't come. Dad had known his time was short as surely as Truman must know they will look for him too, now that PR is unbalanced.

I flop back down in the seat and reread the letter, but I can't find despair, only love and purpose. I owe it to Dad to complete his work; he left it to me like a legacy that I must accept with a full heart.

CHAPTER 29

A tinkling noise pulls me back to reality. It's a com from Clarisse, so I take the call, whether or not I like it.

"I've heard some strange events are going around town, and I want to make sure you're okay."

It's sweet of her, but her concern is so out of character that I can't help but wonder if she's checking to make sure I'm not with Aden.

"I'm fine. Just downtown for a bit."

"I'd like you to come home. I'm quite worried about you being out, especially since our lunch was interrupted. Can you come?"

My frustration comes out. "Isn't your husband there?"

"Elizeus isn't here; he's doing some training for his new job. I don't know when he'll be in." The pregnant pause goes on until she breaks in with, "Come home, Libby."

"Mom, I'm not with Aden, I promise."

"I know, darling. I believe you, but I need to discuss some other matters with you. You also need to bring the necklace."

My mouth goes dry. "What necklace?"

"The pink crystal, Libby. I have one around here like it, and as soon as I can find it... Well, you'll see when you get home."

There's a sharpness to her voice that is not way out of line with her usual saccharine tone, but it sets my teeth on edge. Why does she care about the necklace? She doesn't want Clarity, so it must be something else.

"I know you're there," she says. "I can hear you breathing."

"Sure." I slump my shoulders. "I'll be there soon."

I hang up, and my mind replays what she said. I'm looking for alternate explanations, but there are none. If she knows about the necklace, does she also know about Imposter? If so, she's said nothing about it, just continued on in her fictional world.

I turn to ask Byz and her dad who are showing some new people the mirror, and I find Myrna with a small baby in her hands as she rocks him asleep.

"Looking for something?" Puck croaks. I nearly jump out of my shoes as I shy away from him. My hands cover my necklace, and I shuffle through the crowd, far away from him.

Why do they want the necklaces so badly? Puck is already in Clarity, and Clarisse wants no part of it. It doesn't make any sense to me. I'm missing information, and I doubt I'll get it from either of them.

The letter! The one to Clarisse, the one I found before my own. Dad might mention something to make this situation easier to comprehend. I pull it out of my pocket and tear through the envelope.

It's not meant for me, but I've been in the dark long enough. I open the trifold and read:

Clarisse, my love,

I know you don't want any part of my world, and I understand you have things the way you want them. I know, too, that you are an independent woman, and I can respect your wishes.

Liberty is also old enough to decide for herself. I'm making better progress on Clarity every day, and I want her to choose reality before it is forced upon her.

I know you are against this, and I'm sorry we couldn't come to an agreement, but on this subject, there is no middle ground for compromise. We have held her back for all of her youth. I can't keep her uninformed about her future options.

We have raised her well, and she will make the best decision. We need to trust her.

Forgive me for this offense, because I love you dearly. I want to do right by you and our child. Clarity will come. I hope it finds you well.

Elizeus

Nothing about the necklace. But just as I've thought, Clarisse doesn't care to find an alternate reality; she is blissfully happy with her current one. The question is, what would she do to keep it?

A terrible thought occurs to me. Could Clarisse be responsible for Dad's disappearance? She loves PR enough for it to be a motive. Then there's the Red Star on our house, what it might suggest about her. But if so, where's the opportunity? She was at home when I came in that night, so she didn't have the time.

At least, I thought she was home. That's what she told me. But I went upstairs and went to sleep. I didn't actually see her at first.

Maybe she wasn't there when I arrived. She would never stand up Della LaClare if there was a meeting, but that would explain why she didn't answer the door for the police.

I shake my head. Until I can find out for sure, I need to stay away from her, and I'm already planning on avoiding Imposter.

My head is spinning. I'm not sure what to make of it all, but there is the very real possibility that I could be wrong, too. Dad gone. Imposter reassigned. But because I can't place Clarisse at that time, it doesn't mean she can't be placed at all. And if that's so, then maybe Dad is the same. Just because he hasn't shown up at home doesn't mean he hasn't shown up elsewhere.

And that sliver of hope is driving me crazy.

I can't stay here with Puck at the church, and I'm not going home. I need to get out among the people and figure out the mood of the citizens, so I com Aden. It's time to bring him into the fold. Maybe he can help me make sense of all this.

I com and ask him to meet me at the ice cream shop. When he says yes, I slip out through the back door of the church. I need some space and some help.

The ice cream shop seems as good a place as any to find a few locals gossiping about the PR failure. I take a few minutes to get there, but he takes longer. Even with his bike, he lives further out where his dad does hydroponic gardening. Farmers are a valued part of the community, and I wonder if he already knows they use PR to make the food look more appetizing than it is, or if he realizes the good food has a PR treatment on it to keep people from eating it.

Still, it must be cool to have a job that so many people depend on. I didn't realize how much Dad did until he disappeared, and that's sad. He and Mr. Lawson have been making life seamless for everyone, all the while plotting away to get us all back to reality. That's an important job, and I'm proud of him in a way I never thought to be before.

When I arrive, the ice cream parlor isn't particularly busy, but there are many people on the street wandering around. When Aden arrives, I ask him if it's okay for us to sit outside and eat our ice cream. He agrees.

We take a round table farthest from the door and dig in. He orders chocolate sludge, and that's what it is. Most of the ice creams look the same, but there was one called "Palisades," cream with a golden swirl in it. I notice as we exit the parlor that another woman has it, too. She must have heard me order, because she looks at me and smiles. It's so funny that these people have been hiding in plain sight for all my life. I feel like I've been let in on a grown-up secret.

"How was training this morning?" Aden asks. He's about to take a bite of the sludge, but I can't let him go through with it. In a panic, I push it off of the table and onto the ground.

"I'm so sorry, Aden. I'm such a klutz." I place my ice cream in the center of the table. "You can help me eat mine."

With an unasked question in his eyes, he looks down at my unenhanced ice cream. From the disgusted expression on his face, he will not be having a bite of mine.

"It's okay," he says, looking back at the ice cream parlor door. "It's just that it looked so good, and I only get the ugly food at home."

That explains why he's so bulky compared to everyone else.

"Academy was fine," I say, trying to change his focus. "Well, honestly, I didn't go. I wandered around for a while."

His face grows grim. "That's two you've missed this week. They'll hold you back a year if you miss any more, and you'll have the worst pick of jobs. Why would you skip again?"

"I couldn't bring myself to go in and sit in there all morning. I have a lot of stuff on my mind."

"You must have been thinking about me. I'm very flattered, but I'm not worth risking your livelihood over." He's got a goofy smile on his face. He's telling me a joke. Not a very good one, but he's trying. I don't think he's ever done that before. Maybe a side effect of today's glitch.

"How was your day?" I ask, and his face immediately drops. "Anything weird happen?"

He shakes his head. "We need to leave it to the programmers. They'll have it fixed in no time. I was at work, though, and everything got a little crazy. Suddenly, people were overly tanned with strange hairstyles and wild clothing. There were a couple of fights, as people couldn't figure out who they were sitting with. It got pretty hostile.

"And forget about the building. It looked like it was barely standing. And the food? Well, I won't go there. It was unbelievable."

"I was at home with my mom," I say, feeling him out. "She closed her eyes through the whole thing as if nothing was happening. My house looked a wreck, too. What if that's the way things really are?"

"You can't think that way." He looks down to the sludge again, then back to my ice cream and to the parlor door. "It was a glitch. I bet they have it all fixed up by now. Though I suspect that someone will get fired over it. The sun was a yellowed haze. That can't be reality, else we'd all be about to die."

"I don't know..." I say slowly. "Let me ask you this. What if it *were* true?"

He shakes his head. "But it's not."

"But what if it were? Would you like me if I didn't look the same?"

"What kind of question is that?" He jerks his head back like I've wounded him. "You look fine, Libby."

His answer sounds like a no. I really hope that isn't the case, because the world is about to take on a whole new look. He doesn't really know what he's saying yet, but it's the best he can do for now. Or is it?

"I'm going to get some more ice cream," he says, standing.

"No, wait!" My urgency throws him; his eyes widen with surprise and he freezes like I've pulled out a weapon.

"Okay!" He holds out his palms, suggesting I calm down.

I take a big breath, unable to let him go on like this. "I want you to do me a favor. It's kind of weird."

His face scrunches up, but his eyes are alert. "Sure..." he says uncertainly.

"I want you to put on my necklace." I'm trying to gauge the look on his face, but it's such a mixture of feelings, I don't know what to make of it until he speaks.

"Guys don't wear necklaces."

"This isn't for fashion. It's a reality check." I discretely slip off the necklace, and the light softens to PR's perfect sun. Staring into his real eyes, still green but with brown flecks, I know I might not see that look again. "I want you to see things as I do, and I know that sounds a little odd, but humor me."

"Okay."

Deep breaths. I stand up and walk behind him. "This necklace is kind of a big deal, so don't make a scene." I wrap the necklace around his neck, not bothering to latch it.

He jerks back as he takes in Clarity.

"Hey!" He puts his hand on the table as if to stabilize himself. "That's what it looked like this afternoon. Did you cause that?" The accusation in his tone is hard to miss.

"No, not me."

I hold the necklace as he takes in the scenery. He doesn't say anything.

"Look down to where you spilled your ice cream."

His head tilts, and again, he pulls back.

"You almost ate that, but I couldn't let you do it. Now look at mine."

"That can't be right..." he mutters.

"It is. This is reality with no PR enhancements. It's called Clarity."

When he's looked all around him, he tries to turn to see me, but I'm behind him, holding the necklace. "And you? Do you look the same?"

I close my eyes. "No. I look different, too."

He cranes his neck, but he's in no position to see me. Tugging my hand, he signals for me to move in front of him.

Here goes nothing.

Holding both ends of the necklace with one hand, I step around him.

His eyes go wide, and it leaves me breathless. I'm not sure what his expression means, but I'm terrified to find out.

"Oh," he chokes out. "Your skin is like the others." He looks down at his own arms. "What do I look like?"

"You look different, Aden."

I take the necklace off him and walk around the table. He looks at me with horror as I sit, trying to look natural as I replace the necklace. He must have a million questions, but the only answer I have for him is that it's all been a lie. All of it.

"Look, I don't know what's going on here, but I don't like it."

"It's not going away, Aden. We'll have to adapt."

His jaw tightens as his anger swells. He pounds his hand against the table. "No. We have to fix this glitch. I don't know what you've gotten involved with, but I don't want any part of it."

He looks at his arms and hands again and shakes his head. "This is crazy. I'm out of here."

As he stands, he pushes his chair back forcefully, the screech drawing the eyes of everyone nearby. He doesn't care, though. He takes off back toward the farm.

I should be mad, but I feel a little sorry for him. He took it about the same way I had, so maybe he needs a little breathing room.

CHAPTER 30

I don't finish my ice cream because I'm busy people watching. The whole street is full of people who would usually be smiling and carefree, but something is off about them. Their mouths are a little too tight, their shoulders are tense, and their eyes fixate on their surroundings as if everything could morph at any minute.

They most likely got their taste of Clarity this morning while out on errands, volunteering, or at work. But for the trial this evening, most people will be home. Some of them will see their family for the first time and be absolutely horrified at what they see. Strangers in an unknown space with no rhyme or reason. A complete reversal of the reality they were so sure of minutes before.

Tonight, I won't be with Clarisse and Imposter when they get their first good look at each other. I wish I could witness Imposter seeing Clarisse absolutely gooped with paint and dressed in horrid clothing. Clarisse will definitely know Imposter isn't her husband. If she opens her eyes, that is. She's worn the necklace before, so she's seen him. I'm sure of it.

I can't afford to think of them now. They'll have to sort it out. I'm going to watch tonight through the cameras they've set up in the church that will record what's happening in the city center.

I wonder what Dad was thinking as he anticipated me seeing the world for the first time. Had he been as nervous as I am now? I may never know, but I'll die trying to figure it out.

I'm no closer to the truth than I was a few days ago and don't have a clue what happened to Dad, but my thoughts are leaning toward the police and Puck—or both.

I close my eyes, sending a silent message to Dad to help me. He must have left a clue somewhere.

Coming back to a question I've wondered before, I turn the problem over in my head. Why had he taken me to the carousel when it would have been just as easy to show me at home?

Maybe he wanted to show me something in the park. Maybe the clue is still there.

I gravitate back to the bench where I sat with Dad, but there's someone already there. I stop beyond them and look at the carousel. It's the same way Dad had me face before he turned the necklace. He might have wanted to show me something, or maybe he just needed a moment before he showed himself. I might never know, and it breaks my heart that Dad's last message to me never made it through.

I turn toward the man who's sitting where Dad was that night. Beyond the bush behind him is the sidewalk, filled with pedestrians continuing with their usual routines. It's all still new to me, but nothing stands out as unusual.

I turn in a circle. Then I see it. On the building beyond the carousel, right behind the bench: a giant Red Star.

Like the others, it has five points. That can't be a coincidence, but I don't understand what the significance is of the red. Several people have made it clear to me now that Red Stars can't be trusted, but I have yet to meet anyone except Clarisse. Is there a larger truth I'm not privy to?

The man on the bench must get sick of me hanging around, because he packs up his things and scurries along.

The building is behind the thick black bushes, but I think I know which one it is. I jump on top of the bench and look over the bushes to read what remains of the faded storefront: "THE CLOCKERY." It's Puck's hideout.

It's a sign. An omen. But of what? I walk around and look at Puck's door again. There's no sign that anyone's there, but it isn't as if I could tell before. And after last time, I don't feel comfortable knocking again.

I walk into the alley, and the tall homeless man who caught my leg earlier is visible from where someone has left the gate open.

"Hello," I say.

He makes a rumbly noise that is a cross between a "harrumph" and a "what?" I don't want to get close to him, because I don't want him to grab me again, but I speak up so I can ask him a question.

"Are you using PR?"

He screams at me, making me jump backward. "I don't have to use it if I don't want to! You people don't live any better than me, you just don't know it. I'll fight you if I have to. I don't want to be hooked up on your technology again. Be warned."

"I don't want to hook you up!" I interrupt before he can yell anymore. "I don't have it either. Well, technically I do, but it's all being interrupted at the moment. I can see you. I see you as you really are."

"Well, good for you, then. Will you kindly close the gate so I can sleep?"

I take a step forward; I'm not ready to close that gate yet. "I will, but I need to know a few things, and I think you might be helpful."

He dismisses me with a wave of his hand. "I don't have to answer anything."

"No, you don't, but I would be thankful if you did."

His forehead wrinkles, forming dark, dirty lines across his brow. He has gray eyes, but the rest of his features are awash in dirt.

"Three questions," he says. "No more."

I can do that. I'll have to be careful to get the most information out of him, but not overtax him, so he'll stop answering. I ask the most obvious question first.

"What can you tell me about the pinstripe man?"

The man looks both ways, as if to check whether someone is listening. "Puck? He's my friend, but sometimes I don't like him. I used to argue with him. But without good food, I'm too weak to do anything now. One day, his ways are going to catch up with him. That is, if the others don't get him first."

"What others?" It's out of my mouth before I can stop myself, and I might just have wasted one of my questions.

"The other people without the tech don't like him because he doesn't want everyone to see. He's pretending to be a good guy to all sides, but he isn't. He likes to milk people out of their money, selling junk as fine treasure, and sometimes he's mean to the rest of the people who want to make everything better. They threw him out of the planning and painted a big Red Star on the front of his building as a warning. I heard him tell the police officer that one day. I think they're working together."

As soon as he mentions the police, I remember the double Red Star on the station. The police and Puck. They must be working together.

That also explains why he was at the church. He's pretending to be like the Yellow Stars. I wonder if Mr. Lawson knows.

Wow. I knew this was all messed up, and that the Watchers had a conspiracy to keep us ignorant, but it hadn't occurred to me that there might be insiders playing the same game—especially the police. Maybe they know exactly where Dad is? Puck or the police may have taken him for his role in PREP.

My blood boils, and my fingers clench. I can't let them get away with this.

"That's two questions, but I'm tired and hungry. Do you have anything for me to eat?"

"I don't, but I can bring you something tomorrow when everything dies down. I think I can get my hands on some good muffins if I ask nicely, and maybe some fresh drinking water."

His eyes are bright now. "That would be... really good."

"Okay, last question. What do the other colors of the stars mean? If red is bad, a warning, what about the Blue and the Yellow?"

"Blues are the academics and historians. They're processing the information and recording it for the people that come after us. Until recently, they didn't think the community was ready to quit PR. But they're the ones who're working with Lawson to make the switch from PR to Clarity easier; they're working on sewer and water treatment, food production, and protection for the sky. You have to be really smart to be one of them. I'm not that smart."

That makes sense; Shy did say he was a researcher. "What about the Yellow?" I ask.

He shakes his head and holds up four fingers. "That's four questions. You said three. I can count."

"Answer this last one, and I'll give you a surprise."

He waves me off. "I don't like surprises. Sometimes they're bad."

"This one is good. It's candy."

He must think it over because his face clenches. "Show me."

I pull out the lollipop Byz gave me earlier.

He eyes it for a moment, then his gaze falls back on me, though it's softer now. "You might be one of the Red Star people. I don't know you."

"I think I'm a Yellow, because I think the Yellow Stars are trying to get rid of PR so everyone can survive together. If that's what Yellow is, then that's me."

"Yeah, Yellow. Yellow is good." He gives me a dopey grin. "Can I still have the lollipop?"

I leave it with him. It's time to visit the library and get more information on the Blue Stars.

CHAPTER 31

I've got about three hours before I need to go on lock down at the church. That gives me plenty of time to stop by and see if Shy finished with his meetings. Plus, I'm dying to know what went missing.

A few eyebrows rise as I jog that way. Walking is usually sufficient unless you're running late, and everything is so well-timed that almost no one is ever late.

By the time I'm halfway there, my breath is coming in heaves. I've never thought of myself as out of shape. I walk almost everywhere, but I'm not accustomed to jogging.

Then it hits me. It's not just me, but the haze over the city. The air is choking me, and moving faster upped my intake. It takes me a few minutes to get my breathing under control, but I don't let it stop me.

When I get to the library, I hop up on the porch, look around for witnesses, and rap three times fast, three times slow, hoping the knock is recognizable as being from a person grounded in Clarity. There is no answer, and I listen at the door for voices. None that I can hear.

The shrubbery is thick around the building, but there's a little room to squeeze behind it so I can look through the windows. At a desk, Shy leans forward, his forehead resting on a book he was reading. He must be taking another nap.

"Shy!" I tap on the window. He doesn't move.

I try the window, but it's locked. The rest are the same, and the door is secure. I bang at the window, and he doesn't move.

Not good.

Picking up a broken brick, I break through to the lock. With a quick turn, it rises enough for me to open it all the way.

"Shy?" I whisper as I climb through the window and make my way to his desk.

A quick nudge does nothing to wake him, so I feel for his pulse. There isn't one. On the floor is a bloodstain. Following it up, I see the knife in his stomach.

An icy chill runs up my spine.

Turning on my com, I'm about to call the police when I remember the Red Stars. Yates said there had been a break-in at the library. In that case, he definitely knows. Or worse, he's the one responsible.

The room is tidy, not like a break-in at all. Whatever was stolen, the thief must have known exactly where to look. The question is whether Shy was killed during the break-in or after, but I'm guessing by the dark color of his blood that it happened at the same time, though Yates hadn't mentioned a murder.

I need to be with someone I trust, and right now, that person is Byz. She'll know better how to deal with the situation.

Instead of comming, I head for the church. Following the yellow stars, I notice the blue and red ones too. No double stars like the library, but there are many smaller buildings along the way. I run all the way to the street with the church and then sneak to the back and knock on the door; three fast taps, three slow. No answer.

I knock again, making sure the pattern is clear. Nothing. I lean against the door in exasperation when a small figure comes around the side of the building. It's Byz.

"You're early," she says. "But that's okay."

"I can't get in." I swallow my frustration. It's not her fault.

"That's because you're using the last knock. It's a precaution we use." She knocks fast four times, followed by two taps. The door opens, and we're inside.

I can't explain it, but I feel so much safer here than anywhere else. Outside is ripe with potential danger, but here it feels safe and homey.

Byz guides me over to one of the wooden pews and lets me rest for a minute, but I'm too frantic to stop for more than a few seconds.

"I need to see your dad, Byz. Something's gone very wrong at the library, and I need to let someone in charge know. Is he here?"

"He is, but he's very busy. Can you tell me what happened and then I can relay the message? Mom and I are the only ones he'll let in the office."

After hearing the details about the library, Byz's frown is deep, her face pale, and her lips pursed.

"Let me see what he says," she whispers.

I watch her move across the room; she looks back at me twice. The feeling of being safe here is suddenly threatened. It's not that I don't know who to trust, which is certainly an issue, but it appears Byz is in the same situation.

She stops at her mom and whispers something in her ear, but it can't be the whole story I told her. She hasn't had time to say more than a few words. But her mom nods, opens the old door for Byz, and closes it behind her.

Part of me is relieved to have that terrible revelation out of my hands, but as the numbers amass in the room. I'm wondering if anyone here already knows. I might not be the first person who happened by the library and got more information than I'd hoped.

A feverish chill runs over me. I find someone's coat at the end of the pew and slide it around my shoulders. All I can do is wait and hope that everything turns out all right. It'll be a few hours before they interrupt the signal again, and then the truth will be out for good.

Part of me wishes we could make it permanent now. Tear off the blindfold and have everyone come back to reality. That's not really in my hands, though. I'm not aware of the big plan, and there are probably very good reasons for the way they're doing things.

Anxiety about Shy, the coming trial, and Byz's distrust make me stop and take deep breaths. Time ticks by, and I notice a few people in the pews who are loners too. I don't have any idea how long they've been aware, but it's fairly clear by the way their eyes scan the room that this is their first visit to the church, and they're not comfortable.

I say nothing about what I saw in the library, because I don't know how important Shy was to the PREP plan. I'm grateful to sit here, even if I feel a little out of place, because the Realists are planning to integrate the community back to Clarity.

When Myrna comes in, Byz's mom, Alaina, leans forward and whispers in her ear. I remember Myrna's hug, and I want to run and give her one, but as soon as she pulls away, both she and Alaina are looking at me with hard eyes. Myrna motions me over.

I stand up, but Myrna does not meet me halfway. She has me walk the whole distance, so I'm pressed into the dark corner with the two of them. Myrna grabs my shoulders lightly to get my full attention, though she already has it.

"What exactly did you see?" Myrna asks, her breath heavy, but sweet.

I tell her about Shy, the break-in, and the police.

"Things have changed drastically," she says. "Elizeus and Shuyler's absences must be related. Red Stars, I'm guessing. We'll need to watch out for the few Red Stars left. They shouldn't be any more of an issue than they are now, but Shuyler's death also diminishes some of the support systems for Clarity, since he was actively helping us."

I nod, uncertain what else I can add.

She continues. "I don't know who the next in line is, but without a leader, more of the Blue Stars will choose PREP goals over the greed of the Red Stars. At last, they'll be putting the people over the science."

Myrna throws her hands on her hips and looks sideways at Alaina. "Has anyone told Truman yet?"

Alaina nods. "Byz is in there now explaining what she can, but I'm sure he'll want to talk to Liberty, too."

No sooner is that said than Byz exits the door and comes straight to me. The look on her face is light, and it offers some release, but there is a tightness in her smile that makes me wonder what she's thinking.

"Your turn."

"Should I be scared?"

"Of my dad?" The laugh is genuine. "I hardly think he'll hurt a hair on your head, Libs. He's just worried."

I nod and make my way toward the oaken door. When I tap, there's no answer. The wood is too thick for him to hear me. I rap harder and hear a muffled voice on the other side. Hoping he said "Come in" or "Enter," I turn the handle and peek inside.

Mr. Lawson is sitting at a massive table with seats all around it; it's obvious this is the meeting area for all the leaders in the Yellow Star community. The room makes me feel smaller than I already do, and the size of the table isn't helping.

"Come down here with me, Liberty." He pushes out the chair on his right with his foot. I hesitate.

"Your dad was always a cautious soul, too. Let me ask you this: if you can't trust me, then who can you trust? I'm not being mean here, but I'm the one person who's carrying on your dad's work so you can live in the real world with the prospect of a longer life."

It makes sense, but there's something off-putting. I notice that his chair has a tall back where the rest of them are mid-rise. He is sitting at the end of the table and there's no other seat like it. At the very least, that implies that Dad and Mr. Lawson weren't equal partners. One was over the other, and if that's the case, then for all I know, Mr. Lawson took Dad's place.

"Who was in charge?"

"I'm in charge now. No one else knows how the interrupter works."

I shake my head. "No, I mean, was Dad in charge or were you in charge?"

"We worked together…" he says as I continue to stare him down, "but your father was boss before his untimely disappearance." He sighs. "Look, Liberty, I know you're hurting, but Elizeus was my best friend. We've shared this secret for what seems like a lifetime."

What he says is true, but not the full picture. I want to know more. "But your family has been aware and my family hasn't. You must have disagreed on that to some extent?"

His jaw sets firm. "Elizeus agreed with me. Your mother is the one who wanted you sheltered by PR."

"Well, I don't want it."

Mr. Lawson nods and taps the table with his finger. "I can finish what your father started, if you like. Take PR away from you. You won't need the necklace anymore, and you'll be aware of everything like you are now. But once you switch over, you can't go back.

"That's what your dad wanted for you—your whole family to be free. You would have been if your mother hadn't denied him at every turn. He didn't want you to grow up confused, so he allowed you to live in the same world as your mother."

"I know he wanted me to know…" My voice sounds weak, so I speak up. "It was in his letter to me."

"Yes. Don't think it wasn't torture for him, though. For the last few years, it's been harder and harder for him to leave the office." Mr. Lawson lays his palms on the desktop. "Pretending everything was all right and being worried that he'd made a mistake in letting you believe. It's really what got all of this going. He wanted you to see what he saw, not to scare you off, but to work beside him and the Yellow and Blue Stars to correct it."

That's a lot to sink in. It explained the sigh at the end of the driveway everyday Dad came home. It explained all the weird "what does this look like, taste like, smell like" questions he asked over the years. It explains everything except for what happened to him.

"Will you take away my PR?" I ask before I even realize it's coming out of my mouth. I didn't know I had decided what to do, but as soon as I say it, it feels right.

Mr. Lawson looks at me and smiles. "Your dad would be so proud of you."

CHAPTER 32

I'm sure he's right, but the praise feels wrong coming out of his mouth. His family has already taken this plunge, so of course, he approves.

"How do I do it?" I ask.

"Well, there are two ways to make it permanent. You can ride it out with everyone else, and it'll be permanent in a few weeks, or we can have you fully turned right now."

"What would be the benefit of speeding up the process?"

"Well, for one, we need that necklace back. There are a few key people that we feel will make the process go faster because of their leadership roles in the existing community. If we give your pendant to someone influential, they can start paving the path to a new normal.

"Second, there will be people looking for that necklace, and as long as you have it, you are in danger. I think that might be why Shuyler was killed; he had one, too."

I put my hand over the pendant. "Dad gave something to my mother that would endanger her?"

His head crooks to the side. "Your dad didn't give you that necklace?"

"No, that one was ripped off my neck the night Dad disappeared. This one I found in his study in an envelope addressed to my mother."

Mr. Lawson shakes his head. "Your dad probably never meant for either of you to keep the necklaces. I think he wanted to give you a glimpse of the changes and the reason for them. After that, I believe he intended to bring the necklaces back here. It's amazing you've kept one of them this long. One of them going missing, however, is concerning. You said it was ripped off. Would you happen to know by whom?"

I drop my gaze to my tacky shoes. I do. "Puck. The pinstripe man. I think he took it."

Mr. Lawson mutters under his breath something that sounds like a curse. "Puck is a dangerous huckster. He'll sell the necklace to the highest bidder, or more likely, replicate it. It doesn't matter to him if we have Clarity or not. He can take advantage of the confused in either scenario. If Clarity never comes, he'll be able to sell his junk to the public. And if it does, he'll sell his hoarded supplies to the panic-stricken. Either scenario makes him rich and powerful. But he prefers the people to be ignorant. It makes his scheme easier—or at least it did until the Realists figured out how to disrupt the signal."

I'm not surprised about Puck now I understand the Red Stars a little better.

Mr. Lawson stands and walks to the door. He opens it and motions someone forward before making his way back to the table.

"Puck is trying to infiltrate the Yellow Stars. I've warned all the regulars about him, but there are a few who think he's sincere. I think he's either trying to sabotage us or take over the whole operation." He sits back down. "Do you want to go permanent or do you want to wait the couple of months of chaos?"

Biting down on my lip, I consider the options. There's no real reason to wait, especially if my goal is to help Dad's plans become a reality. Literally.

Byz enters the door. "You asked for me?"

Her dad beckons her closer. "Yes, I thought your friend might need some advice about whether to enter Clarity permanently. I thought you could answer some of her questions."

"No need," I say with my head high. "I want my PR removed. How long will it take?"

"The interruption starts in a about an hour, so we can't do it before then. How about tomorrow afternoon?"

That seems like forever away, but it's not like I don't have the necklace.

Mr. Lawson continues. "Until then, you need to stay here. I cannot stress enough how valuable those necklaces are. Hold tight to it, because if you lose your sense of Clarity, you'll lose much of your resolve. The pull of PR is nearly irresistible."

He stands and motions me to the door, and I get up to leave.

"I really need to attend to other matters in getting the interrupter ready, but if you have any more questions, Byz can answer them." He pulls the door closed behind me before I have an opportunity to ask any more questions.

I stand staring at the door, speechless, until Byz pulls me toward the pews.

"Don't mind him, Liberty. He's just really busy. He and your father worked hard on PREP, and it's important on a lot of different levels."

I let out a long sigh when my com rings. I hold up a finger to Byz and hear Clarisse on the other end as I answer.

"Honey, when are you coming home? I'm making dinner tonight. Spicy torpedoes."

I shudder at the thought. "It'll be later; I'm with a friend."

Byz looks up and smiles at me.

"You're not with Aden, are you? We didn't have time to talk like I wanted to this afternoon, but I really hope you're keeping to yourself."

There's definitely an accusation there. "I'll be safe, mother, but I'm really not with Aden." I'm tired of this discussion already. "I'm working on a project with a friend."

"Is it an art project? I could help!" Her enthusiasm rips through my ear.

"No, it's not. It's an assessor project."

"Oh, yuck. Hey, did I tell you your father will be away for a few weeks? He had to leave quick, and I know he missed saying goodbye."

That's doubtful. The man wasn't as much my dad as he was a complete stranger.

As Clarisse talks, I excuse myself from the rows of pews to a storage area behind the stage. "I really need you to come home, Libby. It's not optional."

"Yeah..." I sigh. "Okay, I'll be there." I hang up before she can get another word in and lean against the shelves of bottled water. My gaze slips to the light streaming through the window to my left.

"Okay..." I mutter to myself and stand up straight. "Okay."

Ignoring Mr. Lawson's warning, I slip out of the coat and slide open the window. I won't be gone long, and I won't do anything to jeopardize their mission. But I'm still investigating Dad's disappearance.

After edging over the sill, I quietly close the window behind me. I don't know where I'm going, but I do know who I'm looking for: Imposter. I've got questions, and I need some answers.

CHAPTER 33

The heat is oppressive as the false moon hangs precariously in the dusty haze. I don't see many people, though. This close to dinnertime, people are tucked in their houses, a few in restaurants. Soon, they'll be second guessing the food in front of them. They'd be wise to do so.

Keeping my eyes open for Imposter, I pass few people, but they're oblivious to me in my plain clothing. I see a few couples along the way, too. I bet the sun is shining on them, bathing them in its glorious light, instead of baking them alive.

The carousel is silent at the moment, but after dinner, it'll run until eight o'clock when the darkness begins. The precarious bulk of metal sways with the wind. It's hard to believe I've admired this particular piece of junk my whole lifetime. The unicorns have lost their horns and some of their feet. The firetruck hangs crooked. Even the benches used for adults holding small children look as though they might crack under the slightest weight.

In the blink of my eye, the world reverts to PR. The moon lights up, the breeze cools, and the carousel is in perfect repair. I turn circles, trying to figure out what's happening.

Honestly, a great burden lifts, and I can breathe freely for the first time in days. I want this to be real—Dad sitting on the park bench waiting for me—but it's not. Still, it tugs at me, wrapping around me like a shield.

I must resist it.

I take the necklace from under my blouse and turn the top. Nothing happens.

Then I remember: Byz warned me I'd have to take it off and charge it, but I don't know how. Hopefully, she'll be able to show me when I get back this evening.

Something grabs me by the arm, and I yelp, expecting it to be Puck, but it's not. I turn around and see Dad.

"Libby," he says. "You've got to help me."

No, not Dad. It's Imposter. I struggle against his grip as he continues. "They want to send me away, but I can't go back. Can't. I waited years for my chance to get here. Is there somewhere you can hide me?"

"Who's sending you away? To where?" I ask, pulling my arm roughly from his hand.

"Can't explain, but I can't go home, and I can't go to the police." He's peering over the bushes as if something might jump out at any moment.

I frown. He has some nerve coming to me for help. "What did you do to my dad?" I demand. "Show me where he is."

He shakes his head violently. "I never met your father. Swear. Help me hide."

"Why should I? You pretended to be my dad, *and* you threatened me."

"I had to," he says, his plea in his eyes as well as his tone. "Didn't have a choice. Everyone on the other side of the river wants to be here in PR. We don't have it over there." He turns back to the bushes. "I've messed it all up. I'm so sorry, Libby."

"Oh no. There he is!" He dashes out of the bushes and toward the riverside, where the ship docks.

I turn to see who is following him when I feel something pull at my neck, jerking my body backward. A searing burn cuts across my neck, followed by a snap. My stomach drops, and my hand flies to my throat. The necklace is gone.

I spin around and watch Puck running in the opposite direction. I give chase but lose him at the police station, and now that I'm in PR, I'm a little more obvious. People are staring.

When I turn to try the Clockery, I spot Lieutenant Yates heading my way. My instinct is to run, but that makes me look guilty, and I don't need any more help with that.

"I've been looking for you," Yates says as he nears.

I roll my eyes and mutter, "When are you not?"

Thankfully, he doesn't hear me. "Follow me."

"My necklace is missing." I stand my ground. "I have to find it."

"A necklace is the least of your concerns, young lady. You've got bigger issues at the moment."

I know where he's taking me, and it's the last place I want to be. But when I angle my body away to make a run for it, he puts his hand to his hip. There, I spot a hard, black baton.

He wouldn't hit me, would he?

With one hand on his baton, he extends his other toward the police station. I let out a long sigh, plaster on an innocent smile, and head through the doors.

The police station is a lot nicer in PR, and when I go in, there's a large waiting room, complete with a coffee center. I go to the front desk, and the sergeant calls me by name.

"We've noticed that no one has seen your father since this morning. Normally, I wouldn't notice without a complaint filed, but this time, we were surveilling him. He disappeared."

They probably want to murder him, like they did Shy. They have to know Imposter doesn't know anything, but he's also a loose end. For a split second, I feel sorry for him, but it doesn't last long. Imposter's not my primary focus. He'll have to fend for himself.

"We want to ask you a few questions now you're here. We're concerned about your safety."

I know I have little choice in the matter, though the woman is at least pretending to be sweet. I nod, and she walks me around a large partition and guides me to a couch in a small room.

She doesn't wait for me to sit as she starts. "There were some unusual activities this afternoon. Did you notice anything out of the ordinary?"

This is a tricky question. If I say I didn't notice anything, that's even more suspicious than saying I did.

I decide to tell her the same story as I told Yates, explaining my first experience with the dusty window panes and the crack. I tell her, "In a few seconds it was over, so I thought I'd imagined it. When it happened again today, I was a little more alarmed, but it only lasted a few minutes. My mother insisted it was just a glitch, and my friend says the programmers are probably already working on fixing it."

The sergeant quirks her cheek to one side. She really is quite beautiful in this reality. Everything is.

"Interesting." She scribbles something on her pad. "And your father and mother, when was the last time you spoke with them?"

I'm honest. "I saw my mother at lunch, but I haven't seen Dad since late Tuesday." *I saw Imposter only a few minutes ago*, I mutter in my head.

"You've been in here several times to ask about your father. Do you still think someone else took his place?"

I could lie again, but I just told them otherwise. "Like I said, Dad disappeared three days ago. I wasn't aware someone attacked him until the police officer brought it to my attention. The next day, an unknown man came in and took his place. He is not my dad—at least, not the one I grew up with." I'm trying to sound positive, but the fact is, if Dad's not dead, where is he?

"There's no file of your father missing before today. The officer checked, and he was accounted for at that time. What is it that makes you think that's not your father? There has to be more than using a nickname."

I grit my teeth; how many times will I need to go over this? "He called me Libby, he smells funny, and he can't answer simple questions about our family history. *It's not him.*"

"Interesting." She says it, but she yawns while she writes it all down. By the time she puts down the pen, I've caught her yawn too.

She tilts her head and looks me in the eye. "Have you been sleeping well?"

I look at her slack-faced, not knowing what her angle is.

"Sometimes when we don't get our rest, our minds can become very creative. That's why standards call for at least nine hours of sleep. Without it, the world can be very confusing."

There's no way I'm going to buy into that. *Sorry, hon. Your dad's fine. You're having a nightmare that you can't wake up from.* Please.

She stares at me, allowing the conversation to become much more uncomfortable, but I don't give in.

"So now you are actively looking for my dad?" I ask, to be certain. "Let me ask you this... Have you investigated the person who commed in my dad's assault that night? It wasn't me or my mother, and if the police officer had no body, whose authority did they use to come to such an assumption?"

She looks up from her pad. I've gotten her attention. "Normally, we could have traced the number right away, but this com came from an unknown device, and the signal originated in the park. It was the voice of a young girl." She pauses. "Did you make the call?"

"No!" I say a little too loudly. "I mean, no. I didn't know about it until the police came to my door and woke me up."

My suspicions curl up inside my chest, but it won't do any good to ask what the girl looked like or the age, so I jump right in to the obvious question.

"What did the voice say?"

"I don't remember exactly. I'd have to look that up, but the file went to the archives when the case closed. Whoever it was said the victim was a friend of the family."

Young girl. Friend of the family. Hadn't Byz told me she had used an emergency call?

I put my hands on my cheeks and lean my head back. Part of me wants to scream. Is nothing as it seems?

Byz.

CHAPTER 34

They ask a few more questions about Imposter's activity over the past few days, but I give them vague answers. If they're going to lock me up, they're going to do it whether or not I squeal on Imposter, and I see no benefit in ratting him out.

The woman asks no questions about Shy and the break-in. That's suspicious in itself, but I'll worry about that after I figure out what happened to my dad.

Thankfully, they let me go, and I take my new worries out of the police station. Not for the first time, something is definitely going on. I don't have a clue what it is, but it's happening right in my midst. No one is being clear with me, which makes me angry. This whole situation is ridiculous.

I'm going to get answers if it's the last thing I do, but it's going to have to wait a little longer, because the interrupter should start soon, and I don't want to be caught in the confusion.

My house is the closest place to go. Despite the insulting innuendos, I need to give Clarisse another chance at doing the right thing, at choosing Clarity. It'll make the transition much easier. Dad would have wanted that for her.

I could run. But now I'm aware of the low air quality, that seems like a bad idea. Instead, I speed walk. I rush past the carousel and take large strides down the road toward my house.

When I arrive, all is quiet.

"Mother," I call, hoping that maybe she's gone and I can wait out the trial here.

After no response, I relax and sit on the couch to wait out Clarity. My mind is on so many things. Byz was there when Dad was assaulted. Puck has the necklace. Probably both necklaces. My mother is a Red Star. The whole town lives in a delusion, and someone has killed the lead researcher. Too many things are happening at once, and I miss Dad.

My mother rushes from the bedroom across the living room and blocks the door. She is holding a hairbrush, and as soon as the door is closed, she points it to me. She looks like she is laughing, but there is something off about her. In PR, she is back to being absolutely beautiful, and I dread seeing her painted face in a few moments.

"Where have you been?" she asks, but it sounds grating. "And don't tell me you were working on a project. The lady from the police department commed and told me you were there, going on about Elizeus's disappearance. She was rather concerned about you, so she wanted to let me know to keep an eye on you."

I don't know what to say to that, but I'm not surprised. I now know her connection to the police station has to do with the Red Star.

"Something's not right, Clarisse. Things aren't what they appear. The man who came home from the conference and training is not Dad. He's an imposter, but I'm having trouble proving it without a body."

Her eyes are slits as she smiles. "There are lots of things that are hard to understand about this world, but your father isn't one of them. He loved you dearly, and he loved me, but he couldn't leave things as-is. He wanted me to give up the life I've worked so hard for."

Again, Clarity is an obstacle for her, something to get past, not something to acclimate to. But at least she acknowledges it. It's a start.

Dad must have told her some or all of this.

"You think I didn't know?" She shakes her head and sighs. "Of course. After eighteen years together, and it's pretty obvious when someone pretends to be your husband. I'm not an idiot. No one ever gives me enough credit."

The words are slow to come, but as they rise, they fumble off my tongue. "So, you've known all this time that Dad disappeared. Why didn't you tell me? Why aren't you helping me figure things out?"

Tears prickle my eyes, but before I can say anything else, it happens. The broken-down house I've known for days is back and in complete disrepair.

Clarisse has her eyes open this time. Her white-painted, ancient face is decorated in red lipstick that makes her mouth a perfect O, her eyes are shaded with what looks like charcoal, and her hair is twisted up with various clips. Her designer clothes look like she took them from a trash heap. It's almost comical, which multiplies with the sly smile on her face.

"This is us, mother. This is who we really are."

"Speak for yourself," she says. I look down at her hand, but instead of seeing the hairbrush she was holding in PR, I see a long, sharp knife with a silver handle. My heart leaps into my throat, and I quickly jump over the couch, putting something between us.

"You can't hurt me! I'm your daughter."

I flick my eyes around. The door to the garage. No, it'll take too long for the door to lift. She'll catch me easily that way. I need to get through the front door. Unfortunately, that's where Clarisse is standing.

"My daughter, as you've pointed out, has been a lie, which was all right until my husband wouldn't let it be. He wanted me to see him and you for who you really were." She gestures from my feet to my head. "I have no obligation to this version of you. I don't want you like this."

"What?" But the truth is, I know exactly what she's saying. I wish I didn't.

She continues. "Your dad was relentless, so I had him replaced. It's easy enough to do with the right influence, and I have plenty of that."

"Did you do something to him?" Something tickles my cheek and I reach up to wipe it away. My hand comes away wet. I'm crying, partly from anger, partly from fear, and partly from grief.

"No, honey." She wipes a tress of hair out of her face. "People won't hurt someone because you ask nicely. Murder is a serious thing. You can't rely on anyone else—not even the crooked police. No, your father would never stop, so I had to stop him myself."

She flicks the knife, and the light glints off it. "I knew he wanted to tell you. I felt the necklace when you and I hugged after school on Tuesday. He thought I didn't know, but he underestimated me."

She jabs forward, and I jump, but she's too far away to reach me. "I overestimated you, though. I thought once you had a look at Clarity, you'd see how awful reality was and turn off the necklace on your own. After all, you are my daughter. But I gave you far too much credit."

She's walking toward me and the couch, knife out. If she vaults over, I won't have much of a chance to get away.

"He tried to give it to me, that necklace, but I never wanted it. I don't want to live in this catastrophized world. I want to live in peace, creating my art, and living a life of perfection. Why would anyone want anything else?"

She sets her shoulders back, proud of herself. "I wanted it for you too, you know. Elizeus gladly traumatized you in the name of truth. Truth is relative, though; my truth is not here in this old, unattended house. My reality is beautiful, and I don't intend to give it up lightly."

I'm listening to every word she says, but I'm having trouble getting past the word 'murder.' Everything else is a silent hum as that thought tumbles in my head over and over.

"But it's more than that. Puck told me about the Clarity trials, and the police have been keeping a close watch on you. They've all kept good tabs on you."

She's done something to Dad.

"But your dear dad wasn't content to ruin it for the three of us; he wanted to ruin it for everyone. I couldn't let that happen."

"So you hurt him?" I back closer to the table. "But how?" At this point, I still can't imagine she would have the audacity, much less the strength, to carry through with killing Dad. He's the man she has loved for eighteen years. And hauling him out of the park would have been impossible.

"It was easy because of you." She points, the blame landing on me instead of herself. This is the real Clarisse—no facade. "I followed you both, and when you took off, your father ran after you. As soon as he passed the bushes, I bashed him over the head with a unicorn horn I stole from the carousel. It was enough to knock him out."

I cast my eyes around again, though I still keep Clarisse in my peripheral, trying to think of my own weapon. What's here to defend myself? What would Dad do? The tears are blurring my vision. I knew this was coming. Somewhere, I've always known.

She laughs, sardonically. "I couldn't have budged the muscular PR version of Elizeus, but as he was, he was small and slight. I pulled him into the bushes and hid him until I could get the transport around to load him."

"I... I thought you were at home when I got home."

"Afraid not." She sneers.

She takes a step forward, and I want to run, but I need to hear this too. I need to know what happened. "But... he loved you. Perfect or not, he loved you as you were. Didn't you know?"

She laughs again, sharp and humorless. "If he'd really loved me, he would have left me be. He wanted to save the world from perfection, and I wanted no part of that."

The knife is twitching in her hands. I need to get out of here, or at least distract her. I move toward the stairs, keeping the couch between us.

"And the man I brought in! You know, they don't have PR across the river. They wait in line for a chance to come here. It was his fresh start to come here and be his best, but he was no Elizeus. He shared no interest in my work, didn't care one way or the other about you or me. He was completely on PR, but he wouldn't stop asking questions about Elizeus."

"You didn't kill him." It's a statement, but she takes it as a question.

"No, I threatened him with exposure to the police, and he ran. Just as well, because he was too close to us to keep secrets and too distanced to count for loyalty. He would have ended up dead had he not made that decision. I might have encouraged him a little."

Clarisse rounds the couch, and I don't know what to say anymore to stop her. I run and hide behind the kitchen table instead, where food and fashion panels are spread out. I look for a weapon of my own, but she made soup, and soup spoons aren't exactly deadly.

We revolve halfway around the table, when she realizes I'm the faster of the two of us. She pulls up the knife and throws it at me. I duck, and it sails past me into the living room. She's about to run and get it when I pick up her newest panel. I take a spoon and punch a huge hole through the middle of it.

"Don't you dare touch those!" she says, grabbing one while I pick up another and jab the spoon through again.

As she grabs her precious panels, I take off for the front door, slamming it behind me. The street is busy with other people lost in reality. Clarity is a hard adjustment to make. The ones that aren't arguing are snooping around as if the whole world is brand new instead of old and malnourished.

I can't have Clarisse follow me out here. There are too many people to get hurt.

I stop on the porch as I hear her thunderous feet approach. She pulls the door in, and with all my might, I kick it in on her. I'm hoping for enough force to knock her down, but I hear her cry out. I peek through the open door to see her covered in blood where the knife must have been knocked back into her torso.

She's on the floor, and I'm about to lose it completely. I can't believe I just stabbed my own mother. I reach down to see if I can help, but she opens her eyes and glares at me.

I run.

CHAPTER 35

Past a few arguments and through the confused and crowded streets, I run to the only place that matters. The place where I last saw Dad, the place where this nightmare began. I'd give everything up, forget Clarity, anything to have him back.

I fold over on the bench and let the tears come in streams. Clarisse tried to kill Dad, and he probably had no idea who attacked him.

How could she have done it? He loved her despite everything. He loved us, no matter what. But Clarisse, she can't love us fully. She doesn't want us as we really are.

I'm succumbing to deep heaves when a shadow falls over me. I open my eyes to see Puck, a giant smile on his face. He lifts his eyebrow at me and beckons me forward.

I don't move. Through my tears, I say, "She tried to kill him. Clarisse thinks she murdered Dad. And then she turned on me. I've lost everything now. It's all gone."

"Well, well... welcome to Clarity!" he says, gesturing his arms wide. "Nothing is as it appears."

I wipe my eyes, though the tears are coming in torrents. "And you? You stand by and let this charade continue!" My voice grows firmer with each word as some of Clarisse's assertiveness flows through me. "I want the necklace. Both of them."

When he doesn't move, I stare through the blur of tears. "Now!"

He looks at me, and the edge of his smile makes me lash out at him. With both fists, I push him back. He opens his mouth to defend himself, but I don't give him the chance. I push him once more, saying, "The necklaces don't belong to you, and you don't need them, anyway. You already see the world as it is."

"Yes, I do," he holds his hands out, blocking me from his chest. "But if Clarity must come, I've had to figure out something else."

It's been close to fifteen minutes and soon, PR will return. I need one of those necklaces, at least until I get my tech removed. I can't afford to get lost in PR now. I've got to stop Clarisse. Though when the glitch is over, Clarisse will probably look for me.

Clarity is the only answer. Dad's work is the means by which I will avenge him.

"There's no way around it. You've lost, Puck. Clarity is coming in waves, but it's coming. Soon, everyone will be working together to salvage what's left of this world and figuring out a way to sustain and improve our environment. It will all be better then."

"You would think, girlie." His eyes are slits. "You've lived in a gilded world your whole life. You have no idea of the strife that will happen when people understand that goods are scarce. People will steal, maim, and kill to get their share for their family."

I want to tell him he's wrong, but I don't know that. Look at what's happened to Clarisse.

My sorrow diminishes my ability to think. It leaves me speechless, overloaded.

He smiles at the doubt that must be written all over my face. "That being said, I have big plans. I've been storing supplies for a long time. If Clarity comes, I'll make a fortune out of selling my supplies for exorbitant costs. Do you know how much power that will give me?"

My voice rises, but I don't care anymore. "You are the type of person they built this program to feed! The greedy, the stingy, the basest among us who would have it all or nothing. When Clarity becomes real and we work together, you'll see a lot of changes."

A girl on the path stops and looks at the bench. Puck smiles at her, and it's halfway friendly until she leaves.

"You know nothing about human nature, child." He speaks through gritted teeth, looking around to see if anyone is watching us, but they must be wrapped up in their own dilemmas. "You've got a lot to learn, but not me. I've done my research. People are diabolical. So what if I beat them to the punch?"

I have no idea if he's correct. It's not impossible. I've seen the best side of life, but I've also seen the best side of people. But Clarisse is proof of what he's saying—and the police. Even Mrs. Devonshire chased her husband with a broom handle.

Perhaps when things aren't at their best, people aren't at their best. Plus, there will be some disequilibrium. I can see that not all houses are equal now, and not all things as lovely as others. With inequality will come some level of unrest.

"Did you know what happened to my dad? Did you know my mother tried to kill him?" I realize I'm holding my breath as I wait for his reply.

He smiles wryly, shaking his head at me. "I've seen your mother around, and she is fully immersed in PR, as are most people, but she takes it over the edge. She's afraid of losing it, and if that's the case, she's known all along that it isn't reality. It was easy to make her an ally."

He smiles, twirling his finger around in the air. "You've seen how we live. The people will not be happy to find out where they're living, what they're wearing, and most definitely what they're eating. When they realize they're all little dried-up raisins, they're going to miss PR. Not only are they going to be angry with the Watchers but also the people who took out the programming."

I piece his words together.

He's right. It's the perfect motive for Dad's disappearance, Shy's death, and Clarisse trying to kill me. Dad was the leader. There must have been plenty who wanted him dead here. But the Watchers might also know his role.

Puck turns and heads back toward the buildings, but I follow him with my question. "What do you know about them? The Watchers?"

I barely get the words out as the world transforms for me again. I am back in PR, talking to the dapper pinstripe man. The sun relents, and I turn to watch the people, still confused. A hush settles over the street. The people smile, so glad to see what's familiar to them at last. It's a relief for me too. Reality is trying to destroy me. But I can't afford to think that way. No longer is the illusion beneficial. I know too much.

"It's back, I see. I can tell," he mumbles, laughing. He gestures outward. "The PREP program is wrong not to pull the plug all at once. They'll drive the people mad with the constant change in setting. But, if your kind are determined to do away with PR, I may as well be their savior. I can put the program to an end so we can fully operate in Clarity.

"But to answer your question, the people who have created this alternate reality are living an alternate reality of their own. They have stolen the best of our resources and stock-piled them for when the world becomes uninhabitable. They live a perfect life, although limited to the biome. I don't know exactly where they are, but they watch from high above the river."

I follow his finger as he points to the moon over the city center. It's perfect now, but it's also recording us. Watching our every move.

"How do they get our stuff? How do we supply them?"

"The river, of course. The captains travel in between, but even they have never seen them. They merely dock, and machinery of-floads the supplies. I've asked them to make inquiries, but they're not dummies. They know what will happen to them if they act suspect, and they're too set in their ways to want to stray from PR."

I'm finally pulling myself together when we cross Main Street and step up on the perfect sidewalk. I'm listening to him closely, when a transport moves through my peripheral. It's speeding, but I think little of it until it turns the corner and immediately swerves onto the sidewalk where we're standing.

Puck pulls me up onto a nearby staircase as my mother takes out everything in her way and crashes into the concrete steps. She tries to get out of the transport, but she has wedged herself too close to the building.

My scream is shrill, even to me. The tears, the fear, the uncertainty, and the truth zap me instantly. I scream again when Puck shakes me hard.

"Much as I'd love to stay and chat with you, I think it might do us both well to get out of here. I will see you soon." Puck chuckles as he turns and heads back toward the south side of town.

I don't disagree. I need to get to a safe place, too.

Following Puck in the direction of the police station and church, I struggle to keep up. He's much faster with his long legs, and it doesn't take long until I'm wheezing. I turn into an alleyway to catch my breath, cursing the restricted air.

The hulking man that I gave the lollipop is there.

"Are you okay?" he asks.

His eyes are kind, stopping me in my tracks, and I let loose the pressure I've been building since this all began. "No. I'm not. The world is a lie. Dad's not here, maybe killed by my mother. And she's trying to run me over with her transport, and Puck... I thought he was evil, but he just saved my life."

He lets me cry it out for a few minutes before asking, "Do you know where you're going?"

"I do, but I'm uncertain how to get there without being seen."

"You tell me where you want to go, and I'll get you there, but it'll take a minor sacrifice."

CHAPTER 36

He takes me into the alley and walks to the old refrigerator behind Puck's back entrance. He pulls something from it, handing it to me before we step through the gate. I'm holding various items of clothing, but all I can see is the beautiful suit on top.

He takes it from me and explains. "For when I need attention. It works like a charm. I can get into any restaurant in town. But that's for being seen. You want plain clothes for being unseen."

He pulls out a pale-yellow crocheted blanket and a t-shirt with a hood.

"Dial down your color saturations and put these on. They look especially drab in PR."

The items look nondescript, but also clean. As I slide them over my dress, I'm hoping they're not filthy in Clarity.

"There we go; now you'll look like someone different if your mother passes us along the way, and being with me will help throw her off your trail."

A weight lifts from my shoulders, and I smile weakly. "I can't thank you enough. Puck says people are all bad, but you're very kind."

"I'm returning the kindness you showed me when you didn't have to. Consider us even."

I'm so relieved that someone removed from the ambition of PR and Clarity is kind that I almost reach out and hug him.

He takes me behind the city center toward the mall before turning right and taking us on a parallel path to the library. I'm grateful there's no sign of Clarisse. It's getting darker, but the moon shines brightly as the evening settles. People are returning to their homes, deluded until the signal disappears again. I'd like to make it to the church by the time the darkness settles, and from what I can tell, we're making good time.

"What's your name?" I ask, making small talk.

"It's Mitchel, named for my dad. He was raised with PR, just like me. I came into Clarity later. If I were to have children, which isn't looking likely, I would make the switch right away. I'd show my child the real world. For now, I'll share it with you."

His eyes are soft and his manner gentle. I believe him completely.

He takes a bit to tell me how things were before as the plagues and wasting came through the communities, killing most of the people that inhabited at least our area. He couldn't say beyond that, because opportunists took over the media, seizing control.

"They herded the survivors in mass droves to here in the south. We took over this small community after the virus obliterated it. I'm sure some of the original people have ancestors here today, but mine are all gone."

Mitchel is walking fast, and I have to speed walk to keep up with him. In PR, the climate is nice, but I'm still panting. His long stride gives him an advantage.

"How is it that you don't have PR?" I ask.

"My father removed mine when I turned thirteen. He said I was old enough to handle the real world and help make changes. A doctor cut the PR programming from me." He pulls back an ear to show me the long scar that runs from behind his ear to his lower neck.

He must notice the shocked look on my face, because his mouth turns into a big O. "Don't worry. They don't do surgery these days. Instead, they make a slight slit in the skin and coat the tech with a metal. That's all it takes. But I'm glad they took mine, because I think the metal is dangerous."

He stops at the intersection and points to our right. On the corner of the next street, I can see the library. We're almost there.

"I'm sorry about your dad." Mitchel says. "He was a good man."

I only nod; there are no words.

He's quiet as he leads me to the church. When he gets there, he points as if he's fulfilled his duty.

"Aren't you coming in?" I tug his hand, but he doesn't move.

"You'll find that there are good people in PR and out. But you'll find bad people on both sides too. Be careful who you trust. Good luck," he says and turns.

"Thank you!" I call after him, but he's out of hearing distance, and I dare not speak any louder.

I'm suddenly very hesitant to go inside. His warning hangs in the air, and I try to think of who inside would be untrustworthy. My immediate concerns go to Mr. Lawson and Byz.

The police all but spelled it out for me—Byz saw Dad attacked and made the emergency com that night. Why wouldn't she tell me if she was innocent?

Then there's Mr. Lawson. He must know Byz was there. From what he said, he must have been there too.

It's a lot to take in, but it's the only place I really have to go. My house is no haven, and Puck has marked himself as an opportunist, even if he saved me. The church is my last refuge.

I knock on the door using the four sharp raps, followed by two short taps on the door, and it swings open to reveal a strange woman.

"Here you are!" she says, rushing me. This has to be Myrna. She looks different in PR, but still as friendly. "We spent most of the afternoon guessing what became of you. I know it's very hectic in here, but no one saw you leave."

With a shrug, I dismiss it, not bothering to tell her I climbed out the window. But when Myrna pulls me into a big hug, all fight leaves me; I cry on her shoulder, and she hugs me tighter.

When the tears die down, she grabs my shoulders and looks into my eyes. "What is it, dear?"

"Clarisse tried to kill Dad." I suck in a whimper. "She tried to kill me, too."

Myrna pulls me into a hug again and lets me cry some more.

When I pull away, Byz and another woman, probably her mother, are standing there, looking worried. Byz grabs my hand. "Where did you get off to?"

"I went home for a while. I had to see Clarisse to help her through."

Mrs. Lawson quirks her eyebrows. "How did that go?"

Myrna senses Mrs. Lawson's sarcasm, shakes her head, and motions her elsewhere.

Byz still has my hand, but I yank it back. "I talked to the police, and they told me about the emergency call."

Her face freezes, worry lining her forehead.

"You told me that night you came to my house that you recently made such a call." I look into the face I trusted. I want to yell at her, but I'm too hurt.

"Don't worry, they didn't know who you were, but I did." I refuse to cry for her. "You knew that my mother did something to my dad, but you said nothing. Why wouldn't you tell me? How could you let me go to her, knowing how dangerous she was?"

Byz takes a deep breath before answering. "I should have told you, but I never imagined she'd go after you. You've had little to do with PREP, and you're her flesh and blood. But..." She leans her head forward. "She didn't kill him, though. Your mother attacked him and dragged him into the bushes, but he was crawling out the last I saw of him. He was alive, but she had left by then."

My hope is in neutral, so worn from ups and downs. All I can do is listen.

"I commed the police immediately, using the emergency device my dad gave me in case I ever got into danger," she says. "By the time the com ended, your dad had disappeared. I wasn't sure if he'd gotten up and walked away. I didn't know, but I knew the police would come, so I had to leave immediately. I really know as much as you do about what really happened to him."

"He was alive!" I knew it! "Then what happened to him?"

Byz shrugs as if it's the hardest question she's ever had to answer. "I'm sorry I didn't tell you, but we hadn't spoken since we were kids. I didn't know you well enough to know how you'd react. You reminded me of your father, but I couldn't be sure you weren't like your mother. By the time I realized you were okay, it felt too late to tell you. I knew you'd distrust everything I said. I told you the truth, but I left some of it out."

Swallowing hard, I take a deep breath. "I want the PR removed, or covered, or whatever you do. I don't believe in this world anymore, and Puck stole my necklace."

Her face falls, but I'm beyond caring at the moment. I continue. "Dad disappeared, and my mother is insane. I don't want to end up like either. To make the right decision, I need to know the facts. All of them. If we're going to make things better, I have to get rid of PR. No more lies."

"I'd like that. I'll talk to my dad," says Byz.

We both watch as Mrs. Lawson moves across the crowded room to whisper to Myrna.

Byz tries to distract me. "Don't worry, though. If all goes to plan, we can arrange it in the morning. If you're sure?"

"It's the one thing I'm sure of," I tell her. I'm determined to see Dad's work go on. It's almost as important as finding out what happened. After all, he's lived the cause his whole adult life.

"We have to stay here for a while, so we'll be sleeping here. Let me show you where I am, and you can share space with me."

I follow her to a rack with soft pink blankets and fluffy pillows. It beats my ratty bedding any day.

I grab one of each as Byz shows me a spot behind the farthest mirror. There's so much on my mind that it's all I can do to nod at her. I spread out on the floor to get some sleep.

I don't know how long I lie there, but my brain is so full of new information, good and bad, that I can't seem to grab hold of a thought to examine it.

The uncertainty of Dad's death breaks my heart, only to send it soaring again with the possibility he could be alive.

Then there's the utter insanity of Clarisse. I shudder as I push away the image of her bashing him on the head and brandishing a knife at me.

Also, the truths that Byz has hidden from me. All of it too much to bear, bouncing around my head, one thought colliding with another.

Perhaps tomorrow my world will stabilize, and I'll free myself of the fake reality that's covered me my whole life.

Before drifting off, I imagine my dad. He's smiling at me. But from where?

I cry softly until all is quiet.

CHAPTER 37

M uffled activity wakes me up, and I take a minute to remember I'm not at home—as if the hard floor beneath me isn't reminder enough. I roll over to get a few more minutes, desperate to catch up with the deficit of sleep, but as I do, a shadow rolls over my face, and I have to look.

I expect someone to be hanging over my head, but there's no one there, so I look around. PR is off. I know the instant I see Myrna and another woman putting blankets over the windows, blocking the light from coming into the room. I don't think much about it. Not until Byz pulls my blanket off me and hands it up to Myrna.

"Hey!" I complain.

I normally wake up in a great mood, but not today. First off, I cried myself to sleep, so my eyes are thick and puffy. Second, I'm not in a stable environment, and it's getting to me. Today will bring more changes. I close my eyes, happy to have my pillow.

Byz reaches down and shakes me. "Get up."

I don't want to comply, but when she tugs the pillow from under my head, I realize I slept on a balled-up sweatshirt. There's no way to go back to sleep. I pull myself up on my elbows and look around.

Someone has shoved the mirror along the back wall, and I'm curious why, but it's not nearly as pressing as my need to use the facilities. Standing up and stumbling toward the bathroom, I have to leave the door open, because the electricity doesn't seem to be working, and someone has covered the window with another blanket. I have to pull it back to see where to sit.

A police siren blares down the road. Thankfully, it's heading away from the church.

Something is up, but I don't know what. It feels off, so I wash my hands and go back out to find out exactly what's going on.

As soon as I'm out the door, Byz hands me a trash bag full of something light. She carries one too.

"C'mon." she says. "We don't have much time. People are already leaving their houses."

I follow her. "What's going on?"

"PR is off."

"I thought that was going to be from noon until two."

She nods, eyes big.

"So? Can't they turn it back on?" I ask.

She leads me out the side door onto the front lawn of the church.

"No," she says and pulls out a wad of trash and starts throwing it to the ground. I know I'm half asleep, but even so, this is weird.

"What are you doing?" I ask as she walks a few steps and throws some more litter on the ground.

"We have to make cover. They're on the streets much faster than we expected, and we thought we had more time. When the people realized PR is off, they didn't wait it out in their homes for as long as we thought they would. They're out, looking for someone to blame."

"Why would they come here? It looks like an old abandoned building."

"That's not the problem. They're going to notice our lawns are litter free. They're going to stand out like a sore thumb, so we need to trash this one up if it's going to be any kind of safe haven."

I jump in and start helping. "What about the stars? How are you going to cover that up?"

"We can't really cover it up, but Dad went out first thing this morning and added new ones, so it would confuse people if they realized the code. He's only doing the yellow though. The Blue Star and Red Star people will have to be on their own. There isn't time for him to do all three."

We empty both trash bags, but it still doesn't look as messy as the other yards. Even if it did, the trash looks new compared to the other people's houses, whose junky lawns include trash that yellowed with time. It's washed out and weather worn.

Byz points to a house across the street with even more trash than the rest. "C'mon. We'll take some of theirs. They've got plenty to offer."

We grab our bags and fill them up again, transferring the trash to the churchyard.

A loud scream down the street.

Byz grabs my hand. "We need to get inside before someone sees us."

She turns to the side door and does a new knock, but I only catch the last of it. It ends with three sharp raps.

As soon as she opens the door, Mrs. Lawson takes the bags and pats Byz on the shoulder. "Good job, girls."

Inside, it's dark except for a few lanterns. I can barely see, but I guess everyone else is in the same situation, so I don't complain.

Byz pulls me back to the sanctuary and finds us a seat on the last pew. The others are slowly filing in, and it's the first time I realize how many people are here.

"What happened? Did your dad turn on the interrupter?"

"No, he didn't do anything. Someone else must have cut it off. It could be someone from the biome or someone here. There's no way to know which. We expect people to become furious when PR doesn't return, so we'll wait here until most of it blows over. Then, we'll go out to the community and discuss changes. It'll be risky, but there'll have to be a leader, and we'd prefer it be someone from the Yellow group as opposed to the other two."

"Your dad?"

"Maybe. My dad is very persuasive, but I don't think he wants to be the leader. If I had to bet, it'll be Myrna. She's never met a stranger, and no one can link her with the assessor's department. It's what I'd do at least, and judging from the way Myrna is taking charge, she's considered it, too."

"So we wait." I puff up my cheeks, my head not comprehending exactly what's happened. "For how long?"

"No telling. We may be here a day, a week, or longer."

My stomach rumbles. "Wait, is there enough food for us all to hide here? We'll starve to death if it takes a while."

Mrs. Lawson slides into the pew in front of us. "We don't have an abundant supply, but I'll be darned if my people are going to starve to death. Fortunately, we had already started stockpiling what we could in advance of permanently interrupting the PR signal. We have a few friends that got us a good amount of water, and we've managed to can a lot of produce. We don't have a lot, but we have dried beans for protein. Another shipment was to come in tomorrow, but unless something changes between now and then, we probably won't get it."

"Is there something to eat now?" I ask shamelessly. I'm starving.

Mrs. Lawson points toward the side door. "On the table by the side entrance are a lot of wheat crackers I made this week. Until we get an accurate inventory of the food we have, we'll have to suffice with them. We need to ration what we have, and we can't do that without a good count."

"Okay," and I'm up, heading toward the vestibule, where a woman with a baby grabs some crackers then sits down to nurse her child. I wonder about the child's generation. Will there be enough resources or enough time to set things right? It's too soon to tell, but I know it'll be close.

I count out eight crackers and cross over to the nursing woman. Before I can start nibbling, my stomach groans loudly, and I realize I haven't eaten since the ice cream parlor yesterday.

Aden! He's woken up to his PR disabled too. I'm so glad I told him. At least he has a good idea of what's happening. It'll be up to him to calm the others in his house. I wish I could reassure him.

Oh, who am I kidding? I wish he was here to reassure me.

Someone bangs at the door to my right, making me jump. It's three strong raps and three taps. I have no idea if that's the correct knock or not, so I look at the mother who nods at me to let them in.

When I open the door, Mr. Lawson comes in and quickly closes it behind him. He's so fast, he almost runs me over, but I step out of his way before I'm squashed.

"Sorry," he says when he realizes. "Hey, there's a guy outside calling your name down the street. Do you know who that is?"

Aden. Must be. I nod.

"Whoever he is, he needs to go home. It isn't safe out there. The people are coming out of their houses. There are about to be a lot of angry people on the streets, and I don't want to be among them until things calm down a bit."

"You think they'll calm down?"

"At some point, I think they'll decide that working together will be more beneficial than working independently. But it won't surprise me if a wave of violence precedes it." He pulls cans of spray paint out of the pockets of his vest. He must have used at least five, though he might not have brought all the cans back with him.

"Do you think it'll be enough?"

He follows my eyes to the paint and shrugs. "It's better now than it was, and the trash on the lawn helps, but the building itself is in better repair than most. We'll be lucky if we ride the violence out."

I nod, crossing my arms, trying to feel safe, but it's not happening. I'm not safe. No one here is. Mr. Lawson can't protect me, even if he wants to.

I sit next to the woman and nibble at my crackers until my mouth is completely dry.

"Is there any water?" I ask her.

"Only thing I know of is the restroom and kitchen sinks," she says. "I can't speak to the water quality. I haven't checked the refrigerator yet. May be worth your while."

I take a minute to find the kitchen in the back of the church, but there are two people sitting at the table. They don't look welcoming, and the short one harrumphs as I enter. I decide not to greet them, and they return the favor.

When I turn on the faucet and watch the rusty-looking water pour out, a shiver runs down my spine. I've been drinking this forever, so it won't kill me, but I'm not ready to give in yet.

I open up the refrigerator, but inside is not food. Instead, I find medications. Some sort of inoculation would be my guess, but I'm not sure. No luck for anything in there.

I open the freezer and find plastic bags with bricks of ice inside. The ice is clear, so it's my best bet. I pull one out and slam it against the counter a few times until a few edges break off, but most of the ice stays intact. I pull out the broken pieces and put them on my tongue.

Now, I have the interest of the other two, who watch me intently. They stare so long that I hold the bag out to them to see if they want a piece, and the man with his back against the wall takes it and passes it to the other man across from him. After he gets his piece, he hands it to me, and I seal it and put it back in the freezer.

I'm about to leave when the taller man says, "You're Elizeus's daughter, aren't you?"

"I am, but... I mean... No, no, I am. I *am* Elizeus's daughter."

"We heard he's missing. I want you to know he was a good man working to benefit everyone in the community. He worked hard to get us here, and he didn't have a lot of support to start with. He and Truman had to take a lot of risks to get people involved, but their efforts were worth it. The time has come for Clarity."

I nod. Not knowing what else to say to these strangers.

The short man joins in. "He was an excellent leader and a kind man. Our leader was good too, but someone got to him before this could happen?"

"Your leader?"

"Yes, the Blue Star leader, Shuyler, was killed yesterday. He was starkly against Clarity at first, but he'd done enough research to realize we needed everyone fighting for the planet. He was changing minds, arguing that the research was useless if there was no one to appreciate it. He was an ally of your father, and we all thought highly of him."

I want to thank them, but if I talk about Dad, I'm going to cry. My mother has turned into a monster. Or maybe she was one all along, and I'm just now seeing her for who she is. But Dad, he had been my champion. He tried to bring me back to reality, despite my mother's protests. I don't know exactly why it took so long, but in the end, he wanted me to join him in the cause. That's got to be the reason my mother tried to murder him.

A loud bang shudders through the building. I dart out of the kitchen, back to where everyone is gathered around the pews. Again, somebody bangs on the chained double doors at the front of the building. Whoever it is definitely doesn't know the knock. It could be anybody, but it's not one of us.

As I pass through the sanctuary, a brick comes through a stained-glass window. It knocks down the blanket and spreads white light around the room.

CHAPTER 38

"Don't panic," Myrna says. "It may be random vandals."

We're all hoping she's right. The dust dances in the light from the uncovered window, and the terrible haze is pouring in.

Another brick. A different window. I can't figure out which was hit until the two men from the kitchen run into the sanctuary and announce they've been seen.

The knocks sound like hammers on the big wooden doors of the sanctuary. There can't be just one person; it has to be at least three to four people. Maybe we can handle them. Maybe.

The door shakes on its hinges. It's too old and heavy to stand much longer. Though the doors are thick, they were probably meant to fortify the building instead of keeping out masses of people.

Everyone runs away from the doors, but I stand there in frozen fascination until Byz grabs my hand and tugs me to follow her farther in the building. I'm confused, so I acquiesce as she drags me behind.

When at last she stops, I know where I am. We're in the storerooms, and we aren't alone. Others have come to gather supplies too. One is Mrs. Lawson. She tosses things to Byz to put in her pockets, but I don't see what they are until I get to the box. They're small bags of nuts.

I stuff my pockets. There are gallons and gallons of water here, but none small enough to take, so I have to skip this vital resource. Thankfully, Byz is filling her thermos.

"Here," she tosses me a few small bags of a mixture of oats and grains.

When we finish, we run back up toward the sanctuary, and I head toward the side door where several people have gathered.

"No, this way," says Byz, leading me to the wide sanctuary doors, which are about to come down.

"Hide behind here and when everyone floods in, we can be a part of the crowd or leave behind them."

We stand close to the wall as the door slams onto the ground, thickening the dusty haze. A hoard of people comes through the open space. Byz pulls me behind them, and we become our own scavengers. Others pour into the space from outside. There are probably about forty here now, and I hope they don't know each other, because then we'd really stick out.

The pink-pantsed man from Byz's house must be the leader; he's the first into the sanctuary. When he sees it's empty, he turns around. Byz pulls us behind someone for cover.

The man's voice booms. "There's got to be something here. I've watched people come and go from this building for weeks, and I don't think they were here for training. Split up and yell if you find something. We'll divvy it up if there's enough."

"What if there is not enough?" a woman with a bandana says. Her eyes look hollow, and I wince when she looks my way.

"If there's not enough," he smiles, "we'll have to fight for it."

I hope for the hollow-eyed woman's sake he considers it enough to share, because she looks like she needs nutrition now.

The leader barks orders, telling who to go where. I hide behind Byz as he sends her back toward the back room, which is good because we need to get out of here.

Byz must come up with the same solution, because she heads straight for the side door, stopping for a second to fill her pockets with crackers. I do the same, and soon we're back in the neighborhood, wandering the streets.

Everyone is out now; some are angry, but most are in some form of denial. They look lost, staring from one building to the next, one face to another. Many are scouring the neighborhoods, not looking for a fight, but wanting to see the way things are in this new world.

The angry ones are easier to spot. They move fast and shove past people on the corners. More than a few of them have picked up makeshift weapons, and they get a wide berth from others.

Those who have transports are driving along the streets. Except for the tense-looking drivers, the passengers have their hands or faces pressed to the glass. Their eyes are wide with wonder, though I can also make out fear.

"Where are we going?" I ask.

"I don't know," Byz answers. "I don't know where my parents went, but they'll look for us. I just have to think about where. My instinct is telling me to get away from our house. Everyone knows that Dad is a balancer, and the angry ones are bound to show up there."

"Do you think he did it?"

Byz stops cold and turns on me. "My father wouldn't have done something like this without consulting the base. And he doesn't have the power to turn off the signal, anyway. As far as I know, no one does... or did."

A plea from her eyes urges me to believe. And I do believe she's telling what she knows. And that's good enough. My concern now is the Red Stars and how they must be the cause of the ruckus.

I change the subject. "Well, we can't go to my house. Clarisse has gone completely out of her mind. She thinks she killed Dad. Did you see where she went that night? Or what direction Dad was heading. Anything you've remembered or forgotten to tell me? Anything at all?"

"No, I don't think so. My dad knew your father was going to talk to you, so he asked me to help if you freaked out. He thought maybe someone your age would make it easier to take, I guess. All I know is your dad was up off the ground before your mother disappeared. After the com, I had to leave or put my family at risk.

"I only told the police that someone attacked your dad. I'm not sure what the police found and why they blamed you. In fact, I've wondered whether they were involved. That's all I saw, though. I really don't think your mother hurt him enough to kill him."

If Clarisse didn't kill him, it wasn't for lack of trying. She'll do anything to stay in the comfortable world of PR, including killing her husband and attempt to murder her daughter.

I wonder how Clarisse is handling the change now. Is she curled up in a ball on the kitchen floor, or is she out in the streets threatening everyone?

The thought makes me shiver. She's horrible, but I now see there are plenty who are as desperate as her. They crawl out of their front doors with scrunched faces and gripped fists.

Someone will have to pay for what's been done, and pity on whoever that person is.

My mind is turning circles. Just when I feel like I have some clue what happened, I'm back to square one. But if that means there's still a chance Dad is alive, I can deal with it. He can't just be on a trip, though. Where could he be?

Another transport screeches around the corner, plowing into a female pedestrian on the sidewalk. The people with her pull her onto the nearest lawn, but there's nothing to do. Sol Luna-Nueva has no emergency response, other than the police. They'll be lucky to get her to a domicile before she dies.

As the transport passes, I get a look at the driver.

It's Puck in his ridiculous pinstripe suit.

CHAPTER 39

The asphalt clears as Puck pummels through. I feel the need to follow him, but there's no way to keep up. If anyone wanted to manipulate the signal, he would be the prime suspect, because he has said that the PREP people shouldn't gradually reveal Clarity, but permanently expose it. He said he had a plan, and he also has the most to gain with his hoarded supplies.

The weirdest thing about it is he seems to be running from something. What? Has someone figured out he's responsible?

I watch his transport slide around the curve, narrowly missing another group of people who have to throw themselves onto the nearest lawn. I have no idea what's in that direction, but it can't be much farther to the river, and there's nowhere to cross except the main gate on the bridge, but that's closer to the mall.

A thought occurs, and it suddenly makes sense to me. Puck wanted the necklace so desperately, but at first, he had hidden his desire from me. He didn't want me to see what he was doing. But he must have been in the park the night Dad disappeared since he had both necklaces. Getting it from me would be much easier than stealing it from Dad. Puck was waiting for me to get it. He knew I was too weak to protect it.

Byz yells from behind me, because I've strayed too far in the other direction. "Hey, where are you going?"

"I think I know who did it!"

"You know who turned off the signal?" she asks.

"Not sure about that, but I think I know who's jamming the signal, and I think I know why."

I'm halfway down the street before I realize I'm running. I notice because of how difficult it is to breathe.

Byz calls behind me, but I can't make out what she's saying. My rage is murderous; Puck took the one person that ever wanted to see me grow. He literally wanted me to have the world so we could save it together.

The transport is out of sight, but I'm determined to find it. I hear Byz still calling out my name, but I've got to get to him. It's got to be me. No one else has lost as much as I have.

A woman ahead of me pulls her son onto the grass. She mouths the words, but it's Byz's voice I hear shout, "Watch out!"

I turn back just long enough to see Clarisse plow down the road. She could be after Puck or she could be desperate to get somewhere, but all of that is derailed when she turns her head slightly to the right and sees me standing there.

I'm not her perfect little girl anymore, but she knows my face. My real face. Her eyes are wide. She recognizes me from last night, when she tried to kill me.

She screeches to a halt, stopping several yards in front of me, and steps out of the transport.

I recognize her too, but as glammed up as she was before, she has really upped her game. She has torn one of her blouses into strips and woven it through her hair. Her face is still painted white with charcoal eyes, but she has added purple to her cheeks. For her mouth, she has painted a little black heart. I can see dried blood streaks on her legs from the knife wound.

She's wearing the trash bag dress. It makes her shoulders angular, like the queen on a deck of cards.

In her hand is a long piece of wood that looks like the railing to our porch. She slams the door behind her and the trash bag dress tears. A large bloodstain from the knife wound covers her white shaper. The undergarment accentuates her curves. Is there nothing real about this woman?

But there is. There is something very real, and it's me. If I don't get out of here, she's going to kill me.

Clarisse kicks off her clogs. When I turn to run, Byz's head is pulled back. She turns her head, and I see that she doesn't know what to do, and I don't want to drag her in any further. I leave her there gawking as I move between two houses and through a gate in the backyard. I don't see a way out, but I do see a plan.

Jumping on top of an outdoor table, I land in another yard, which thankfully is not fenced in. The road is in front of me.

Over my shoulder, it looks like I'm in the clear when I hear the transport squeal around the corner. She must have given up on the fence and driven around. I'm running at full tilt when I pass Aden, bumping into him with my shoulder.

"Watch out!"

I've already passed him, so I don't see his physical reaction, but there's a catch in his voice when he calls after me. "Liberty, I've been out looking for you!"

I don't answer him, but the next thing I know, he's running with me, and we're both wheezing. "Look, I'm sorry!"

"Move," I tell him. "My mother is trying to run me over." He jerks me aside, and the transport passes.

"Your mother?" he says, looking back.

I can't say it aloud, because it's too horrid to comprehend her actions. All I know is we need to go before she comes back again. I run toward the yard I just came from, thinking she won't backtrack for me, when Clarisse drops from the fence. The garbage bag dress is completely gone, the bloodied white shaper, the cloth strips in her hair, and her painted face make her look gruesome.

I turn around as the transport pulls around the corner, jamming straight for me. But who's driving it if it's not Clarisse?

When I run again, Aden directs me to turn toward the main stretch. Gasping for breath, certain that I'm about to be runover or tackled, I wait for the hit.

But it never comes.

I take the chance and turn.

Clarisse is behind me, hotfooting it over the street with the porch railing in her hand. She looks maniacal. She must blame all of this on me, but why?

Either way, I have a lead on her, and that's what I need just to get away, since the transport seems to have disappeared. I turn my head and run out into the street, not realizing what's happening until I'm up, over, and on the ground, and another transport is passing me.

Everything slows as I realize I've been run over.

Flat on the hot pavement, I lie. I'm looking at the haze and the giant eye in the sky that watches over us. I don't know if I can, or even if I should, move.

The best I can do is turn my head toward the sidewalk. In the crowd, no one comes to my aid, as if I have some type of contagious catastrophe. They circle around me as they walk down the street. I don't think anything is broken, but I don't know how that can be. I stay still, anyway, hoping all of this will go away.

Aden catches up with me.

"Liberty, are you all right?" His voice is desperate as he takes off his shirt and wraps it around my leg. I can't see the injury there, but I moan in pain when he lifts it.

"Am I alive? The transport—" I can't finish my sentence.

"I know. I saw you roll off the hood. It's a wonder you weren't killed. If it hadn't been going so slow, you'd be dead." He looks both ways down the street. "We can't stay here. Do you think you can get up long enough to get out of the street?

"No, no!" I don't know whether I can reach the grass, but my legs feel crushed, too sore for him to carry me. I survey to see how far the sidewalk is, and it's too far. I couldn't make it even if I crawled.

"Here, let me carry you." Aden picks me up from underneath with one arm under my shoulder and the other under my hurt leg. I'm screaming with pain, but the sound seems so distant. I know that doesn't bode well for me.

Pulling my hand down, I take some pressure off where he's holding me when I see her.eh

"Watch out!" I yell as Clarisse clubs Aden sharply on the head with the porch railing. Together, we fall over into a heap and sprawl on the pitted asphalt. He scrambles on top of me, and I'm confused about what he's doing until Clarisse clubs him again.

He's protecting me!

The blood from his head wound is dripping on my forehead when she hits him a third, then a fourth time. The last blow is too much as she hits him at the base of the skull, and all his weight comes down on me.

I'm trapped, but protected. I can't stay here, and I don't have the strength to remove Aden. Clarisse's shadow comes over us as she grabs Aden's torso and shoves him aside. She smiles at me, but there's something bestial about her eyes.

I flip onto my stomach and crawl as best as I can, using one foot and my elbows to propel me. I'm barely moving, but I keep at it.

"Look at my baby girl," Clarisse mocks me. "Out in the real world. Are you enjoying it so far? This is the world that Elizeus planned for you, planned for us all. And he got what he wished for. Isn't this what you wanted, too?"

I want to tell her that I want Clarity, that I want us all to face the future together, but all I can do is huff as I keep moving. No one would want this.

"You're an idiot, like your father. There's no saving the world. Instead, we can choose to live beyond it. We could be happily in PR, if you and your father didn't mess it up with those stupid pendants."

I'm almost to the grass, and I grit my teeth as the gravel from the asphalt tears into my elbows and knees. I don't know who

I'm fleeing from, her or traffic. Both seem to be insurmountable problems.

"Look at me," she says, and on instinct, I do. She's a specter in her tight-fitting shaper. Her feet are dark with tar, but for a second, I notice that her hair has fallen, and it drapes in soft curls around her painted face. This was my mother. Clarisse. If she ever had anything redeeming, it's now gone. She is hardened, like the road beneath me. I turn away and crawl some more.

"You're such an ungrateful child. You literally had everything you wanted. Was that not enough for you? All your needs were being met, and you had a cozy life ahead of you, but you had to seek *them* out and turn off your own future."

The shadow on the road is on top of me now. She's within striking distance, and there's nothing I can do about it and no one else has the presence of mind to save me. I roll over and see her hand with the piece of porch railing raised high.

All this, and I feel peace roll over me. I'm real. A genuine person with real needs and concerns. I would have changed the world if she had left me alone. I can see a brighter future for those who walk around me.

In the distance, I hear the squeal of the tires. If they're going to hit me before she can take me out, all the better. Someone needs to derail her before she can do any more harm.

"You didn't murder Dad," I manage between huffs. "And you can't stop Clarity."

"Ta-ta, Libby." She smiles. With all her violence, the flash in her eyes tells me I'm done. She brings down the club, but before she reaches me, the transport arrives out of nowhere and smashes into her and then a palm tree on the main strip.

Clarisse is gone, and I can't breathe.

Now it's my turn, but instead of revving up to me, the transport stops short with a loud screeching of the brakes and the transport door opens. Byz steps out from the driver's side.

"Are you all right, Libs?"

I shake my head, too exhausted to speak.

"You! Help me!" Byz commands to a man on the sidewalk. He tries to keep walking, but she won't let him ignore her. "You get over here or so help me, I'll get in this transport and mow you over as well." It's enough to make him compliant.

"Aden?" I pant. We can't leave him here.

She shakes her head. "There's no time to get to him. We've got to find my parents and figure out what's happening. Your mother won't be bothering us anymore, but we still have enemies about. Don't forget it."

"I won't go without him." I try to say it firmly enough that she forgets I'm powerless at the moment.

She groans, but relents.

"You," Byz directs the man. "Help me get these two in the transport."

I watch their shadows as they lift Aden. Byz can't hold him up, so the man drags him across to the passenger's seat. I feel myself lifted in the air and set in our backseat. The tattered seats are rough on my face, but I straighten out my leg the best that I can.

There's a scuffle outside of the transport. Something bangs against the hood. I hear a muffled struggle outside the window, but I can't lift my head to see what's happening. My limbs are heavier than my eyelids, and the pain is a blanket covering me.

The driver door opens and closes, but before the engine runs, I hear a small, stifled laugh.

"I've been looking for you, girlie. Now, it's getting Realsies. I want to show you something," Puck says as I feel a small pinch in my arm, followed by nothing.

Chapter 40

When I open my eyes, I'm in a cylindrical room, darkened except for a pinpoint of light at the center of the ceiling. A loud hum echoes from the walls; it hurts my ears.

I feel like I've been runover, which reminds me that I have. My legs feel too far away, disconnected. My shoulders ache, and my back feels locked down. I try to sit up and feel my muscles balk. They needn't worry; my hands, and probably my legs, are strapped to the table.

What's going on? I listen and hear nothing over the hum. Alone, for now. Puck must have put me on the table. Heat rushes my face as I realize he may have left me here to die.

This room is a remnant of the old world, and you can tell it's seldom used, because it's beyond the rot of PR, and black vines cover the walls. Even with the vines, the air smells stale, making my breath shallow.

I can't stay here.

A shadow to my left. I slowly crane my head in that direction to see a glass booth. Puck is sitting in a chair. It looks like he's reading. He must feel my eyes, because he looks up.

A speaker clicks on in the room, and Puck's voice echoes off the walls. "Ah, now you're awake. I was hoping you wouldn't miss the show."

"What are you doing?" I say through gritted teeth as I try to move my arms again.

"I'm doing you a favor, girlie. Your father worked for this his entire life. He may not have wanted my support, but you've helped me to decide. I'm ready for the world to open its eyes. For us all to have some equilibrium. Yes, the people will need clean air and water, and especially the goods I have stockpiled over the years.

"I thought it fitting that you would be the one to share this day with me. We've used each other very well, and now it's time to make this jaunt of ours permanent."

It's clear that he used me, but I'm not sure what I've gotten out of the deal.

"My dad. It was you..."

He dismisses me with the wave of a hand.

"That's for later. For now, I'm blocking the signal. Don't you want to know how?" His grin is wide. He's been waiting to tell me this, but I hurt all over, and I'm in no mood for his games.

He waits for a few seconds and then tells me, anyway. "Really, it's quite brilliant. The necklace blocked the signal for you, but it wasn't enough to block it for everyone. Thanks to earlier happenstance, I was able to collect all six of them. I've put them together and used them to amplify a signal that's big enough to cover the eye."

"So it's done. PR is over?" I can't quiet the part of me that is thankful, but I hate that I spoke.

"Not quite yet. These signals are being powered by an old generator. It won't hold forever. PR will return without intervention."

"Oh." Even I can hear the disappointment in my voice.

He shakes his head, grinning. "Don't worry, girlie. It will be permanent in a few minutes. I have a surprise for you."

His hands busy with something I can't see in the bottom of the booth. He has my full attention until a loud clunk from above makes me feel like the ceiling is going to collapse. I turn my head up as the noise makes the whole room tremor.

But the ceiling doesn't fall; it opens. The pinpoint of light becomes a sliver. It's blinding after being in the dark room. I squint, adjusting my eyes, but everything is blurry.

"You'll see it in a minute, and it'll be clear what I plan to do."

With no idea what he's talking about, I pull at the straps on my arms and legs. "What are you doing?"

"I told you not to worry. I don't wish to harm you yet. I'm tightening down on any possible interference with my plan." He is fiddling with something below the glass when a lens diffuses the light into the room like a rainbow. The lights are mesmerizing, but I have to turn away from their intensity.

Puck continues as I turn to face him. "I've spent way too long waiting for this moment, and the last three crystal pendants finally let me see the technology your dad was using to block the signals. Of course, I'm not out to disrupt the signal but to eliminate it."

He claps his hands, so satisfied with himself.

"I don't know what you're talking about." Taking a deep breath, I try to pull my hands out of the straps, but my shoulders hurt enough that I can't apply much force.

"No, you wouldn't understand. The crystals in the necklaces make a spectrum that diffuses the signal. It's what I used this morning when I disrupted it." I see

He's staring at me, and I realize he's enjoying watching me struggle. I'm so frustrated that I want to scream, but I don't have the lung capacity to do it.

He continues. "It would seem like the signal was lost if you were to look for it, but I assure you it's there and well-hidden at its source." His eyes return to the panel. "You're about to thank me for taking the crystals. I've had three for a while, and now yours, Alaina Lawson's, and that mother of yours. My, she is a hoot, so easy to manipulate, so desperate to hold on to her delusion. This is what I needed the crystals for. I had to find the last two. I found both yesterday. One was being used for research by the Blue Stars. Then, I took your mother's from you."

"You were the one who killed Shy? Did you do something to my dad?" If he's hurt him, there's nothing to keep him from hurting me. I squirm in the restraints, renewed with urgency.

"The police killed Shy, but I prefer to think of him as more of a self-sacrifice. He was willing to die for that crystal, and that's what he did. A martyr, if you will. He gave his life protecting history, but I'm here to make the future."

"And Dad?" I say.

He waves his index finger back and forth at me. "In good time, in good time."

A shudder runs down my spine. I can't feel my left hip any more. It's gone numb. That's not good.

"The PREP group uses the waves to block the signal in a similar manner, but on a much smaller scale. I am not served by their acclimation trials or the need to block the signal intermittently. Too much could happen between now and then." He's more talking to himself than me now, steadily working on what must be a control panel.

"My situation is much better if the people are desperate for answers, dependent on someone to save the day. I intend to be that person, having acquired as much wealth and supplies as I'm going to need. It is now time for me to gain the power and honor that I've deserved. Don't you see? I'll be the new Deliverer."

My heart stops. He means to take Dad's legacy. "Why would they turn to you when so much bad is said about you?"

"Look back into the light."

I focus, but the sunlight puts a large dot in my eyes. But after several blinks, I realize that the dot is outside my scope of vision. Instead, I'm looking at something round that seems to levitate in the sky.

"The moon!" We're almost under it. How is that possible?

"You mean the eye. Clever, no?" I don't have to see him to know he's smiling. It comes through his voice. "We're in the old observatory off the river. Under the eye."

"Why, though? Why are we here?" I lay my shoulders back on the table. I'm in no shape to get out. A heavy sigh slowly seeps from my lungs.

"This morning, I put all the crystals in the lens I created for the telescope. It's sending a signal that has halted all PR. PREP has now made its goal. Elizeus would be proud of what I've accomplished, and I thought it only fair that you also get to witness it."

"Okay, I've seen it. How about you untie me from this slab and take me home?

"Oh, no, no, no. There's more." His voice is high, excitable. "You and I are about to untether the eye for good. Now that all six crystals are in place, I'm set. The Watchers won't see to stop me. We're going to use a last lens to zap the base of the eye and watch it burn. With the elimination of the false eye, we will make history. Well, *I will*, but you get the joy of taking part."

"They're already eliminating the signal. What makes you think you'll be the one they'll remember?" I'm defending Dad, but I really don't know enough about it to have good ammunition for this argument.

"It's going to eliminate the signal, but it's also going to stop the Watchers from monitoring us." His voice is low and rushed, indicating his frustration with me. "Don't you see? They'll have to leave us alone or send emissaries back to check on their projects and resources, and I doubt they have the strength to stop us all."

The crystal lens moves in a slow rotation, aligning with the would-be moon. The room fills with the smell of something burning, renewing my struggle to get free.

My chest is tight as I struggle to breathe. I can't think about his plan. I have to get out of here.

When I don't respond, he continues. "I'm sure I can get them to give away details of where they come from, and I'm the man that will get it out of them—with the help of the police, of course."

His words are lost in my struggle, but I replay them back in my head and stop again, recognizing a way to stall him. "I know the police are on your side. You may as well tell me the full story."

A frustrated huff comes from the intercom. "Yes, yes. The police are with me. They did what they had to do. Your father wouldn't give them the crystals, so they got rid of him so he couldn't warn the others."

"They killed him?" My voice is strained, like it doesn't belong to me. It's distant and weak.

"No, no, no. I'd never hurt the Captain. They sent him over the river and sent a fake back here. Too bad he wasn't convincing. He won't get a second chance."

"Wait... So he is alive?" Fresh tears pool in my eyes and drip to my ears. "On the other side of the river?"

"In a word, yes. That would be correct," he says, sounding like he is put out from the change in subject. "Don't get excited, girlie. For you, he may as well be dead. He'll spend the rest of his life over there. There's no way to get him back."

The light reaches the outermost edge of the eye, blurred by tears, but I'm fixated as the light moves up the surface.

"In any case, you're mucking up my grand finale. All my life, the eye has watched over me. It's watched my father grow sick and die, and my mother mourn him so much that she died as well. It has watched us all bumbling around in our dream worlds."

I hear the great crystal slide into place and hold my breath as the heat sears up to the point he directed it.

"Impact in three... two... *one*."

The stream of light opens up a small puncture in the eye, penetrating the exterior. Whatever is inside is combustible, because flames come out of the open sore before bursting fully into an explosion of fire.

The flames lick the sides of the eye, melting it in front of me, dropping large fragments into the river. I'm certain I'm not alone in my awe of watching it drop. There's no going back now, no more chance of waking up in that dream world. Gone is the sovereignty of the Watchers. It's a new day.

"Isn't it amazing? I hope you enjoyed it. I wanted you to see it before it's your turn."

"You said you wouldn't harm me!" I force myself up against the restraints with the last of my energy. I need to get out of here.

He laughs as the ceiling closes up. "No, no, girlie. I said I didn't want to harm you yet, and that's completely different. Sharing this is my gift to your father for all his hard work, but surely you can see how you're going to be a liability. I can't have anyone soiling the new Deliverer."

The click of a door handle, and I hear his footsteps around me. "It's fitting that you die in the same way the eye did. You both have been watching me and keeping tabs, but I'm going to be the only one who comes out alive."

When I he's close, I jump, but I'm held down by the restraints. I renew my struggle again, pulling at the straps. He looks at me in the most endearing way. His eyes are soft and his smile sympathetic.

"The final sequence has been set. You've fought hard, but now it is time to rest." He pulls out a small pin from his lapel and turns my head to the side. I feel a slight pressure on the base of my neck. "This pin will attract the lasers now that they are activated. One last jolt of reality for you."

Puck shifts to the side, holding my head in place, but there is something moving in the glass booth. Another flash. I see Aden standing where Puck was a few minutes ago.

Aden's moving quickly for someone covered in so much blood. His face is panicked, and I watch in slow motion as he flips every button on the panel.

Mirrors on the sides come out and direct the light from where the decimated eye was to the mirrors above. The pinpoints of light move down both walls toward the pin. I can see it sear through the mildew as the wall lets off fumes of disintegration.

Aden must hit the button for the retractable ceiling, because it starts to open up again. Puck looks up, but before he can turn, I clamp my teeth around his fingers. It's enough of a distraction that he pummels me with his free hand. I sink my teeth in farther, ignoring the pain and the taste of his dirty skin.

Puck's eyes roll up to see the ceiling. He's now pulling instead of trying to distract me with head shots, but I don't let go. If I'm going down, he's going with me.

The light is just over his head. I clench down as he pulls with all his might. I can't hold on much longer. He yanks his hand free, and as he does, he jerks his hand into the laser above. I smell the burning flesh and hear him cry out a moment before it sears off his fingers. Holding his hand, Puck runs out of sight.

I scream too as the light closes in on the pin in my neck. The left mirror should stop there, but the right mirror will have to pass over my head to reach its destination.

There's no way for Aden to get to me in time. He's pushing more buttons, but the light is focused centimeters from my head.

I close my eyes, not daring to watch it. My body struggles, but my mind is still. This is the end.

"Don't move, Liberty!" Aden shouts. "We've got to get out."

I open my eyes in morbid fascination, but the light has stopped inches from my head. It's seared through the table and onto the floor, but it's not moving. Aden stopped it.

I breathe out in short little huffs, doing my best to calm myself.

"We've got to get out of here before the observatory goes up in flames," Aden says as I hear his voice move from the booth to the cylindrical room. He cuts away my restraints.

When he picks me up and throws me over his shoulder, my vision tunnels. I watch the floor as he runs outside, puts me on the ground, and wraps his arms around me.

He holds me tight, and it's all that holds me together. I watch my tears fall down his shoulder as we both collapse into the dirt.

I'm not sure how long we lie there before Byz and Mr. Lawson show up. Byz flops down beside me, and Mr. Lawson looks down.

Mr. Lawson asks what happened, but I don't have the strength to answer, and Aden is too busy holding me.

"Hold tight," Mr. Lawson says. "Help is on the way."

Behind him, the observatory burns and smoke curls into the sky.

Byz holds my hand, but she looks so distressed that I can't face her. Instead, I turn to Aden.

"It's going to be okay," he whispers. He picks up his hand and runs it down my cheek.

I look into his eyes, and I know it's true.

Somehow it's going to be okay.

Dad is still out there. Over the river. Alone. And I know I'll do anything I can to find him.

I lift my head in a failed attempt to support myself. When it falls back, I turn toward Mr. Lawson. I want to tell him Dad's okay, that he's just across the river. But if I do, I'll just put my father further at risk. The last thing he needs is a bunch of Yellow Stars rushing the bridge, trying to get him back.

No, my father gave the world back to me, and it's my turn to return the favor.

"Rest," Aden says, as I squirm. "You're going to need it."

I quit fighting. I am going to have to rest, but not for long. I've got so much more left to do. My dad doesn't even know that it's his turn to count on me.

I won't let him down.

Thanks for reading!

If you enjoyed the book, the sequel will be available soon. Check out the preorder at jlynnhicks.com.

Also By J Lynn Hicks

Clarity Chronicles
Clarity
Tenacity (Sept 2022)
Authority (December 2022)
Unity (March 2022)

Daughter of Rebellion Series
Upload
Overload
Payload

ACKNOWLEDGMENTS

There are so many people to thank.

First, thank you to my newsletter list and followers. I write with you in mind.

My developmental and line editor, Liz Cartwright, helps shape my crazy ideas into a consumable format. My books wouldn't be the same without her.

My cover designer is Daphne Zane, and I'm in love with the covers she made for this series and easily her biggest fan.

Thank you to my critique partners, Maria Mojica and Amber Cole. You helped me iron on this first book and your feedback has been invaluable.

To my writing group at the Jackson-Madison County Library, thank you for being there.

Any host of online networking groups, but specifically 20Books, 365 Writing Challenge, and Unleashing the Next Chapter.

To my writing besties, the ones that can sprint for days. Much gratitude for Amber Cole, Jessica White, and Sonja Frojdendal.

My writing companion, Alicia J Chumney, brings me levity.

To you, who read this far, I give my humble gratitude.

Thank you to my husband who gives me time to do my thing, and my children and extended family that support my journey.

Mostly, thank you God for helping me out of the pit I was in and setting me back on track. You're last on the list, but first in my heart.